THE SHOW HOUSE

a novel

DAN LOPEZ

The Unnamed Press
P.O. Box 411272
Los Angeles, CA 90041

Published in North America by The Unnamed Press.

1 3 5 7 9 10 8 6 4 2

Copyright © 2016 by Dan Lopez

ISBN: 978-1-944700-03-4

Cataloging in Publication Data available upon request.

This book is distributed by Publishers Group West

Cover design & typeset by Jaya Nicely

For Mom & Pop
& Cal

PART ONE

Entre One Summer y Another Winter

I'LL WAIT FOR IT HERE, THADDEUS THINKS, CONTEMPLATING the long, rectangular pool. A few dead leaves float on the surface, some bugs. He makes a note to call and have it cleaned as soon as they return next week.

He can see Cheryl through the sliding glass door, seated at the kitchen table balancing the checkbook, receipts spread out neatly to her left. He'd like to go inside and sit with her—maybe tell her that they should schedule an appointment with the pool-cleaning service—but she prefers to be alone when dealing with the finances. Anyway, she promised to bring him a glass of chardonnay and a ham sandwich as soon as she finishes. All he has to do is wait, but he's too nervous about tomorrow to sit still for long, so he walks around the yard, kicking palmetto fruits off the concrete slab and onto the grass as he goes. He just has to get through these next few hours, he reminds himself, and then they'll be on their way to Stevie's house and everything will be fine. His breathing is labored; his joints crack, but it feels good to move.

The breeze bends a low-hanging frond from a nearby palm to the surface of the pool, and with some effort he drops to one knee alongside it. He dips a finger in the cool water, sending ripples lapping against the scummy blue tile. Too cold for swimming. Haltingly, he drags himself back to his feet. Drying his finger on his pants, he heaves a sigh. Ordinarily, a heater keeps the water pleasant year-round, but last night Cheryl shut it off in anticipation of the exterminators' arrival—no sense in wasting money on something they won't be around to enjoy.

It's not just the water that's cold. By Apopka standards, it's a chilly night. But he doesn't mind. Winter in Central Florida can reinvigorate what the long summer has stymied. Yes, he thinks, as he strikes out across the patio with renewed vigor; the cold weather is just what they need. He stubs his toe and stumbles on a root that has cracked a row of pavers. "Something new to fix," he mutters. But he doesn't scream. There was a time when he would've screamed, when he would've thrown things and hit things like an enraged child. Cheryl always calmed him down in those moments. She's the only one who ever could. She's saved his life in a million little ways like that over the years, and though he doesn't say it nearly enough, he's thankful for that, for her. But he doesn't need her help tonight. Maybe it's the meditation videos he's been watching on YouTube, or maybe it's a natural result of age; either way, he's mellower these days. The rages seem to have at last abandoned him. So what if a root has cracked some stone? It was probably time for a renovation anyway. This whole backyard has gone to pot. Take these two weathered lounge chairs, for instance. Ferreted away in a corner, they see more rain than sun, and what's the point of lounge chairs if you can't catch some rays? He's been lazy about upkeep, has allowed things to slide. But that's finished now. Things are going to change.

Using the moon as an approximation for the sun, he shoves the lounge chairs into a V formation. Their flaky legs leave chalky trails on the concrete slab. He wipes away the grime that has accumulated, perhaps for decades, on the mildewed vinyl slats. A small table—its opaque surface pockmarked by water stains—fits nicely between the chairs.

He eyes the arrangement for symmetry, nods with satisfaction. Then he takes a moment to catch his breath. It's a start. A few minutes—that's all it took, and some focus. Simple work. He tests the pool once more. Again he dries his finger on his pants before walking away. He taps a porch sconce. A handful of dead bugs tumble off the sun-yellowed plastic cover. "Good, good," he mumbles.

When tomorrow goes well, the rest of the week will be a piece of cake, and then it's only a matter of time before Stevie and the whole family will want to visit to use the pool, and won't it be nice to have everyone here together? That's what backyards and pools are for, family, and really, all in all, this backyard isn't in bad shape; it just needs some attention.

A string of tiny bodies scurrying up the back wall catch his eye. Leaning close, he watches them file into a minuscule fissure between the stucco and a paint-speckled outlet. Termites. Their white bodies stream into the dark recesses of his home. He lumbers over to the wall-mounted garden hose nearby and gives it a sturdy yank (the hose is old and the plastic often sticks). It releases from its cradle with a squeal. With his free hand he fishes his reading glasses from his breast pocket, then studies the nozzle, moving it back and forth until the tiny faded glyphs etched along the rim come into focus. He settles on a powerful jet setting and fixes his sights on the intruders. Tomorrow the professionals will deal with the rest of them, but tonight he can have a little fun. He squeezes the handle and drowns the termites in a whitewater torrent.

"*Hasta la vista,* baby!" He grinds the fallen into the wet concrete with a toe.

Satisfied, he slings the hose back onto its cradle, letting the loops sag like a belly.

The sliding door whooshes in its track and Cheryl emerges wearing a shimmering nightgown offset by a pair of threadbare Minnie Mouse slippers. "What are you doing?"

"Huh? Oh, termites."

She nods and thrusts a plate at him. "Here," she says, and he's confused for a moment. It's only when she hands him a glass of chardonnay that he remembers that he's been waiting for her.

"Sit with me a minute," he says, tapping the lounge chair. His fingers leave dirty prints on the wineglass.

She remains standing. "Put everything in the sink when you're finished and don't stay up too late. The exterminators will be here first thing in the morning. I want you well rested for tomorrow."

He nods and returns to his wine. Sipping it theatrically, he praises the hints of citrus, all the while waiting for her to sit beside him. Anticipating it. "What an intoxicating beverage." He shoots her the mischievous eyebrow. "Is that a new nightgown?"

"No."

"It looks great on you."

He purses his lips for a kiss. Instead, she kisses a finger and lightly taps the corner of his mouth. He tastes the minty flavor of her oily hand cream.

"I'm going to bed," she says. "You should, too."

"Oh?"

"Not like that. I'm tired."

He folds his chin into his neck like a wounded anhinga. And for a moment he seems to have pinned her reclusive tenderness, because instead of marching straight inside as she often does, she lingers by a second set of sliding glass doors, this one leading to their bedroom.

"Thaddeus?" Her tone, if not outright sweet, is at the very least significantly less guarded. "Tomorrow, promise me you'll behave? It's a very nice thing Steven and Peter are doing, letting us stay with them."

For the first time all night (for the first time in many nights) there's softness in her voice, and, thrilled, he smiles at her, gives her his fullest attention. It's that simple, he thinks, a kind word. An acknowledgment. What any man would want from his wife. But just as quickly the softness hardens into a trembling anxiety bordering on anger.

"I think Steven's finally ready to move on. When I think of all the time we've wasted—"

"Remember when we built this pool?" He knows to interrupt her when she tenses. He doesn't have many tricks, but he has this one and it usually works. "Stevie got so mad because we had to rip out that... that tree—what was it called?"

"Kumquat," she says cautiously.

"Kumquat. Right." He takes a large bite of the sandwich and struggles with it for a minute. Crumbs catch in his stubble. "We'll be fine," he says, smiling. "No big deal."

"Promise me you'll behave. Please."

He nods. "Stevie's a good kid."

A sudden breeze sets the palm fronds chattering and she clutches her gown at the throat. "Just be yourself tomorrow, huh? Only maybe a little more subtle."

"I should do something special for them. To thank them for the hospitality. Maybe I'll buy them a boat. You remember how much Stevie loved fishing when we went to the Keys."

"He's never liked fishing."

"Sure he did! He loved it."

She rubs her temples. "Where are they going to keep a boat? They don't live on the water. Stop inventing things. Besides, you already bought Gertie that doll."

He scratches his chin. "Those were good times. You remember." He smirks at the memory. "Something really great."

"You've done enough. Just be nice. That's the only thanks anybody needs right now." As if closing a box, she folds her hand and turns to enter the house. "And don't stay up too late. It's getting cold."

He wishes her good night, but she's already inside, so he finishes his sandwich and wine before digging around in a terra cotta planter for his stash. Cheryl always hides it in the same place for him, so it'll be easy to find.

The pipe isn't much to look at, just a heavy piece of glass a little bigger than his palm, the bowl chipped and darkened from years of use. He's had better pipes, but he likes this one best because it was a gift from Stevie. It might have been a souvenir from someplace Stevie visited in college. He seems to recall a foreign name, long faded, painted alongside the carburetor. Who remembers the particulars? The important thing is that it was a gift, and he often imagines sitting here with his son, their feet dangling in this pool, passing this pipe back and forth like greedy friends stealing a sliver of midnight for themselves, something to hoard just between the two of them. If only they could, then perhaps the decades of animosity would fade away. Perhaps then they could move past the minefield of being father and son and instead be simply two men together in their commonality.

But that won't be tonight. And tomorrow is for Gertie, he thinks as he inhales. The sky flattens. For a moment he imagines snowfall. It's not unheard of—rare, yes, but not unheard of. Do they have snow in the country where she's from? Cambodia? Vietnam? China? He doesn't know. He blinks and the snowflakes disappear. At any rate, there's not a lot around these parts. He drifts off, dreams a bit about dolls and weed and Cheryl and Stevie, comes back and drifts off again, repeating the cycle as the temperature drops then rises. And continues to rise and rise.

YOU SHARPEN THE KNIVES. THERE ARE SEVEN. MONDAY through Sunday, an ambitious purchase made before you truly understood the way to work. In that way you were naive. In that way even seduced by the capitalist drive, the allure of a better life through acquisition. The fluorescent light above your head flickers. Light then dark. Light then dark. That will need to be fixed before the open house tomorrow. You make a note, then return to the knives. Occasionally, a blade slips off the whetstone and you nick the granite counter.

You won't use the knives. That exquisite boy with the cornrows showed you a better way. You took to the visceral bond of a tight grip like ink takes to paper. But the act of whetting a blade remains important. The rhythmic skill brings you peace, prepares you for the night. In this way, you are a fisherman or a hunter caring for your tools. It's a ritual and rituals are important.

You're not unusual in any outward way. You could be anyone as you slip into an old pair of high-top sneakers. Your black hair, while habitually dull, drapes across your brow conventionally. Your legs are a bit too long for your trunk, maybe, but that's nothing a vertical stripe can't fix. You bite your nails. Realistically, this is a fault. A bad one. Your fingers are unattractive. They catch on fabrics. Streamers hang from the ragged edges, which are a liability in your line of work. You must stop biting them.

Wool is out of the question. You grapple with the closet. The door slips off its track again (that's something else you'll fix). A velvet blazer will do. It's creased from how it was folded in your pack. No big deal. Slip it on.

Keys are next.

Find them. Clip them above the left pocket. Your jeans are tight.

Cologne. Watch. Kefia. The remainder, too, follows an order. Perhaps it's fetishistic of you to exhibit this penchant for order, for exactitude. How silly to care. How uninspired. Outside the clubs, they are careless: they spit; they laugh—

But they die.

People think they know you, that they know everything. Yet they understand nothing.

Can you feel it? Of course you can. A chilly current flows through the air, a variety rare enough in Orlando. Tonight is certainly a night for a sallow, fidgety boy with a stutter, most likely blond. Someone translucent, like the clarity of winter in the City Beautiful.

Pick a location.

Already, you feel the spring of hardwood beneath your feet, the banal conversations between songs. You dance. You will dance.

Location.

Parliament House is impossible. You went there last Friday. This week there will be too many questions. Have you seen him? Tall. Sunglasses and a topknot. Parents, boyfriends, everyone worries. And you'd just as soon avoid the entanglement.

Location?

Independent Bar.

Park the car. The stereo hisses into submission. The door is not far, then you are inside. Goth music. Black walls. Pop music. Red walls. The wristband—yellow tonight—rips your arm hair. First, a drink. Then skip upstairs for a perch above the dance floor. Above everything. You are above everyone.

Even now, the work remains a rumor. Some are afraid to go out, yes. But not here. Surely they're safe here. If they travel with friends and don't pick anybody up... They're wrong.

"You need a drink," he says suddenly. He saw you before you saw him. He approached you. Spoke.

"What did you say?"

"You need a drink."

"Have one already," you say. You jiggle a glass.

"You don't get it. That's cute, you know?" He stands. Bowlegged. Cocks his head to the side and grins. His teeth like a printer's stamp pressed into his thick lower lip. "You need to buy *me* a drink."

"Says who?"

"Ask what I want." He's Puerto Rican with a stainless steel lip ring, a tight shirt, and a concave abdomen.

"No," you say. He won't do for tonight.

But he's persistent. He slides onto the neighboring stool and presses his thigh to yours. "You're salty, papi, but I won't hold it against you. Vodka cranberry, by the way." He extends a hand. "I'm Alex."

"What a coincidence," you say. "Me, too."

You shake hands, noting the wide, sinewy finger pads like a frog's toes. A callus catches you below the thumb. Tonight he's safe, but maybe some other night he'll be appropriate. You disappear and a moment later fit his hand with a plastic cup from the bar.

"Drink," you say, and he does, thanking you. You grin, satisfied with yourself. You spit in that drink.

"Wanna go home?" he asks.

"Things at home aren't so good right now."

"What's that?"

"Nothing. Not tonight."

Making your vague excuses—the bathroom, a friend waiting— you walk away. You've already wasted too much time with him.

The night progresses swiftly once you've refocused, and before long you spot your perfect boy dancing alone. He is translucence incarnate.

The rest comes simply. Your left hand meets his right shoulder. Your lips mesh. Can he taste you? No. You lack a distinct flavor; you are a perfect reflection of him even in this way.

"Matthew," he says.

"No shit. Me, too," you say. Your place, a string of things you say. He agrees.

And then you're both gone, slipped into the night like a knife into its chock.

FEW KNOW BETTER THAN LAILA MORALES THAT SLEEP, AS A luxury, is best enjoyed by the overworked. But all luxuries expire.

In the darkened room she stirs. Wispy tendrils of an amorphous dream—something on a ship, maybe? Or in a car? Or was it an airboat? And wasn't that an old colleague, a lab partner?—dissolve into her subconscious like a slick of blood diluted in water.

Blackout curtains keep the sun out, air-conditioning maintains a constant temperature, but nothing counteracts a full bladder. Biology wins every time.

The stir deepens, lengthening until wakefulness breaks over her all at once with a race of the heart and a sharp intake of breath.

Squinting, she automatically seeks out the phone on her nightstand, dismissing, unread, the notifications cluttering the display. It's ten A.M.

Her first conscious thought is *Alex*.

Her second: Bathroom. Now.

The second, more insistent, compels her to move.

She shuffles across the worn Berber, flicks the switch in the en suite, and yawns her way onto the toilet. She scrolls through her calendar. No work today at least, and for a moment she luxuriates in the blissful relief of a free Wednesday. But that doesn't mean there aren't tasks to accomplish. After weeks of tracking, projected forecasts, and escalating warnings, Hurricane Natalie is nearly upon them. They'll need water, at least a few gallons each. She keeps empty jugs in the truck for just such an eventuality. Gas, too, for the truck, while she's at it.

She flushes and moves to the sink, brushes her teeth, gargles, spits. Dries her hands. She'll need Alex's help with the shutters.

That's the sticking point. Downstairs she can handle, but she doesn't like climbing ladders so her bedroom window presents a challenge.

Alex.

Hers is not a large place. It's small, actually: a one-bedroom town house with a whisper of a screened-in patio. But it's hers and it's enough for one person. That's the problem, she thinks. It's not one person anymore. Not with Alex crashing on her couch. Indefinitely, Laila reminds herself. Two months in and the arrangement still irks her. "Please, mi'ja, it'll be just for a while," Alex's mother, Esther, had insisted over the phone while Alex pressed in beside Laila, shouting obscenities at the phone. A hastily packed duffel bag slumped at his feet. *Things at the ancestral home have degraded.* That's how Alex put it when she persuaded him to calm down and present his side. "He doesn't listen!" Esther interrupted, prompting Laila to take the call off speakerphone. "I don't know what to do. If your father were here—" Tears prevented her from continuing. Laila didn't so much relent as embrace the inevitability—Alex was standing in her living room, after all. She weakly mustered the strength to ask: "How long is a while?" She'd wanted to add that she had her own life and that she liked it just the way that it was, but between her brother and her stepmother, the family hardly needed another diva. For the sake of harmony she held her tongue. "I don't know," Esther said. "Just until he settles down."

She'd been through this before and the parallel is not lost on her: a decade as an only child, the doted upon pride of a small, well-to-do family. The role suited her. It was enough. It was quiet. She had her routines, a life with room enough for a mother, a father, and her. Then her parents divorced. Her father married Esther soon after. Then Alex came and crowded things. Seventeen years later he's doing it again.

She sighs, steeling herself against the chaos reigning beyond her bedroom door, her inviolable sanctuary. (*Meaning off-limits to you.*) Downstairs she expects to find a trail of discarded fast-food containers, their contents half consumed, littered across every surface from the kitchen counter to the couch, where her brother's thin, naked body will be sprawled, long limbs reaching like a spider's across the balled-up sheets of his ruined web while a snore bubbles his parted lips. ("Coño, Alex! I don't wanna see your dick, man." Was it too much to ask that he put on a pair of underwear at least? "Yo, why not? It's a nice dick." She finds herself smiling at the memory. How is it that Alex always manages to make her smile, even when he's being a little shit?)

But instead of that, when Laila descends the stairs she's greeted by silence.

Silence and a long shaft of sunlight scorching through the half-moon window above the sliding glass door leading out to the patio. The light traverses an impeccable interior before resting on a tidy couch where Alex should be. In his place, she finds folded sheets and neatly stacked pillows. How is it possible? She remembers seeing her brother when she got home last night after inventory. Somewhere around two A.M. she navigated the collateral damage of his late adolescence, guided only by the amber glow of streetlight filtering in through the blinds. Alex had been asleep, and not wanting to disturb him—and, let's be honest, she was exhausted, little more than a withered twig in a lab coat after twelve hours on her feet—she silently grabbed a bottle of water from the fridge and an oatmeal cookie sandwich from the pantry, before retiring to her room, pausing to kiss her brother on the forehead. "Good night, papo," she whispered. He had been home. She saw him. Didn't she?

"Alex?" She sniffs the top pillow and lurches. It's damp and redolent with a tangy mix of sweat, grease, and musk—the sharp scent of teenage boys. He definitely spent the night. "You home?"

No answer.

Though there are few places to hide, she checks them all. The half bath in the foyer is vacant. The kitchen empty. The patio undisturbed.

He must've gone out. But this early? And where? And why? Alex is not one to rise before noon for any reason. She can recall only one instance in which he got up in the A.M. without a lot of hassle: the morning of their father's funeral. But that was an exception, one she prefers to not dwell on.

She checks her phone to see if there's something in the long list of notifications she ignored. Sure enough, a text: **going out**. No further details. She counts herself lucky that he bothered sending that much. Esther never got even that small courtesy when he ran out on her, and now she's persona non grata after sending him to live with his sister—like that's some great punishment. If anybody should be pissed at Esther it's not Alex.

The time stamp on the message reads 8:30. Something is definitely up. What does he have to do at 8:30 in the morning? It's not like he has a job. She opts for the light touch when texting him back.

Cool come home early k? Need ur help with the shutters luv u

She might get into it with him tonight, explain (again!) the importance of letting her know where he's going to be and impressing upon him the merits of basic civility toward those who love and care about you...

But today is her day off and she's determined to keep it for herself. She will waste no more energy on worrying about her selfish brother. It's a quarter after ten and the only thing she wants right now is coffee!

THE FROG-CROAK SOUND OF DUCT TAPE TEARING JOLTS him awake.

An army moves around him. Men go in and out of the house, shouting at one another to mind plants and to tend to various pieces of equipment arranged throughout the limestone patio. Some climb onto the roof, where they stitch together heavy yellow tarps with rows of alligator clips, while others feed a tube under the tarp and test seals. Overnight, his sedate home has transformed into a midway abuzz with activity.

Cheryl hands him his coffee. "Here. Drink," she says, her voice stripped of whatever softness it possessed the night before.

"The doll?" he asks, clearing his throat and wiping the sleep from his eyes. His pipe, long extinguished, rests on the hard bubble of his gut. His entire body aches.

"In the car with our suitcases." She stashes the pipe in its usual place. "They're just about done. We should get going." She helps him to his feet. "You're sweating. I told you to come in last night. Now you don't even have time to change."

"I'm fine. Never better. Feel like a million bucks." He stretches himself like an elm scratching at the sky and stomps his feet to get the blood circulating. He shakes his body like an earthquake, rolls his neck, windmills his arms, and cracks his back. And in one bearish gulp he empties the coffee mug, announcing his satisfaction with a yawp.

The foreman peeks out from beneath the tarp. "Hey, lady. We're about to close 'er up. If you forgot anything, now's the time to get it."

"No. Go ahead," she calls back.

But before he can duck inside, Thaddeus beckons him. "Just a few questions!"

Thaddeus turns to Cheryl, who busies herself returning the lounge chairs to their original positions, mumbling something about UV and sun bleaching. "Do you have the doll?" he asks again.

She sighs. "In the car. Along with our suitcases."

The foreman waddles over, tossing a glance at his loitering crew. He checks something on his phone, then looks up at Thaddeus. "I went over all of this with your wife. What do you need?"

For a long time Thaddeus doesn't speak, only stares at the yard.

"Hey, guy, you got a question or what?" The foreman squints in the early-morning sun. He's a large man, and already a tributary of sweat marks the valley of his spine. He smells of mulch and high-endurance deodorant. "Yours ain't the only house we got today. Ain't even the only one we got in this neighborhood. You'd be surprised what bad shape a lot of these old houses are in."

Thaddeus purses his lips. "How long until we can use the pool?"

He shrugs. "Should be fine now, unless it's broke. We only do the inside. Inside." He points at the house for emphasis. "Look, I left a pamphlet with your wife—"

"This pool," Thaddeus says. He wraps an arm around the foreman's shoulders and drags him along the perimeter. "The contractor—a good-looking lady-contractor, couldn't have been more than twenty-five—she wanted to charge twenty thousand for it. Do you know what I told her?" He grins, awaiting a response.

"Look, we really need to get started here—"

"I said, 'No way, Josephina!' Ha!" He taps the foreman's chest. "I could do the job myself for half that if I knew about construction."

"Yeah? Good for you. Like I said, I gave your wife the rundown. Just avoid goin' inside and you'll be good—"

"'Materials alone are going to run twelve grand.' That's what she told me." Thaddeus narrows his eyes. "Okay, so I told her I could go as high as fourteen thousand. Hey, two grand's just a weekend in Vegas anyway, right? But it wasn't enough. 'I have my crew to think about,' she said. We went back and forth for twenty minutes. I don't have to tell you about negotiating." He gives the foreman a knowing nod. "Finally I said, 'Fifteen thousand. That's my final offer,' and showed her the door. And what do you think she did?"

The foreman glances back to his crew and motions for them to seal the house.

"She said, 'You drive a hard bargain.' But she took the job. I liked her style, so I said, 'What the hell, with the five grand I'm saving I'll start a scholarship to help more girls like you go to trade school.' I can't help it; I'm a feminist. When the job was done I gave her an extra two hundred bucks for her trouble. No big deal."

The foreman slips away, and moments later a quiet hiss signals that the gas has begun to fill the house.

"Let's go," Cheryl says.

But the limp tent sputtering to life transfixes Thaddeus. It morphs and undulates like a lava flow. Forms rise in the fabric only to collapse as the gas reaches toward equilibrium. "It's just the wind," Cheryl says, but he ignores her. His home is turmoil. Right now poison pours over Cheryl's clothes and into Stevie's old room. Next will be the garage, or would that have been first? Ultimately, the order matters little to him. Gas will eventually coil around everything like a cat setting down for a nap: his law books in the attic, the photograph in the family room of Stevie leaning over the rail at Niagara Falls pretending to slip, the Hawaiian leis from a family vacation he can't quite remember, entire drawers full of odd knickknacks and fading memorabilia that attest to a life well lived, tangible proof of memories made even if the memories themselves rise more sluggishly and infrequently than they used to—all of it, ultimately, choking on gas. But how many of the termites?

He stays awhile longer, watching the tent. Then with a cough he turns to Cheryl. "They'll do a great job," he says. He knows that they'll go above and beyond because he took the time to build a rapport with the man in charge. And in business, as in life, it's the relationships that matter. "A fine job," he says. "No problem."

Cheryl looks down at her nails and taps her foot. "Can we go now?"

"Whatever you want, heart of my heart."

Taking her hand, he kisses her on the knuckles, but the static charge has barely left her skin before, wide-eyed, she yanks her hand away.

"I may have accidentally touched the poison," she whispers, half apologizing.

Orlando feels like an extension of Apopka. Or maybe it's the other way around. A mall looms in the distance, and before that a multiplex cradled by a handful of shops. But mostly the streets are wide and residential. If a difference exists between the neighboring cities at all it's in the way faux-Spanish architecture dresses up the vernacular of simple midcentury bungalows in Orlando to a greater degree than it does in Apopka. Thaddeus is having a hard time navigating it. It's been years since he's been in the suburbs beyond downtown.

"Lot of new construction," he says.

"Uh-huh," Cheryl says. "You're going to want to make a left at the light. It's the one with the waterfall."

He maneuvers into a turning lane, dutifully engages his directional signal, and waits. Traffic roils from the horizon like salmon on run. In Apopka traffic's not so bad, or maybe it is and he's simply accustomed to it. (The streets by their house, at least, are familiar.) An oasis pools in the middle distance. A final car swims through a long yellow light, then Thaddeus proceeds, on Cheryl's direction, passing smoothly through a portal of blue tile and lacquered calligraphy spelling out the name PALM FALLS WEST. At the end of a long drive flanked by hedges and iron lattices stands a security kiosk, built with unassuming white concrete that could just as easily be calcified runoff from the eponymous waterfall.

"Gated community." He whistles. "You didn't tell me they lived in a gated community."

"Yes, I did." She removes her sunglasses and places them in her purse. "All the new ones are gated."

"I would've remembered something like that."

"What do you want from me? I told you."

The white gate opens before they reach the kiosk, but he stops the car and lowers his window anyway. "Good morning!"

A guard leans out of the kiosk. "You can go right on through, sir," he says. His uniform appears freshly bleached, the epaulets newly stitched. Even bent over, the polyester holds its crease. He waves at Cheryl. "Nice to see you again, Mrs. Bloom."

Cheryl returns the gesture. "Hello, Byron."

Her smile is bright, boarding on flirtatious, and Thaddeus wonders if he should be worried. He'll have to look into that later, but right now there's work to be done.

"We're visiting my son, Stevie, and his partner for the week," Thaddeus says. "Do you need me to sign anything?"

"No need, sir." Byron smiles. "Mrs. Bloom is on the list. You can go right in."

"I'll sign whatever you need."

"He said it's fine," Cheryl snipes, maintaining a pained smile.

"Just so everything's on the up and up. I know how gated communities can be."

"Thaddeus, let's go."

He relents, raising his hands in surrender. "Hey, man, okay. She's the boss. I just do what she tells me to."

"Yes, sir."

"Keep up the good work, huh?"

"Yes, sir. Have a nice visit."

Thaddeus reaches for his wallet, but Cheryl stays his hand and gives the guard a quick wave. "Thank you, Byron. Thaddeus, drive."

"Yes, ma'am!"

The immediate interior of the complex houses a cabana and a modest pool. From there the layout quickly segues into a series of winding lanes and sidewalks. Some end in culs-de-sac; others skirt roundabouts and branch off into labyrinthine blocks with plenty of meandering green space. The homes are all two-story off-white units with trim in peach, seafoam, or light gray. A few look freshly painted, others recently pressure-washed. A traffic sign reminds motorists to be vigilant of children at play. The overall impression is of something clean and new. "Some place," he says.

Just being here seems to have elevated Cheryl's mood. As soon as they turn the corner—or, rather, slalom along a lazy curve—she spots the house and taps him on the arm, pointing it out. He's happy for the contact, even if it's fleeting. "Here we are! Just pull into the driveway."

Uniform rows of violet and white perennials adorn the bottom of the house. Pagoda lights trim the front walkway, and stacked river rocks create a neutral border between the saturated green of the grass and the robust brown of the wood chips piled high throughout the flower beds. A juvenile oak sprouts from the center of the lawn.

"Some yard. Must be making the gardener rich."

"Oh, the homeowners' association probably takes care of it." She flutters out of the car.

"Homeowners, huh?"

He shifts the car into park and steps out with a wince. These days driving always puts a crick in his knee, and sleeping outside last night didn't do him any favors. He bends the knee until the pain recedes, then hobbles around the driveway.

She extracts a handful of letters from the mailbox. "Peter's still at work, but Steven said to just let ourselves in." She hands him the mail to hold while she goes around the side of the house. Lazily, he flips through the stack: a few bills and a catalog from a furniture store he doesn't recognize, that's pretty much it.

"Stevie's not here?"

"He's at the real estate office all day, then doing his volunteering. I told you all this already."

"Oh."

"He'll be home later." Then speaking to herself: "There's a key hidden over here somewhere."

After getting the bags from the trunk, he wanders over the lawn. It's softer than what they have in Apopka, which is stubby, coarse, and often yellow in the winter. This grass, by contrast, is almost blue.

"Some lawn," he mumbles.

Cheryl returns, holding up a key and smiling. "Found it!" She kisses him on the cheek. "Come on, quit staring at the lawn and grab the suitcases. I have to disarm the alarm and I never remember the code. Oh, I'm so excited!"

"Oh"—the kiss still warm on his cheek—"I'll come all right!"

Palm trees line the deck of Stevie's house, barks painted white against insects. Cheryl is upstairs while he paces aimlessly; dusk can be the loneliest time of day. She'd grabbed him as soon as he dropped their bags in the guest room, needing him for the first time in months. "Do you want anything special?" he'd asked, unsure how to proceed after such a long absence. She hadn't deigned to answer, leaving little for him to go on but a cryptic shrug. He didn't press her further; instead, he improvised, and they had a magnificent time.

And now he finds himself drunk on it still, stumbling around Stevie's backyard, letting the decor wash over him and already missing the warmth of her skin, the scent of heat in her hair. Her smooth back has maintained its perfect line through the years—a sculpture that never tires of posing. She even kissed him before dropping her head dreamily onto a fresh white pillowcase that still retained a vague latticework of creases from the linen closet. "They'll be home soon," she said. "And I still need to get dressed." She suggested he get some air, her voice tinged by that familiar indifference. But she must have noticed it sneaking back in, because she kissed him again and softly added that she was feeling tired and might take a nap.

"Whatever you want," he'd said, afraid of ruining the moment, and he repeats it now to himself as he circles the pool, which is better than theirs in every way: the still surface reflects the window to the guest room where Cheryl keeps her own counsel, the adjoining hot tub mocks him with its effortless warmth. There's a gas barbecue, too. He twists the knobs and tests the starter before shutting off the valve and opening the hood. Drops of charred fat speckle the burners, but the grill sparkles silver, clean—of course. "Whatever you want."

The labored whine of the garage door opening calls him inside.

It can mean only one thing. In a moment, his idle curiosity about how his son's family lives evaporates. There's no need to wonder, he thinks as he scrambles across the deck and into the house, because he's about to find out.

Inside, he pauses at the landing long enough to call up to Cheryl. "They're home," he shouts, but he doesn't stop to wait for her. Rushing on he stumbles over a leather ottoman. Catching himself, he calls again: "Cheryl, Gertie and Stevie are here!" As he says it, he can't believe it. His voice shakes with anticipation and maybe even fear. Stevie is about to walk through the door. After three years, he's about to walk through that door, and all will be forgiven.

He zips past the dining room and through the laundry room. One and a half inches of beveled, stained oak is all that separates him from absolution. Tonight will go well. Tomorrow will be a breeze. Smiling, arms outstretched, he prepares to embrace his son, the past forgotten, and to greet his granddaughter. He's seconds away now; he can hear a key scratching at the deadbolt from the other side, a muffled curse accompanying it. Impatiently, he turns the lock himself before throwing open the door.

But instead of Stevie with Gertie in his arms, he finds Peter weighed down with groceries. Disappointment at not finding his son momentarily blinds him to Gertie's presence, but there she is, too. Little Gertie. Hurdy-Gertie. The girl he recognizes only from photographs. Her legs splay across Peter's midsection. Her straight black hair hangs down like streamers from his arm. She bears little resemblance to the girl in the photos, however. She's so much bigger for one thing, and asleep, it's hard to find the same animated features. The fact of her race remains absolutely clear, though. There's no mistaking that she's adopted, yet the closer Thaddeus looks the more he senses something vaguely familiar in her face, maybe somewhere around the hairline, and for a moment he entertains the notion that Stevie, Peter, and Cheryl have colluded in a lie about her adoption in hopes of keeping him away for these past three years, but it seems too outlandish even for Stevie, so he dismisses the thought and just like that it's gone entirely, as if he'd never even thought it.

22

They must've exchanged greetings because Thaddeus feels words form in his mouth. From the end of a long velvet tunnel all Thaddeus hears is a deafening din until Peter asks a question that pulls him back into synch with the world around him. "Can you hold her?" Bogged down with grocery sacks and with Gertie, he can hardly move. Thaddeus manages a nod and holds out his hands. To think that last night he was just some old man beside a pool, and now, less than twenty-four hours later, he's not only meeting his granddaughter but being given the opportunity to hold her. His eyes mist.

Peter slips her into his outstretched arms. "Say hi to your grandpa, baby." And that's as much ceremony as he puts into the exchange. Gertie continues to sleep uninterrupted.

"It's okay. Don't wake her," Thaddeus whispers. "She's probably had a big day."

"Careful. She's heavier than she looks."

"She ain't heavy. She's my brother."

Peter shoots him an odd look, which Thaddeus hardly notices.

"Just an old Hollies tune."

How many nights beside the pool have been spent imagining this first meeting, rehearsing scores of scenarios? He had so many reservations, so many fears. What if he wasn't cut out to be a grandpa? What if he dropped her? Would he even be able to love an adopted granddaughter? And now she slumbers in his arms, bigger than he could even imagine, a real person, but still tiny and vulnerable in every way. He could've saved himself the worry, he thinks. He's a natural.

"It's good to see you, Thaddeus." Peter leads the way to the kitchen. "It's been too long."

"Three years."

He stacks canned goods on the granite counter and slips a slab of something wrapped in pink butcher paper into the open refrigerator. For a while they don't say anything else.

"Anyway, water under the bridge," Thaddeus says at last. "You look different."

Peter folds the empty grocery sacks and places them into a drawer. He looks down at himself and grins. "I can't tell if that's a compliment."

In three years Peter's look has changed completely. The wild dark dreads he wore in the past have been replaced by his natural shade of russet blond, trimmed close to the scalp and revealing a rather severe widow's peak. In place of the grimy yellow glasses, which were always far too big for his small face, he's substituted a stylish pair of wire frames. The clothes mark the biggest change. Peter used to wear lots of things with safety pins and ironed-on badges, a style far too youthful for him even five years ago when he and Stevie first started seeing each other. Now his patterned, understated button-up neatly tucks into a pair of pressed tan slacks. No more black boots either. Those he replaced with soft leather boat shoes.

"A compliment," Thaddeus says. "You look good."

Peter smiles. "I guess I grew up, huh? Who would've thought?"

Gertie squirms. Whimpering, she pushes against Thaddeus's shoulder.

"Uh-oh, what's the matter, beautiful, don't you like your grandpa?"

"No, she loves her grandpa." But Peter scoops her out of his arms all the same. Cooing, he kisses her on the head and she calms down. "She's probably just having a bad dream. She gets them sometimes. Steven thinks she's reliving something from the orphanage, but I think it's just something she ate. It's okay, Gertie, Daddy's here. Shh."

"Will you look at that..."

A new serenity washes over him seeing Peter with Gertie. He's here now, in this house, with his family. A moment ago he held his granddaughter and later he'll get to hold her again, and then maybe in a week Peter, Stevie, and Gertie will be at his house and they'll all enjoy the pool together. Maybe they'll even visit Disney World together, as a family. Cheryl will be kinder to him now. They can finally put the past behind them. For the first time in three years Thaddeus can envision a happy future.

Then Gertie screams so loudly she startles him.

She transforms into a dynamo of sleeping rage. Her fists pound into Peter's shoulder and her feet slam into his hip. She wails. Thaddeus scrambles toward her. "What's wrong?"

"It's just a dream." Calmly, Peter rocks her. "It'll pass. We just have to stay calm."

The staircase rattles in the adjacent room as Cheryl comes rushing down. "Wait!" she shouts. "It's okay. I'm here. I'm coming!"

Her cries further agitate Gertie, who redoubles her tantrum, but Peter is able to wake her and as soon as he does she stops screaming. Her eyes immediately rest on Thaddeus, and at first she seems startled by this stranger and her mood threatens to spill over into anger again, but Peter kisses her cheek and tells her it's okay. "Say hi to your grandpa, sweetie."

Thaddeus playfully sticks out his tongue and makes a trumpet of his thumb pressed to the tip of his nose. Though she remains suspicious, she lets slip a hesitant grin that soon blossoms into a gregarious smile.

"Ha!" His granddaughter just smiled at him for the first time!

Cheryl charges into the kitchen, a stricken look on her face, but she stops short when she sees them all huddled by the breakfast bar. "Peter?" She grabs her chest and exhales. "What a relief. When I heard screaming I thought it was Steven—" She crosses Thaddeus with a withering gaze. "I thought something happened."

"We're fine," Thaddeus says.

"Just a bad dream, is all," Peter adds.

Gertie sucks her thumb, her gaze shifting back and forth between Thaddeus and Cheryl, a stranger and a friend. She's done crying, for the moment at least, and Thaddeus decides it's a good sign.

"What a relief," Cheryl says. Turning to Gertie, she pouts and slips into baby talk. "Your grandma just got worked up over nothing."

Gertie squirms, wanting out of her father's arms. He sets her on the floor, then takes a seat at the breakfast bar. "It's okay. We're used to drama around here."

"Nothing to worry about," Thaddeus reiterates. "We're all fine." Then to Cheryl, he says, "Stevie isn't here yet."

"Wait," Peter says. "What do you mean Steven isn't here?"

HOW MANY MEALS WILL A CAN OF BLACK BEANS YIELD, realistically? Can two people subsist on sardines, peanuts, and sofrito bouillon for a week without killing each other? What if those people are siblings—does that make it better or worse? Laila shakes her head at the impoverished state of her pantry. "And what if one of those siblings is a selfish food hog?" she says, sifting through empty cartons of food that Alex couldn't be bothered to throw away.

It's bare bones. The Pop-Tarts she bought on Monday are gone ("What? I like having a midnight snack, yo!"), so are the tortilla chips ("I get hungry watching TV!"). A lonely pack of instant miso soup and a half brick of rice round out the supplies. Anything that requires cooking is safe from Alex's ravenous maw. And it's a good thing, too. The chicken legs and thighs in the freezer will go into the pressure cooker tonight along with a few frozen veggies. That way, at least, they'll have one good meal before the storm knocks out the power and they have to eat like refugees.

Hurricane Natalie picked up speed overnight and the television playing in the background updates the storm's progress every fifteen minutes. The eye is now expected to pass over Orlando sometime around midnight. Residents are advised to stock up on provisions and remain indoors. "Duh," she says. If Alex were here he'd have something snarky to add. Could it be possible that she misses his presence around the house? The news cuts to a shot of the shore at Cocoa Beach. Tourists in clamdiggers wander through the frame. A despondent would-be surfer paddles out into the placid water. A typical day in paradise. "It's calm now," the meteorologist on the scene reports, calibrating the cadence of his delivery to trace the fuzzy boundary between intimating a need for panic while dispelling the same. "But later this evening we expect seas of—"

Laila switches the television off and tosses the remote onto the couch. Another moment and they'd be cutting to stock footage of a swell cresting over the breakwater while some idiot fisherman in a slicker casts a line into the surf.

"I'll deal with you in a minute," she says, shutting the pantry.

She rinses the coffeepot and washes her mug, then dries her hands and heads upstairs.

Pulling back the blackout curtains in her room allows the late-morning sun to fill the space like a vessel, illuminating, in the process, her secret shame. Alex embraces his messiness, but with her it's a furtive endeavor. Clothes drape over an antique armchair in the corner. Dirty coffee mugs colonize the nightstand. Grooves in the carpet delineate a collection of favorite paths around the room, an atlas of forgotten vacuuming and too few shampoos. Her simple dresser is a layered moraine of accumulated living. Purchased (for a lot more than she cares to admit) specifically because its clean lines evoked an aspiration toward orderliness; instead, the dresser's plain surface has become an archaeological wealth of jewelry, bills, magazines, and makeup. This is the real reason Alex is banned from her bedroom. She doesn't want to confront the hypocrisy.

She grabs a pair of clean panties from the pile on the chair, depositing in their place the yoga pants she slept in, and slips them on. Her jeans, freshly laundered and neatly folded two days earlier, peek out from beneath a sweater she optimistically considered wearing on a recent chilly morning. Her favorite tops lie somewhere in the pile, too, though no doubt impossibly wrinkled. Rather than sort it out she pulls a fresh blouse from the closet, not a favorite but serviceable in a pinch.

A quick pass with the hairbrush and a splash of facial toner, then she's back in the kitchen to survey the pantry again—this time with a pencil in hand.

Determining what provisions to buy is surprisingly tricky.

Ideally, hurricane supplies consist of food one typically eats, staples that won't collect dust on the shelf between now and the next storm. But how much tuna will they realistically consume? How many lentils before she's sick to death of soup? And who's to say how long she needs to plan for? The power could be out for a few hours or several weeks, or not at all.

She drops the pad in her purse, then heads for the truck.

Lines at the store are long and the shelves picked over, but an encyclopedic knowledge of the aisles and aggressive shopping cart skills give her an edge. She scrounges together just about everything on her list and is back in the parking lot in record time. She rewards herself with a tall Americano and a trip downtown. After fighting the masses for canned foods, bottled water, batteries, and butane, she's in need of some frivolous sophistication in the form of a visit to an art gallery. It's the kind of thing a cosmopolitan single gal might do with a girlfriend if she didn't have to work twelve-hour shifts six days a week, all while babysitting a teenager. She should text the girls, her locas. When was the last time they all met up for lunch or a drink? Ha pasado—*way* too much time.

She parks the truck in a garage and filters into the pedestrian wave fattening the sidewalks. Office workers return from late lunches and delivery vans idle on curbs. Birdsong competes with the Doppler howl of a passing motorcycle. Somewhere cars honk and fungal fingernails panhandle. Grease and discarded vegetables ripen to a cloying bouquet in alleyways behind restaurants. A tension lifts from her shoulders and a slink slips into her step. She opens the door to the gallery and is greeted by a chime.

A small sculpture, no larger than a paperback, sits on a simple podium in the center of the space.

It intrigues her.

From a distance the sculpture's convex surface appears smooth, but closer inspection reveals a landscape of intricately carved glyphs. Written and rewritten in an unfamiliar language, the carvings are a kind of palimpsest, impossible to decipher. What's more, the distinction between sculpture and podium is illusory. Both are part of the same stone.

She catches the attention of a gallerist poised behind a desk. "Are these real words?"

The gallerist walks over and assesses the sculpture with her for a moment before responding. "Some are, like this bit in Sanskrit. Some are gibberish"—he indicates a series of symbols on the far slope of a bulge—"others are borrowed from invented languages found in literature—Elvish and Klingon. That kind of thing." He slips her a smile. "Let me get you a catalog."

While he's away, she circles the sculpture, examining it from various angles. "It's beautiful. I've never seen anything like it. Are those paintings by the same artist?"

"Mm-hmm. The whole gallery. Everything you see. She's local, but I'm sure we'll lose her to New York soon."

He presses something the size of a European fashion magazine into her hand. Presumably, this is the catalog. She gives it a cursory glance, then tucks it under her arm and takes a phantom sip from her long gone Americano.

"It's really stunning."

"Take a look around." He holds out a hand for the empty cup. "I'll bring you a fresh one. Regular or decaf?"

She smiles. "Regular. Cream. No sugar. Thank you."

He disappears into a back room, returning a moment later with a mug of steaming coffee. It smells delicious and she hazards a sip, burning her tongue.

"Careful, it's still hot. I'm Peter, by the way, the owner."

They shake hands. "Laila."

"Nice to meet you, Laila. Do you live in the area?" As they chit-chat, they drift toward a triptych on the far wall.

"I do, yeah. I'm never home, though. I work too much."

"What line of work?"

The triptych hangs together haphazardly, but each individual canvas is subdivided into orderly diamond grids. The same glyphs that skin the sculpture appear here scaled down. The work is exquisitely detailed. "I'm a pharmacist. Is this painted?"

"Partially. A randomizing algorithm generated it. All the symbols are fed into a database, then the algorithm flows everything into a template. The results are then printed onto canvases prepared with different washes." He indicates the variations in each of the paintings. "These three are my favorite in the whole show."

"They're the same markings from the sculpture."

"That's right."

"They're beautiful."

"I think so, too. There's something so current about it, but also classic."

She compares the texture of the canvas to the flatness of the ink, trying to recall some trivia from her art history class in college, but nothing comes to mind. She shakes her head. "I could never be an artist. I'm not that creative."

"Then tell me about being a pharmacist," Peter says. "Was it something you always knew you wanted to be?"

She laughs. "God, no! My father was in fashion and everybody figured I'd go that route, but it didn't appeal to me. When I got to college I realized I had a knack for chemistry, so I went into pharmacology. People think pharmacists are just glorified retail clerks, but there's more to it than that. There's a whole side of it that's about compassion and pain management. That's what I like about it most. I like working with people."

"That's very interesting." He tucks a hand into his pocket and seems to study her as if she were part of the show, another of the artist's intricate creations. "How's the coffee? Did I get it right?"

"It's perfect. Thanks." She takes a sip and this time she doesn't burn herself. "What about you? What made you want to open a gallery?"

"Oh, that's a boring story. I got into it by accident. I'm really a reporter, but I know a little bit about art so here we are. We'll see how long it lasts."

"Wow, and I thought I worked too hard. Reporter and gallery owner—that's ambitious!"

He shrugs. "It's not as hard as it sounds. They're both really just about talking to people. I manage to get home at a decent hour," he adds with a grin. "I wouldn't do it otherwise."

She finds herself on the verge of confessing that between work and life, she always chooses the pharmacy. But her stepmother's voice is in the back of her head. *You don't know this man. Don't be telling him your business.* As much as she hates to admit it, Esther is right. Confiding in strange men—that's how you get yourself into trouble. She should tell Alex that. Just because he's a guy doesn't mean he doesn't have to watch out around men.

She lowers her eyes to the coffee and says, "That's admirable."

Just then her phone rings; its synthetic chirping shatters the calm of the gallery and startles her. Apologizing, she scrambles to fish it out of her purse. It's probably Alex calling her back. If she misses his call, God only knows when she'll be able to get a hold of him again.

But it's not Alex calling. It's Bill, the pharmacy's regional manager. "Shit. I should—"

"Absolutely." Peter raises his hands and retreats.

She waits for him to return to the desk before taking the call.

"Hey, Laila," Bill says. "Got a minute?" The incessantly cheerful cadence of an ad for store-brand pain reliever playing in the background quickens her pulse. Whether out of fear or excitement, or a mix of the two, remains unclear.

"What's up?"

"I know you just went through inventory last night, but—"

He doesn't even need to finish the sentence. "Which store?" she asks.

"Sanjay's in Apopka," he says, the words rushing out in a sigh of relief. He won't even have to ask; she's volunteering.

"Apopka?"

"Sorry, I know it's not ideal, but his wife is on call and they don't have anybody at home with the kids because of the hurricane. I'd ask somebody else, but I need somebody that can jump right in and you're the best."

She sighs into the phone. Like always, she'll agree. She hates how quickly she relents, but it also fills her with pride that the district manager thinks of her when he's in a pinch. What is it with this pathological need to please? Is it daddy issues? Something else to discuss over drinks with the girls. At some point.

"It's going to take me a while. I'm out." *Living my life,* she wants to add, but she doesn't.

"That's fine. He's at the store now and can stick around until you get there."

"All right, fine, but you're going to owe me."

"You're a rock star! How long till you can get there?"

She checks her watch and calculates the drive time. "Give me an hour."

"We can work with that. Thank you."

She drops the phone into her purse and snorts.

Peter circles back hesitantly. "Is everything okay?"

"I don't know if you have kids or not, but if you're on the fence you should do it. Apparently, they're a get-out-of-jail-free card."

He folds his arms and grins. "I hope that's not the only reason to have them."

"Sometimes I wonder." She runs her hand through her hair and considers the show catalog. "You know what? I really like that sculpture, so I'll make you a deal. I have to run right now, but if it's still here on my next day off, I'll buy it."

"All right, it's a deal." They shake on it. "It was really nice meeting you, Laila. Stay safe out there today."

"You, too."

"YOUR PARENTS HAVE BEEN WAITING FOR YOU ALL DAY,"
Peter says as Steven walks through the door.

Like Peter, Steven seems to have emerged from the last three years as if from a chrysalis, newly formed. Gone are the T-shirts, basketball shorts, and flip-flops he preferred in his bachelorhood. In their place, he wears a dark blue polo shirt, tan work pants, and a heavy pair of boots. He's taller and more compact than Thaddeus remembers. Stronger, too. When he lifts his arm to adjust the lay of a backpack across his broad shoulder, his biceps stretches the cuff of his shirtsleeve.

Steven shrugs. "There were a lot of new intakes."

Cheryl swarms the foyer and engulfs him in a hug. Even from his spot on the couch in the family room, Thaddeus can see that the boy is anxious to escape. "Stevie," he calls, but his words are lost in the din of Cheryl's effusive greeting.

"We held dinner," Peter says.

"You didn't need to."

"We were fine. We can take care of ourselves," Cheryl says, brushing back Steven's hair. That, too, is different. When they last saw each other, his hair was buzzed close to the scalp, but now loose curls cascade off his head like kudzu. Once upon a time, Thaddeus thinks, patting his own shiny scalp.

Gertie sits cross-legged on the floor playing with her blocks. She ignores Steven when he bends down to kiss the top of her head.

"She's still awake, I see."

Peter blows out his cheeks. "I tried."

With a sense of resignation Steven ambles toward the family room, his weighted steps a mere shuffle across the polished wood.

This man is not just his son, Thaddeus thinks. He is an adult with a family and obligations. Thaddeus sympathizes with his exhaustion. After all, not that long ago he, too, worked long hours and wouldn't return to the house until late. The particulars of all those demanding years are gone, but he remembers the weariness. In many ways he feels it still. He wants to embrace his son and tell him that it's always difficult at the beginning, but first he has to get up from the couch.

"Don't worry about Gertie," Cheryl says, flitting around Steven like a hummingbird. "She had a long nap. She'll sleep later." A worried frown colors her expression. "How are you? Peter said they called you in today because there was a problem with one of the kids—"

"Yes," Peter says, "we were all surprised when you weren't home earlier. Must've been some problem."

Cheryl ignores the interruption and presses on. "Is everything all right?"

"He's fine," Thaddeus says. Whirling his arms, he catapults his groaning body to its feet. His movements are quick if not graceful. "Stevie," he says, his voice strained from the effort, "have a seat. I was just getting up." A joint pops, and his knees feel unsteady. It's okay. No big deal. "I was keeping it warm." Just like always the fight will be ignored. No one even remembers the details. It was about nothing.

Steven lingers near his mother as they make their way into the family room.

"I don't want you getting mixed up in other people's problems," she says. "You have a family to consider."

Her relentless attention annoys Thaddeus. The enthusiasm she ladles on the boy stirs up an uncomfortable mix of jealousy and empathy. Can't she see that Stevie just needs some space, a small reprieve before diving into a night at home with the family?

"Stevie." He stretches his hand past Cheryl's head. "Give him some room, woman."

But she bats him away with a grunt. "I'm worried about him," she says.

"The boy just got home. Let him relax."

Steven blinks, and Thaddeus takes it for a sign, a call for help. Emboldened, he retraces his steps and pats the couch cushion invitingly. "Here, Stevie, have a seat."

"I just want to know if everything is all right. What's wrong with that?"

"I don't want to get into it," Steven says. His face is gaunt and hollow around the eyes. His clothes smell of industrial-grade disinfectant.

"Can't you see he's exhausted?" Thaddeus says. "Let him sit down. Here, I kept it warm for you."

Cheryl smoothes Steven's shirt, but he slides away from her touch. "There's always a problem, Mom; they're the definition of a problem population. They're homeless youth."

"I know that, but I still worry. I'm your mother. It's my job to worry." She kisses him, and he frowns.

"We all worry," Peter says. He's been mostly silent since Steven came home, but now he calls Steven's attention to Gertie. "Your father brought Gertie a doll."

"Oh?"

On the floor, Gertie sits Talkin' Tina among her blocks. Thaddeus chose the doll specifically because it came with four different outfits, ranging from "dinner date" to "lounging by the pool," and half a dozen accessories to match. He didn't know what Gertie would like, but there had to be something in there that she'd be drawn to. And if she didn't like the outfits, she could talk to the doll. It can say thirteen phrases, among them: "I'm boy-crazy!" and "Shopping is fun!"

Boasting about the doll, Thaddeus says, "I told them only the best would do for my granddaughter."

For the first time in three years, Steven makes eye contact with his father. The look is brief and cold, but not unkind. His thin lips stretch like putty into a rehearsed smile. "A doll?" he asks.

"Yes!" Thaddeus bowls his way into the fold, displacing Cheryl. "The most expensive one they had."

Everything else fades away. He and Stevie are finally face-to-face.

So much about his son has changed in the last three years—and, anyway, he always took after his mother—but Thaddeus recognizes one familiar trait at last, and it's one they have in common: the bend in the left ear. The Bloom lobe has always dragged against his son's neck, as it has his own. Though partially obscured now under Stevie's dense curtain of hair, the genetic heritage endures, and it gives Thaddeus hope that some elemental connection with his son remains intact. And if they have that, he thinks, there's no reason they can't have it all back—rebuild the relationship they used to have. Be a real family again.

The moment passes.

Steven breaks eye contact, and flicking his wrist at the doll, he says, "She already has a bunch of toys."

"We're family," Thaddeus says, craning for his son's gaze. "Don't worry about the money. It's nothing. My pleasure."

"Still," Steven insists, flashing a mercurial smile, "Peter and I, we don't like to encourage materialism."

"One gift in three years, Stevie—"

"Thaddeus." Cheryl lays a hand on his forearm, and her touch immediately calms him.

He raises his hands in surrender. "Hey, okay. I get it. My mistake. Cool as a cucumber. We'll take it back to the store tomorrow. Your mother still has the receipt. We can get her something else. Whatever you like."

Cheryl smiles. "Your father's had a long day."

"Nothing personal," Steven says, looking at Thaddeus. There's a cordial reciprocity in his eyes that falls far short of intimacy.

Peter crosses his arms. "Oh, it's fine, Thaddeus. One more toy won't matter. And Gertie seems to like it." At the moment, Gertie has Talkin' Tina stripped down to a pair of tan slacks worn backward, a tiara perched on her head. "Right, Steven?"

Steven worries his lip. He shrugs the backpack from his shoulder and places it in the corner. "You're right. No big deal." He extends a hand. "I'm sure the doll is lovely."

"Oh," Thaddeus says, surprised at getting a handshake so soon. "You're welcome."

Returning the gesture overcomes him. Stevie possesses a firm handshake. He'd forgotten that. There's so much about him that he's forgotten, but it's all coming back now in fits and starts. Steven further surprises him by reaching in for a kiss on the cheek.

"It's good to see you, Pop."

Cheryl gasps. "Oh my..."

With a smile burning his face, Thaddeus firmly grasps his son's upper arm, feeling the muscles tense under his grip. His eyes mist. Tomorrow will be a breeze. "Come here," he says. Voice faltering, he drags Steven into his chest. He still has a couple of inches on his son. It's the first time they've touched in more than three years and he doesn't want to ever let go, except that at a certain point he feels Stevie squirm, so he relents and pulls back.

Thaddeus grins, playfully wags a finger. "Now don't go getting any ideas. I know how you guys are."

"Thaddeus!"

"It's just a joke. He understands." He claps Steven on the back. "Just a joke, Stevie. You understand. We can joke because we're family."

"For better or worse."

"Steven!" Peter says.

"Just a joke," Steven says, then he cracks his knuckles.

Cheryl shuttles trays of hors d'oeuvres between the kitchen and the family room while Peter plays horsey with Gertie on the floor. Words volley, some loud, some soft, all too rapidly for Thaddeus to keep up, so he sits back with a cracker and a smear of Brie, grinning blankly at everyone. Before leaving the house this morning, he stashed an emergency cache of weed in the car just in case things with Stevie went south. Part of him wants to sneak out to the driveway now to light up—not because things have gone poorly, but in celebration. Miracles happen! After three years he's in the same room as Stevie and Gertie, and they're all getting along. It feels like a dream because he's dreamed it so many times. He pictured the house differently—maybe a bit smaller, humbler—and the neighborhood exceeds anything he ever imagined, but they're doing well, and it appears safe for Gertie, and that's the important thing.

He reaches for the crudités at the same time as Stevie, and when their fingers brush Stevie acknowledges it with a pleasant nod. He serves himself a cracker and a handful of grapes. They both lean back into their seats, and Thaddeus grins. At last, he thinks, like two friends.

"They'll be done with the house by next week," he says while chewing.

Steven flexes his hand, bending the fingers in unison at the second knuckle. "That's quick."

"Maybe we can swing by there tomorrow—you and me—and make sure everything's kosher. Keep those guys on their toes."

"Maybe."

"No pressure. Think it over and let me know. Whatever you want to do."

This newfound intimacy feels fragile and Thaddeus doesn't want to rush things. They have all sorts of time. Besides, father-son conversations are supposed to be casual, aren't they? Nothing set in stone.

Cheryl adds a plate of hummus to the spread. "What are you two talking about?"

"Just some guy talk," he says.

She rolls her eyes but he can tell that she's pleased. "Don't ruin your appetite," she warns, on her way back to the kitchen.

From the floor, Peter asks if Cheryl needs any help. Gertie pokes him until he neighs, and when he does she laughs and pokes him again. Each time he complies her laughter increases. She claps louder.

Thaddeus grins. "Women, huh?"

"She should be in bed," Steven says.

"It's no problem, really," Peter is insisting to Cheryl. "Steven and I cook every night."

Cheryl shakes her head. "So do I." She runs her hands under the tap and pats them dry on a towel. "This is my way of saying thank you—for both of us."

Thaddeus raises a nibbled cracker and winks. Crumbs rain down his shirt.

"You don't need to thank us," Peter says. "You guys are always welcome here."

"*Su casa es mi casa,*" Thaddeus says, chuckling to himself as he closes his eyes.

All around him are the happy murmurs of a family: the splash of water in the sink, the laughter of his granddaughter, the rasp of slacks rubbing against couch cushions, and the porcelain *ting* of a platter as Stevie reaches for another hor d'oeuvre. The floors creak. They swish with the sound of bare feet against the wood. He opens his eyes to find Gertie propping Talkin' Tina against the coffee table and issuing orders in a cyclone of gibberish. Blond locks tangled, her dress rumpled, the doll responds, "Math is fun!" or "The beach is hot!" (the exact line dilutes in the running stream that is his memory). Gertie topples her with a smack. Then she laughs and looks at Thaddeus with a wicked little grin.

"I should've never let her sleep so late this afternoon," Peter says, dropping onto the couch beside Steven. He pinches the bridge of his nose and winces. "We'll never get her down tonight, and this headache won't quit."

"She'll calm down after dinner," Steven says. He selects a grape from the tray, but then places it back. Standing, he turns toward Thaddeus. "Let me show you the yard."

Peter massages his temples. "Your father's already seen it. They were home alone all day."

"I had to work," Steven says. "I don't know how else to say it."

Peter raises a hand. "All right, I know."

Steven remains standing for a moment, blinking rapidly. He bites his nails. Finally, he nods and sits back down. He nervously cracks his knuckles. "So you gave yourself the tour?"

"You have a lovely house," Thaddeus says. "Must be costing you boys a fortune. The real estate business booming?"

"Thaddeus," Cheryl says. "That's private."

"We do all right," Steven says, his face breaking into a puerile grin. "In fact, Peter just opened a new gallery downtown. They're selling out shows."

"I'm just helping a friend," Peter explains. "And there's a tax abatement."

"Oh," Thaddeus says. "Nobody told me."

Cheryl sighs. "Yes. I did."

Steven looms over his spread knees, slowly stretching his fingers against his palm. "The gallery premiered a young video artist this summer—"

"She was a sculptor," Peter corrects, "and a painter, not a video artist."

"I'm sure you've never heard of her," Steven continues. "Two days later she received an offer for a solo show in Brooklyn." He flicks his tongue against his teeth and winks. The naked swagger of it dislodges something unpleasant inside Thaddeus.

"It wasn't two days later."

It's as if a mask slipped to reveal something greedy and decayed. Just as quickly whatever Thaddeus glimpsed retreats, and Stevie appears perfectly amiable. But the uneasiness lingers. What if all of this is a waste, if it's just a game Stevie is playing with him, and in the end there'll be no reunion, no Gertie, and no family by the pool?

It happens again.

He hears Cheryl give her congratulations about the gallery and watches Peter demur, but its Steven's unwavering gaze that holds his attention. He's seen that same lupine eagerness before and it always precedes a fight. Only this time nothing in Steven's expression betrays anger. The look merely suggests a cold statement of fact. *You're nothing,* it seems to say. Thaddeus grows hot with the desire to shout down his son's smugness. So what if he hasn't been perfect? He's sacrificed for this family, for Stevie. As he has countless times over the past three years, Thaddeus asks himself just how much longer must he suffer for something he hardly remembers.

He opens his mouth—prepared to shout—but he holds back at the last minute. Instead, he clears his throat and congratulates Peter on his success. Steven arches an eyebrow. He seems disappointed.

"I guess you boys have done pretty well for yourselves," Thaddeus continues.

He just has to get past tonight. If he can do that then everything will be smooth sailing.

For a long time he and Steven stare at each other in silence while Cheryl and Peter carry on. Even as he leans back into the couch, Steven's gaze doesn't waver.

"Thanks, Pop," he says at last. "It is wonderful."

Cheryl returns to the family room and, leaning over, she kisses Steven on the head. "I'm so proud of you."

Gertie wails and smacks Talkin' Tina. Gritting her teeth and furrowing her brow, she marches toward Thaddeus, dragging the doll by its blond tresses, nearly losing her balance in the process.

"Poop," she says, pointing at the doll.

"That's her new favorite word," Peter explains.

"Talk about a *potty* mouth," Thaddeus says.

Stevie sighs. "That's a very ugly word, Gertrude."

"Poop!" This time she follows it with a smile.

"Do you want a time out?"

Knitting her brow again, she glances between the doll and her father, considering her options. Finally, she crosses her arms and plops down onto the floor in a resigned huff.

"She's got a temper," Thaddeus says. "Must take after our side of the family."

Steven smirks. "You have to be firm, but reasonable."

"Your mother was in charge of that." He pauses and flits his eyes at Cheryl, giving her the mischievous eyebrow. "She was the disciplinarian. In fact, she still keeps me firm, if you know what I mean."

Steven winces. "Gross."

"Hey, man, that's just nature."

"Doesn't mean I want to hear about it."

Gertie screams and tugs on Thaddeus's pant leg to get his attention.

"Gertie, please," Peter says. "Daddy has a headache."

"All right. No big deal." Thaddeus turns to Gertie, cooing, "What's the problem, sweetie?" He leans over to grab her, but she's skittish and retreats behind the coffee table, clutching her doll. "You don't quite trust your old grandpa yet, do you, beautiful?"

"She's developed some stranger anxiety in day care," Peter explains.

Cheryl walks over to Gertie and picks her up without any problems. "You don't need day care, do you, princess?" She tickles Gertie's tummy and Gertie erupts in laughter. "You just tell your daddies to leave you with Grandma when they have to work. Would you like that?"

"She could go swimming," Thaddeus adds. "It's just a matter of turning on the heater, then she can swim even in the middle of winter. We have plenty of towels, too. No problem."

Steven selects a cracker from the tray. "One of the kids at the shelter watched his mother drown when he was seven." He snaps the cracker in half and eats it in two quick bites.

Peter groans. "Steven, please, not tonight. I can't handle another one of those depressing stories." He curls into himself on the couch and unbuttons his collar. "Let's talk about something pleasant. Thaddeus, what do you think of the neighborhood?"

"Very impr—"

"And then last year," Steven interrupts, "his father was run over by a car." There's a cruel sort of excitement nipping at the edges of his words. "You wonder how a thing like that manifests itself when they're older."

"Maybe he'll end up like that serial killer," Peter says, shooting Steven a look.

Cheryl snaps to attention. "What serial killer?"

"It's nothing you have to worry about," Steven says without taking his eyes off Peter.

"He targets the gay clubs," Peter says. "It's been in the paper."

"Well, do the police have any leads? They must have something. Don't these people always leave a calling card or something?"

Peter shrugs. "It's complicated. Apparently."

"It's not even clear that the deaths are linked," Steven says.

"I don't want to hear this." She hands Gertie to Thaddeus and returns to the kitchen. "I'll never understand that kind of thing. My question is always: Where were the parents? You don't just turn out that way."

Thaddeus balances Gertie on his knees while playfully sticking his tongue out at her. He bends a thousand funny faces, and though initially reluctant to encourage his tomfoolery, she eventually claps. After that, each new face causes her to shake more and more with excitement.

"Ha!" Thaddeus says. "Will you look at that, Stevie? I think she's warmed up to me."

Steven glances at him and rolls his eyes. "I'm sure the killer has his reasons."

"For God's sake, Steven," Peter says. "You don't have to defend everyone."

"But it's true," Steven says. "What, you think it's accidental? You think a serial killer isn't trying to make a statement of some kind? I mean, if it even is a serial killer."

"Well, I don't think about it," Cheryl says, grabbing dinner plates from the cabinets.

"And you think that's a healthy approach?"

"How many of those kids of yours go to the clubs anyway?"

Steven laughs. "You think it's one of them? Maybe it should be."

"This is so morbid," Peter says, rubbing his eyes. "And not what I need with a pounding headache. Let's talk about something else. Does anybody want a drink? I think we have some gin."

"I think these kids get totally ignored," Steven says. "Gay people in general."

"Here we go," Peter says, walking to the bar. "Saint Steven and his righteous indignation."

"I always pay attention to lesbians," Thaddeus says, but everyone ignores him.

"Oh, Steven," Cheryl says. "You're being extreme."

"Maybe. But do you know all the hoops we had to jump through just to adopt Gertie? Maybe this killer has the right idea. Kill off enough gay people and society starts paying attention." He pops a grape into his mouth. "After all, if it weren't for the Holocaust there'd be no Israel, right? Or just look at Baltimore, or even here in Florida. People are starting to pay attention to the race problem we have in this country precisely because of public violence. It's unfortunate but it's true."

"Anybody else for a g and t?" Peter asks.

"Right, that's the solution. Just get drunk instead of engaging in a dialogue."

"First of all, I'm not getting drunk. I'm having a drink. There's a difference. But maybe you're conflating the two things just like you're conflating the actions of some psychopath with a legacy of institutionalized racism."

"I'm not conflating anything. I'm merely offering an interpretation—"

"You're ignoring everything we've accomplished! Your mother's right. You're just being difficult."

Steven shrugs. "You can call it difficult if you want, but people respond to bold actions."

Peter rolls his eyes. "So now he's a hero."

"I didn't say that."

"No, but that's what you're implying."

Steven waves away the comment.

"Nobody's a hero," Cheryl says with finality. "Now, come on— everybody to the dining room. Dinner's almost ready."

LAILA PUSHES THROUGH THE FRONT DOOR WITH THREE gallons of water in each hand, the static weight paining her joints. "Alex, you home?" she calls. "Come help me get this stuff in the house. I got called into work. Alex?"

The same silence from this morning permeates the house. There's no sign that Alex has been back. Son of a bitch, she thinks. She's going to have to call Esther.

She sets the gallons down on the kitchen floor and pushes them into the pantry with her feet, then heads back to the truck for the rest of the supplies. Three trips later the Morales household is prepared for whatever Mother Nature has in store for them tonight. Laila, however, feels depleted. All she wants is to collapse on the couch and take a quick nap, but with traffic bad returning from the gallery, now she's running late. Sanjay expects her soon and she still needs to change and drive to Apopka. Drawing on her reserves, she wills herself upstairs to hunt for her work clothes, sequestered somewhere in the escalating entropy that is her bedroom. As she changes, she calls Esther.

Her stepmother greets her with a yawn. "Oh, Laila, I'm surprised to hear from you."

"Were you sleeping?"

"Jorge"—the gardener— "came by earlier. He says he needs to rip out the tree your father planted. Que tiene un bicho o algo, I don't know. Now the county is saying they all have to go."

Her lab coat cuts through the pile of laundry like a vein of marble in a mountain. She pulls it out, dumping half the clothes onto the carpet in the process. With no time to iron, she'll have to rely on the heat and humidity to relax the worst of the wrinkles.

"I'm sorry. That must've been difficult to hear. Did you take anything?"

"Lo que me mandó Dinenberg."

"The Klonopin? Are you taking anything else with it?"

She tears apart her bed hunting for her name badge before finding it clipped to the medicine cabinet mirror. The engraved lettering is chipped from years of banging around in purses and pockets, the color faded. She affixes it to her lab coat.

"Ay, Laila, stop worrying about me. I just needed something to help me relax; it's been a stressful day. You should be worrying about your brother."

"That's actually why I'm calling. Have you heard from him?"

"¡¿Que paso?!"

"Nothing. I just haven't seen him all day. He went out this morning, said he had to meet somebody."

"Where did you say he is?"

"I don't know," Laila says, struggling to keep her response measured. "I told you he said he was meeting up with somebody. He didn't call you or anything?"

"Why would he call me?" Esther coughs, then clears her throat.

"I don't know. Stranger things have happened."

"Do you think he could be in trouble?"

There's an edge to Esther's voice. Mostly she's fretting over her wayward son's whereabouts, but buried alongside that panic Laila detects a subtle judgment. *He's your responsibility now*, she's saying. That subtly puts her in the uncomfortable position of having to defend her brother, who, frankly, she's more than a little annoyed with at present. How does Alex always manage to do this to her? To them?

"I'm sure he's fine—"

"¡Ay, pero el huracán!"

"Yeah, I know. So does he. Calm down—" *Take another Klonopin* is what she wants to say, but she restrains herself. "He's probably just dicking around somewhere. He'll be back. I only called because I got to go to work and don't have time to put up the shutters."

"Work today? With the storm?"

"I got called in. I'm covering for somebody."

"But you have your own things to take care of, too; when are you supposed to have a day off if they keep calling you in like that? I always told your father that I didn't like these hours for you—"

"It's fine. Really. Don't worry about it."

"I'm not worried about you."

"Gee, thanks." She kicks off her boots and jams her feet into a worn pair of sneakers.

Esther clicks her tongue. "You know what I mean. You take care of yourself. Your brother, on the other hand, would lose his head if it wasn't screwed on—"

"He's your baby," Laila says, mimicking the whiny inflection with which her stepmother has justified every deferral to Alex's selfishness for the better part of two decades.

"Exactly."

"He's a seventeen-year-old pain in the ass is what he is."

"He's still my baby. And don't talk about your brother that way."

"Uh-huh. Well, your baby is over here eating all my food and not paying rent. The least he could do is help with the shutters. He knows I don't like to climb ladders."

"Ay, mi'ja, por favor. I'll send you money for his food."

"That's not the—" Laila cuts herself off. Now is not the time. Not when she's already running late. "Look, if he calls you or anything just let him know that I'm working up in Apopka and that I need him to take care of the shutters. Okay? I texted him, but I don't know, maybe his phone died or something. And tell him to call me back! Bye!"

"Wait!"

"What? I have to go."

"Be safe. And call me when you're home. I don't like you going to work on a day like this."

"Okay, I will. Go back to sleep, and try not to take anything else today."

Traffic is surprisingly light on I-4, but she hits a snarl less than a mile away from the shopping plaza in Apopka. The store taunts her from just beyond a red stoplight. There's nothing to do but wait it out, slowly creeping forward with each cycle of the traffic signal. She glances at her phone. Still no word from Alex. Coño, Alex, she thinks, you better not fuck this up. Though she's not one to normally honk, she does so now. "Come on! Move it."

Her phone chimes.

On your way? Sanjay is waiting.

In traffic a block away, she fires back, then tosses the phone onto the passenger seat.

An accident that isn't even on her side of the street backs traffic up in either direction. As if people don't have enough problems in their lives that they need to rubberneck on somebody else's tragedy. When her turn at the light finally arrives, she guns it through the intersection, doing her part to break the cycle.

The store has been picked over. Bottled water and canned goods are conspicuously absent from shelves. (She was right to do her shopping when she did.) The seasonal aisle looks ragged with nobody having had time to tidy up in the onslaught of last-minute shoppers. Her domain—the pharmacy—fares only slightly better. Sanjay is short-staffed and prescriptions are piling up.

"One of the techs called in," he says, dashing between shelves. The remaining tech, Cecily, does her best to ring up a long line of customers at the register. "It's been like this all day," he continues. "I haven't even had time to fill prescriptions. Cecily hasn't even taken her break. And then Rajani has to be on call and there's nobody at home to watch the kids."

She places her purse under the counter, cracks her neck, takes a deep breath, and smiles. "Okay, what do you need?"

She finds her rhythm in short order once Sanjay departs. The flow of new prescriptions abates long enough for her to knock out some of the most urgent scripts waiting in the queue. Ordinarily, she wouldn't be the one counting out the pills. A tech would do that, leaving the pharmacist to verify the fill, but with one tech down and the other chained to the register, the duty devolves to her. She's quick, but she's also scrupulous, since the potential for mistakes is high when taking over in the middle of somebody else's day. She refuses to rush even as returning patients stream in, anxious to pick up their pills before the storm arrives. Landfall is now expected for ten P.M.

"They'll have to close the store early," Cecily says.

Laila glances at the time on her phone. It's going to be a tight turnaround and still no word from Alex. "I hope so. I still have to put up my shutters."

They work steadily for the next couple of hours. The crush of patients wanes. A stack of unfilled scripts still needs filling, but the immediacy has passed. In all likelihood these patients won't be back until after the storm. Laila gives Bill a call, and he confirms that corporate plans to close stores in the area early but has yet to decide on exactly when.

After hanging up she sends Cecily home.

"Really?"

"Yeah. You're welcome to stay if you want to, but I think the crisis has passed. Bill says they'll be closing soon. I can handle things in the meantime. If you have stuff to take care of still at home you should do that."

"Yeah, all right." Cecily rings up the lone patient in the waiting area, then shuts down her till and gathers her belongings. "You sure you gonna be all right, Laila?"

"Yeah, absolutely. Don't worry about me. I'm just going to get through this pile, then lock up."

"All right." As she walks out she calls back: "Hey, say hi to your brother for me, okay?"

"Will do! Stay safe!"

Then Cecily is gone.

She checks her phone again. Still no word from Alex; nothing from Esther either. "Where the fuck are you?" she mutters to herself.

"Are you a pharmacist or a sailor?"

She looks up to find a large, bald man, midsixties, looming over the register. He wears an amused grin and she doesn't like the way he's looking at her at all. Instinctively, she surveys the immediate area. A shift leader straightens shelves nearby should she need assistance.

"I didn't realize anybody was standing there," she says, masking her surprise with a clipped tone that passes for harried friendliness.

"Busy day?"

"Something like that."

"You're not Sanjay."

"You're observant." She lets a trace of an accent color her words. Patients tolerate a higher level of acerbity if you sound foreign, she's learned. It allows them to feel superior even while she refuses to act deferential. "Sanjay left early. I'm Laila." She flashes a smile and goes back to logging scripts in the system.

"Ah, *mucho gusto!*" the man says. "*¿De donde eres?*"

Great, a gringo who can string together basic phrases.

"Puerto Rico," she says. Though she's never been to the island, it's what he expects, and giving him that is easier than explaining the diversity of the Latin American experience.

"Beautiful island. My son loves it. Do you have any kids?"

"I work too much. No time for kids."

He grins. "You're still young. You have time. Don't wait too long, though."

She glances up from the monitor. "How can I help you?"

He rocks back and forth. "*Yo me llamo* Thaddeus Bloom," he says. "I'm picking up some pills... uh... *pastelitos.*"

He just said he was picking up some pastries. A smile stretches across her face, and she chooses to not correct him. "¡Ah, muy bien!"

"*Gracias.* My wife, Cheryl," he continues, "normally gets them for me, but she's busy at the house today. She's getting everything ready for the storm, the *huracán.*"

Laila resists the urge to roll her eyes. "That's good. Smart lady." She types furiously, partly out of experience and partly in the spirit of theatricality. Something else she's learned: purpose and concentration intimidate customers. If you look busy they tend to assume you are busy and leave you alone. "Last name Bloom, right?"

"Like a rose. I'm sure a pretty girl like you has plenty of roses. ¡*Belleza!*" He bobs his eyebrows. Laila fakes a short laugh in the name of customer service, sexual harassment's complicit corporate partner.

"It doesn't look like it's been filled. I can fill it for you now, if you don't mind waiting."

She points to the waiting area, but Thaddeus lingers. "Take all the time you need. I'm not in a rush." He whistles a little tune to himself.

Glancing out the drive-through window, she spots a feeder band working its way across the sky from the east. The bulk of the hurricane is still well offshore, but the first tendrils of the mighty system are already reaching across land. Her mind flashes back to the shots of Cocoa Beach on the news this morning. They're finally getting some exciting footage, no doubt. It won't be long now till Bill gives the go-ahead to shut down and still no word from Alex.

She grabs her phone and fires off a quick message:

Hey papo just checking in haven't heard from you in a minute. lemme know ur alright, k? should be home soon and we can put up the shutters. hit me back

Alex's mercurial nature requires a gentle touch, especially lately, but she's running out of time and patience.

Glancing back at Thaddeus, she adds: **u wouldn't believe the day I've had!!! :/**

Then it's back to work.

The prescription—Fendiline, a common arrhythmia medication—takes no time to fill. In a moment, she counts the pills, prints the label, verifies the count, and steps up to the register. "I can ring you up," she says, motioning him over.

"Wow, that was quick. Such service! I should come here more often."

Her fingers fly over the register keys. "I'll let Sanjay know."

He hands her his credit card and she swipes it for him, then taps the keypad. "Just follow the instructions here."

He labors over each prompt while the feeder band gets closer. If he's not out the door before the rain starts she'll be stuck with him. He'll want to practice his horrendous Spanish on her while she has work to finish.

"It's asking me for cash back," he says. "But I gave you a credit card."

"Hit the red cancel button on the bottom right and swipe the card again."

The feeder band is maybe half a mile away. There's still time, but they have to move a lot quicker than this.

"Let's see here." He takes greater care this time, pausing to put on his reading glasses before peering at the keypad. His lips pucker and he emits a thin, tuneless whistle. "Credit card. Yes, that's what I want. Okay... Is this total right?"

Laila smiles at him with her eyes and bobs her head up and down quickly. Just hit yes, she thinks. Just hit yes.

"Yes."

As soon as he does the register springs into action, the till and the receipt printer clang like a slot machine that hit the jackpot. She slams the drawer and tears the receipt off, practically throwing it at him. "Have a great day!" Then she's back to the computer to finish inputting the scripts. At least this way Sanjay will have a clean start when he returns.

Bill texts her: **Shut down and get home! Corporate gave the green light.**

And just in time. Outside, the sky is black. The first volley of heavy rain pelts the corrugated roof of the drive-through like little explosions.

You don't have to tell me twice!

A PAPER LANTERN SWAYS IN FRONT OF AN A/C VENT, bathing the rustic dining table in diffused light. Only one seat remains next to the highchair and Thaddeus fixes his sights on it, but Cheryl outflanks him and arrives first. Out of options, Thaddeus surreptitiously pinches Gertie's arm, causing her to wail.

"Oh, what is it, princess?" Cheryl asks in an attempt to soothe that Gertie flatly rejects. With a sigh Steven suggests the doll. "Good idea," Cheryl says. "I'll go get it."

When she stands up, Thaddeus slips into her seat. Success!

Cheryl returns a moment later. Doll in hand, Gertie calms down.

"Ha," Thaddeus says. "I knew she'd love it! Didn't I tell you, Cheryl? I said Gertie will love it!" He winks at Steven, who snorts begrudging assent.

"You took my seat."

"What's the difference? Here, sit here." He pats the chair on his other side. "'Take a load off, Benny. Take a load off, Marie.'"

She sits without further protest. "Don't forget your pills."

Peter enters from the kitchen with a pitcher of water, which he sets down beside Cheryl.

"Are you sure you don't need help serving?"

"You've done all the cooking. The least I can do is serve," he says.

While Peter ferries various dishes to the table, Thaddeus arranges a handful of colorful pills beside his plate. "Grandpa's medicine," he tells Gertie. He's unsure what most of the pills do—Cheryl handles the particulars. He just knows to take them. Gertie studies him with silent, naked intensity, and he can't decide if she's curious or suspicious. "Well, the legal medicine, anyway," he adds with a wink.

"Poop," she says, prompting a stern glance from Steven.

With no water in his glass, Thaddeus opts to swallow his pills dry—reaching through the canyon of stemware for the pitcher poses too great a risk; he's certain to knock something over. No big deal, he thinks. Everything's going great. The hard part is over. In a minute, they'll be eating and then they'll be saying their good nights and then the past three years won't matter anymore.

Peter takes his seat and the various dishes make their rounds. While Cheryl fixes his plate, Thaddeus tickles Gertie's chin. She pulls away from his finger to focus on Talkin' Tina.

"We shouldn't allow toys at the table." Steven sighs.

"It's just for tonight," Peter says.

"We went everywhere looking for that doll," Thaddeus says.

Cheryl peels a flake off a roll. "We went to one store."

"Your mother couldn't decide which doll to get. I said, 'Cheryl, it's only the best for our granddaughter!'"

Gertie squeezes Talkin' Tina and the doll emits a garbled but enthusiastic chirp.

"Seems to be something wrong with the best doll in the store," Steven says, while buttering a roll. When he finishes, he shreds some chicken for Gertie. She devours a few pieces, then offers some to Talkin' Tina. The doll declines, and after a moment she pops those into her own mouth to join the small handful she's already stuffed in there.

"She seems enamored of it, at any rate," Steven says with resignation.

"Probably just a loose wire. No big deal." With his mouth full, Thaddeus adds: "Look at that smile. She loves it. Ha!" He breaks into a coughing fit and Cheryl fills his glass.

"Have some water."

He does as he's told, and when the coughing passes he resumes. "Don't worry, beautiful. Grandpa will fix that loose wire for you right after dinner."

Steven wipes Gertie's mouth while Peter brings out a decanter of wine from a bamboo sideboard.

With one hand Gertie grabs her food and with the other she shakes the doll incessantly at her grandfather.

"Use your words," Steven says in singsong.

She shakes her head and points at the doll.

"Is something wrong with your toy?" Thaddeus asks.

"Don't reinforce her negative behavior," Steven says. "The parenting books are very clear about that."

"Parenting books." Thaddeus nods. "You know your mother made me read one of those books when you were little, Stevie."

Cheryl snorts. "I did no such thing. I'm not a masochist."

Steven's fork stops halfway to his mouth. He levels an expectant gaze, but Thaddeus doesn't immediately continue. Whatever he planned on saying occludes in the roving fog that chooses this moment to descend upon his memory. His heart pounds. The words, he knows, are crucial. This moment is crucial because Stevie is indulging him long enough to give his joke a chance. All he needs to do is get a laugh and he's home free, but he draws a blank. His lip quivers. Rather than stammer a non sequitur he fakes a broad, knowing grin and takes a series of deep breaths. He can pass the silence off as a buildup. If he can wait long enough, find some equilibrium, the punch line will come. But as the seconds stretch everybody begins to stare, even Gertie. His eyes dart from one adult to another, searching for some clue, for some funny quirk he can exploit, but he comes up empty-handed. He can sense the punch line is near, but it remains just beyond the edge, lost in the fog. He's tottering on the verge of failure when his gaze rests on Gertie—beautiful little Gertie, stuffing piece after piece of chicken into her mouth. A hard peal of laughter emerges from him. Gertie's face has cut through the fog like a powerful spotlight. Stretching his arms out as if to grab the elusive punch line, he continues:

"The book—maybe you've heard of it—a book called *Everybody Poops*. Ha!" He plays it straight at his granddaughter, drawing her in with funny faces. "You heard of it, Gertie? Huh?"

Gertie absently nods.

"Thaddeus," Cheryl says. "We're at the dinner table."

Steven snarls and stabs at his food. But it doesn't matter because then Gertie laughs, and watching that unabashed joy bloom across her angelic face—knowing he put it there!—makes him feel twenty years younger.

"Another joke." Steven massages his eyes as he talks. The tips of his fingers are raw, the skin cracked. He grunts. "Peter and I are the ones who have to deal with her bad habits on a day-to-day basis. You don't have to encourage her. At least Mom understands that much."

Stretching against the highchair straps, Gertie coughs.

"What do you mean 'that much'?" Cheryl says. "I don't spoil her."

"Gertie's fine," Peter says. "One toy isn't going to spoil her."

Gertie coughs again.

"Kids love jokes," Thaddeus says. "You used to love jokes."

"No, I didn't, and its not one joke I'm concerned about, Pop. It's a pattern of influence."

Thaddeus brushes away his words. "Oh, for Christ's sake, Stevie. No need to make a federal case. I'm very—"

Gertie's cough cuts off mid-breath and turns into a wheeze. Her arms shoot up, and her chin drops down. Most things may have faded from his memory, but what he's seeing is unmistakable. He recognizes the signs immediately.

"She's choking!"

In that quick snap of time, the proper procedure for a choking infant crystallizes in his mind. His duty is to protect Gertie—that much he knows—and propelled by instinct he lunges for her. But everything is in the way—plates, glasses, a bowl of sagging mesclun—and he crashes through it all, sending it spilling into a slick across the table that bombards Stevie, who, anyway, appears stunned motionless. Thaddeus tries to rise, but the table betrays him. The purchase he needs to find his footing is lost in all the mess and broken glass. His hand slips and he topples in the wrong direction, away from Gertie and into Cheryl. "No!" he shouts, as Cheryl screams. All is lost, and for the first time in his life a thought strikes him with immutable certainty: She is going to die. Gertie is going to die.

Peter moves faster than Thaddeus. Darting from his chair, he swoops past him and lifts Gertie from her highchair. He stands her up on the table and positions himself behind her. He forcefully presses his fist into her chest until she spits up a ball of slobbery chicken bits. But she doesn't take a breath.

"Oh, God," Thaddeus says. Finding the purchase that eluded him a moment ago, he rises to his feet. Cheryl is up, too, and peering around his shoulder. Only Steven remains seated, still stunned.

"Come on, sweetie," Peter coos. "Take a deep breath."

Her breathing returns with a violent shudder, followed by a brief collective silence, which in turn gives way to a caterwaul that shivers the remaining glasses on the table and that finally shakes Steven from his trance. He springs from his seat, sending his chair screeching across the floor, then he yanks Gertie from Peter's arms.

"Oh my God!" he says, rocking her, trying to soothe her, but she is irreconcilable.

"It's okay, Steven," Cheryl says. "She's just scared, but she's okay."

"Looks like her eyes were bigger than her throat, that's all. Look who's here, beautiful." Thaddeus shakes Talkin' Tina in front of her face. "You remember the doll old Grandpa brought you, right? You're not scared anymore. You have to be brave for Talkin' Tina."

Gertie's screaming halts as she examines first Thaddeus and then the doll. He squeezes the doll's midsection so that it emits a high-pitched coo. Gertie begins to come around.

"Ha!" Thaddeus smiles, but Steven's fist pounding into the table cuts short the celebration.

"This isn't a fucking joke," Steven screams. "She could've died!"

"She's fine," Peter says. "It was just an accident." He rests a placating hand on Steven's shoulder, but Steven shakes it off.

"Just an accident," Thaddeus echoes. "You just weren't paying attention. Could've happened to anyone."

"I'll tell you what it was," Steven shouts, maneuvering around the table until he's standing right beside Thaddeus. "It was that damn doll!" He snatches Talkin' Tina out of Thaddeus's hand. Gertie immediately begins to bawl. "I was distracted because of this insulting piece of trash."

"Calm down," Peter says.

"Steven, it was an accident." Cheryl sits down. She tidies her place setting before continuing in a soothing tone. "These things happen to every parent. Now, let's just sit down and finish our dinner. If we act like everything is fine, so will she."

"Everything is not fine! My daughter could've died because of him. Why should I continue to forgive him and forgive his insensitivity? Jesus Christ, when is he going to start taking responsibility for his actions?"

"Stevie—"

"It's nobody's fault," Peter says. "That's what we're trying to tell you."

Thaddeus tries to retrieve the doll but Steven yanks it out of reach—the sudden movement further frightens Gertie.

"Just an accident, Stevie," Thaddeus says. "Let's move on. Hey, I got a joke for you! Huh?"

For a moment, he captures everyone's attention—even Stevie's, who goes so far as to shrug, which is certainly better than the yelling. So he tells the joke: "A man walks into a bar and, finding his friend there, he asks: 'Did you see the baseball game last night?' 'Nope,' the friend says, 'but I hear Ramirez struck out.' 'What about the funny car derby on channel eleven?' the man asks. 'Missed that one, too,' the friend replies, 'but I hear the trick transmission really backfired.' The man takes a drink. What are we supposed to talk about? he thinks. His friend hasn't seen any of the things he's seen. There must be something they've both seen. Then it hits him. 'Okay,' he says. 'Well, I bet you seen that sword-swallower on the evening news.' The friend grins. 'Nah,' he says, 'but I hear he really choked!'"

For a long time afterward—too long—everything is silent.

Cheryl slowly shakes her head. "Oh, Thaddeus."

"Hey, don't shoot; it's just a joke." But nobody laughs. "Stevie," he pleads. "Come on, it's just a joke. Just something to lighten the mood."

Steven turns to Peter. "You see?" Holding Gertie close, he flings Talkin' Tina toward the wall with his free hand. His arm is so much stronger than Thaddeus remembers, his aim much surer. There's a brutal crack, and Gertie screams.

"This whole thing was a mistake," he says, and storms upstairs, depositing Gertie into Cheryl's arms on his way.

Peter follows, and for the second time that day Thaddeus finds himself alone with Cheryl in a house that doesn't feel anything like his home.

Thaddeus sighs and folds his hands on the table. "Your son is too sensi—"

"Don't."

Talkin' Tina lies crumpled in the corner, partly in shadow, its dress torn where the shards of its plastic arm ruptured the fabric—a doll's equivalent of a compound fracture. Thaddeus lumbers over to the wall and picks it up. He squeezes its stomach, but it no longer produces even a garbled whistle. Its hair, however, remains as soft as ever, its expression as garrulous. He shrugs and offers Gertie the doll, which she accepts.

"Poop," she says.

And despite everything, Thaddeus feels laughter well up from someplace deep inside of himself. "That's my girl!"

"WHAT'S YOUR FAVORITE THING TO DO?" HE ASKS.
Trellised chains creep up the inseam of his baggy black pants, shushing like a maraca as he paces.

His name is Asher—you know this because he told you at the bar after apologizing for sneezing on you—and his blue hair is spiked at irregular angles. The graying smudge across his brow indicates that the dye job is recent. You watch him out of the corner of your eye as he, in passing, taps a purple fingernail against the surface of the table in the breakfast nook before moving on to the living room. With each stride he abuses the hem of those hyperbolic pants with the heels of his black boots.

"It can be anything," he says. He's congested, and as he speaks he presses the meat of his thumb against his nostrils, first the left side, then the right. This does not, however, deter him from scrutinizing the living room. He touches everything, then scratches the skin of his torso and arms where it's exposed, which is everywhere because his white tank top stretches so low in all places that at any given moment you can see the metal rods traversing his nipples and the unfinished snake tattoo crawling across his rib cage.

"You just move in?" he asks. "This place is empty."

You say that you're in the process of selling the unit and that everything is staged, which is not entirely a lie. This is a stage of sorts.

He nods.

You imagine that he's searching for some indicator of your personality—to determine if you're the kind of trick willing to call the police if he robs you, perhaps for the money to finish that tattoo—but the house divulges nothing. Nothing here is personal. If he were to open the drawers he would find them empty. This is not your house; it is nobody's house, merely one in a string of subdivision platforms from which to launch your work, and tonight Asher is your work.

Aside from the fact that by sneezing on you he invited a certain level of retribution you would've loathed to pass up, you chose him because the manner in which he presents himself represents rage and rebellion, which is what you want tonight. At home, the situation has stymied. But as you mix him a drink of equal parts bourbon and soda with just a splash of GHB, you wonder if perhaps you acted in haste. His questions betray a desire for intimacy and, by extension, a yearning for inclusion that is anathema to your mood tonight.

He finishes with the living room and moves on to the kitchen counter, where he languidly flips through the crisp pages of a home design catalog. "Like for me, my favorite thing in the whole world is snowboarding," he says, "but it's hard to do in Florida."

"Sure," you say, and hand him his drink and a tab. One dance at Back Booth and the promise of ecstasy was all it took to get him to agree to come home with you. Now you're here, and he's a wounded fish, blindly swimming. Easy prey.

He thanks you and leans over so that his chin rests on the counter, then, affecting what he must consider a coquettish gesture, he flicks a surgically forked tongue at you and asks, "So what's yours?"

"My favorite?" Leaving the kitchen, you sit on the couch and beckon him over. "That's easy. It's Asher."

He washes down the tablet with a hearty swig, then sneezes. "Sorry. God, I can't taste anything."

Your smile is coy, practiced. "Bless you," you say.

For a while you chat about nothing. This is the part you enjoy the most. All the pieces are in place and what remains is some casual conversation and to wait. When he begins flexing his jaw you know that the ecstasy has taken effect. That's your cue to tease his fingers with the smallest wisp of a touch. He's got gorgeous robust fingers, the skin freckled and almost translucent the way it often is with natural redheads. Lean in close and whisper: "I'm going to rip you apart."

"You're funny," he says, and curls into you, his spiked blue hair poking your abdomen. The red is still noticeable at the roots.

"You have no idea," you say.

He finishes the last of his bourbon, then turns with a wink to face you. His hands caress your thigh and your arm. He rubs his back into the suede couch cushions and he laughs. "You know what would be great right now? Music! Let's dance. Doesn't that sound great?"

"Sure."

His eyelids droop. You palm his smooth chin and wrap your hand around his sweaty neck. When you kiss him, you taste the bourbon on his cracked lips. His forked tongue curls around your teeth, then he snorts and you detect the metallic tinge of antihistamines in a small drop of his mucus.

He breaks off the kiss in a nervous giggle. "Sorry," he says, "my nose is just pulsing with happiness, I guess."

"No big deal," you say, and taking his hand you lead him toward the bedroom. "Come on." He doesn't protest.

You both strip, then you sit him down on the edge of the bed and tell him to wait as you slip on just the pants from a pair of scrubs and head to the shower.

The first one was a skittish volunteer at a hospital—squeamish at the sight of blood—who came to the club straight from his shift. You had no protocols for your work, only a vague notion that something had to be done and that you were the one to do it, so you were imprecise. You've kept his scrubs all this time as a reminder to be more objective, which is what you are attempting to be with Asher, but his blasé attitude and innate appeal weaken your resolve.

It's important to wash. Like sharpening the knives, showering protects you. And as you lather and then rinse, you study the way your honed muscles move in symphony, swelling and contracting beneath your skin. It has taken three years, but now this is no longer a body; this is a tool. Smile into the mirror. Then smile again until you get it right.

You must get it right.

He waits on the bed, desiring you, wondering about you: wondering, perhaps, what he will tell his friends about you tomorrow because it would've never occurred to him that he wouldn't see tomorrow. You feel the heat of his lust radiate through the walls and it puts a smile on your face, which, upon inspection, appears natural.

You've been gone only a short while, but when you return there's a different energy in the room. He's wearing your discarded shirt and scrolling through his phone. Your backpack, which you had hidden in the closet, is open at his feet and he's holding a pacifier.

"I got cold," he says with a grin. "And your closet's empty. I hope you don't mind."

The pacifier isn't his either. It's yours and it's her favorite one, the one with a picture of Minnie Mouse. You should kill him right now for his forwardness. Instead, you shrug and endeavor to remain aloof.

"Here," you say, handing him a tissue because you don't want his snot on the comforter.

He stares at the tissue for a moment before absently placing it on the nightstand.

Turning the pacifier over in his hand, he examines the chipped picture of Minnie Mouse, her dress worn away at the edges. "Cute paci."

Gritting your teeth, you snatch it from him. "Yes," you say. A vibration starts in your hands. Whatever empathy you felt earlier evaporates. He is nothing. Doing nothing. Fighting nothing.

"That's cool, I guess." Sniffling, he wipes his nose across the sleeve of your shirt.

Leaving the backpack unattended was careless, and now he knows more than you were willing to share. The important thing, though, is to not allow this mistake to derail the work. Everybody fails, but it's how one learns from those failures that define a person's character.

"So," he says. "You, like, do ecstasy a lot?"

"Not really."

"Oh, so then you just love Disney a whole lot." He pounds his fist into his open palm and hops up and down on the bed. "Do you have, like, a hidden shrine to Mickey Mouse or something?" He's giddy with the ecstasy and finds all of this hilarious.

Your palm throbs. Massage it. Take deep breaths. When you are calm, you continue. "Not exactly."

"Then what?" He bites a lip and his eyes widen. "Oh my God, do you have a kid?"

Your patience expired, you tell him ecstasy is the thing, then stash the pacifier in your back pocket.

The banter—or perhaps the heady cocktail of drugs he's consumed—arouses him, and kneeling on the bed, he prowls toward you, the snake on his side slithering beneath the gauzy cotton of your shirt. "See?" His backside slides out from under the hem. "That wasn't so hard." He emphasizes the word *hard*.

Clutching the front of your scrubs in his fist, he squeezes. You take a deep breath, close your eyes, and prepare.

"What say we get these pants off, Doctor?" Accompanied by a chorus of sniffles, the pimples on his cheeks arrange themselves into a greasy grin. He nuzzles into the front of the scrubs, adding his scent to yours, compelled, as all men are, to mark his territory. But he has no claim here, and besides, your scent is only laundry detergent and soap.

"Look!" you shout. Let the color drain from your face and contort your features into a mask of fright. Point frantically at the blank wall behind him. Confuse him. "Look! Look!"

Like a dog obeying, he crawls around to face the wall. "What?" he asks, his voice groggy with chemicals.

The longer he stares at the featureless expanse, the more desperate your calls become and the more sluggish his reaction. You would like to toy with him some more, to extract a few more ounces of frustration from the moment, but your hands are on fire, the tendons pulsing under the skin. You simply can't wait any longer.

Woozily, he rises to his knees, keeping his back to you all the while as he searches the wall in vain. "I don't see anything." He exhales in a long stream; the thick veins in his neck pulse. "Are you playing with me?"

An electric shudder passes through your entire body, and, grinning, you crack your knuckles. Leaning in so that he can feel your breath tickling his hairs, you whisper: "Look closer."

"I don't want to," he says. He's tired of this game and has turned to whining. But it's almost over for him. Your fingers encircle his clammy neck. He won't have to play for much longer. He closes his eyes, and you can feel him go limp in your hands. "What should I be seeing?"

CHERYL PICKS UP A PAPER TOWEL FROM THE KITCHEN floor and places it in the trash. Sunflower seeds, a snack packed into Gertie's lunch, are spilled across the counter. She folds the lip of the bag, clips it shut, and stores it in the cupboard before wiping down the granite. She scrubs egg yolk and pungent hot sauce from Steven's rushed breakfast plate. Without a word to anyone, he'd gone out last night, returning late. This morning he hadn't wanted to get up, but Peter dragged him out of bed just in time to get dressed for work and eat.

"I know I left the kitchen a mess," Peter says from the couch. He's stretched out with an ice pack over his eyes. "I'll take care of it. I just need to lie down for a minute; I'm feeling much better already. I don't know what's wrong with me. I never used to get headaches."

"It's probably stress," she says. "When Steven was little I got terrible migraines."

He sips from a glass featuring the racially diverse cast of a popular children's cartoon, then sets it down on a coaster. A drop slides down the side, passing over a little native girl in a beaded tunic. Cheryl wonders if perhaps the sparkly-eyed girl is Gertie's favorite character, or if maybe it's the dimpled Asian boy holding a soccer ball and laughing. Does she even know that she's Asian? With any luck, these distinctions won't mean much to her generation, but how could they not with somebody like Thaddeus as her grandfather? She shudders at all the racist jokes he'll make in the coming years. If he'll even get the chance. After last night's dinner, there's the distinct possibility that Steven won't let him near her ever again.

"It's too bright in here—that's the problem." Peter crosses to the patio doors and draws the blinds. "There. That's better." He returns to the couch and his ice pack. "You know, you don't have to clean, Cheryl. I'll do it."

"I enjoy tidying up. It makes me feel useful."

She finds a stack of business cards stashed away in the back of the silverware drawer. First glancing to make sure that his eyes are covered, she flips through the stack: a landscaper's card, a card for bottled water home delivery, multiple refrigerator magnets from the same Chinese restaurant. (Do they order from there so frequently because of Gertie's race or is it laziness? If she's being honest, neither option appeals to her.) She goes through the rest more out of a sense of completion than anything else. But her idle nosiness takes a bitter turn when she comes across a card for Gertie's day care. She's offered to watch her during the days more times than she can remember, but instead they leave her with strangers. It's not right. She's family. She's the grandmother, for God's sake. She practically begged Steven to let her stay home with her this morning.

"Really, it's no trouble," she'd said. "I'm happy to do it."

But Steven declined, insisting on the importance of maintaining a schedule.

"Okay, but some variety is good, too, don't you think? We never were that strict with you and you turned out fine."

"Look, I can't get into this right now. I'm running late. You're just going to have to respect our decision. I'm sorry. It's really the best thing for her."

Our decision. The implication worries her. Steven and Thaddeus she knows how to handle, but Peter is an unknown. If she has to worry about him, too, she might be in trouble.

"Well, what about your father? What should I tell him?"

He turned in the doorway and drummed his fingers on the doorknob. Gertie hung from his hip, sucking her thumb. "Tell him I'll see him tonight."

She sweeps the business cards back into the drawer and turns her attention to corralling loose sections of the newspaper.

"I need to get going," Peter says. "I can't be too late to the office."

"Skip work," she says, walking away from the paper. "If Gertie has to be at day care, you might as well take advantage. We never get to spend any time together, just the two of us."

He hesitates.

"Come on," she says. "It'll be fun. I want to get to know you better. Besides, don't you deserve a day off every once in a while?"

"Maybe you're right. Between the newspaper and the gallery—"

"Exactly! Now, you just relax. I'll make you some coffee. The caffeine will help your head."

"Thanks, Cheryl."

"Of course!"

As she waits for the coffee to brew, she wipes down the table and they make small talk about the weather. The latest forecasts predict an active tropical season in the Atlantic, though there's no possibility of a hurricane for several months.

"We have the shutters now at least," he says, sitting up when she serves the coffee. "Natalie got us worried when it came through last summer. There was damage at the shelter. I think it spooked Steven."

She empties and then washes the coffeepot. "You have to be prepared," she says. "That's the important—" She stops midsentence.

"Is everything all right?"

"What's that? Oh, yes, just a hot flash." She floats him a weak smile.

He frowns. "Maybe you should sit down?"

"No, no. It's nothing. I'm fine."

But, of course, it's not a hot flash. The air has changed in subtle ways that she's learned to recognize over the years. Thaddeus is up. She thought he'd sleep for at least another half hour but his cycle must be off. Her pulse quickens. She'll have to tell him that Gertie is at day care. The news will crush him. He was looking forward to spending the day with his granddaughter.

Peter stands up. "Here, let me help you. I'm feeling better."

"No, sit down. I can—"

Thaddeus's arrival silences her. He wanders into the room, humming quietly. "Good morning," he says, addressing the room as if he were speaking to an auditorium and not just the two of them. He moves without aim and stops beside the kitchen counter as if by accident.

"You're up early!" she says. He mumbles something about the weather and having trouble sleeping in a new bed, but she doesn't listen. Instead she makes encouraging sounds to keep him talking while she dashes around the kitchen. Over the years, she's learned that the best way to neutralize him is to keep him busy, so that's what she'll do. She can't allow him to piss off Peter as well. Not after last night. When there's a lull in his monologue, she sets down a glass of water in front of him and presses a pill into his hand. "Here. Take this. It's the new blood pressure medicine. Sit down. I'll bring you something to eat. Do you want eggs?"

His eyes swim up to meet hers. "Where's Stevie?"

"He dropped Gertie off on the way to work," she says, as if it's nothing, as if it's exactly what she expected would happen. Confidence, she's learned, placates him. "He's at the real estate office all morning, then the shelter in the afternoon. Busy, busy, busy! You know how that goes, but he said he'd see you tonight." She smiles and points at the pill in his hand. "Why don't you sit down? And take that already."

He swallows the pill without protest. "I see," he says, then lumbers over to Peter. "What's with you?"

"He has a migraine," she says. "Leave him alone."

"It's just a headache," Peter says.

"Hmm." Thaddeus puckers his lips and scratches his thumb against the stubble on his chin. "Never had one."

She pours a glass of orange juice and drops some bread into the toaster. "They're not pleasant. Come on. Come over here. Leave him alone. Breakfast will be ready in a minute."

"Did you take aspirin? Cheryl, did you give him an aspirin?"

"Of course I did. Did you take your pill?" She watched him take it, but quizzing him forces him to shift his focus away from Peter.

"Yes," he says.

"Good. Drink the water, too. You never hydrate enough. And here, sit down. Breakfast is ready."

Hands in his pockets, he ignores her and continues hassling Peter.

Watching them side by side like that, she can't help but note the vast differences between the two men. One is small and the other large; one is contemplative and the other bombastic. But more than physical traits or even personality, what she notices most is their divergent philosophical approaches to life. Even supine and battling a migraine, Peter projects an aura of selflessness, of collectivist sympathies that Thaddeus completely lacks. He's an anachronism, she thinks: indulgent American patriarch, circa twentieth century. In moments like these, she wishes she could send him to some museum to be cataloged and locked away like a dusty antique cannon, to be decommissioned, disarmed and stripped of the ability to destroy every fragile thing she's built. It would serve him right. But she wavers. It's not entirely his fault; he's just too bulky, too impractical for modern life. He wasn't designed for it like Peter was. She's just the sucker who got stuck with him. But that's age. She selected from the choices she was given at the time and now she has to live with it.

"Thaddeus! Come on. Leave Peter alone. He's not feeling well and your breakfast is getting cold," she says, even though the toast is still in the toaster.

"The aspirin will make you feel better. No big deal."

He's finished with Peter, but instead of returning to the kitchen, like she's asked, he ambles around the room and stops in front of a framed print. "Where's Gertie?"

"At day care," Peter says. "Steven dropped her off."

"I just told you that."

"Oh."

She parrots what Steven said about the importance of maintaining a schedule, glancing at Peter all the while to gauge his reaction. See, she wants to say, I can be a team player, too. But if he's impressed he doesn't let on.

"Why don't you sit down?" she tries again, in a softer voice this time. "Your food will get cold. Do you want eggs?"

He waves her off and continues to stare at the art on the wall: a pastel cascade of curves and fleshy arabesques.

Of course she recognizes the expressionist vagina immediately, remembering when Peter purchased it and how proud he was to find a rare, signed lithograph. She wills Thaddeus to walk away from the print. But he doesn't. He ponders it, tapping a finger against his pale lips.

Move on, she thinks.

He opens his mouth but remains silent. Hesitantly, he points at the painting before arching an eyebrow. At last he shrugs. "Modern art. Not my thing."

"What a shame," she says, masking her relief. "Now, do you want eggs or not? I don't have all day."

He doesn't answer, but she makes them anyway. Otherwise, he'll eat only toast, and the doctor's orders were very clear about taking the new medication with a full meal.

"When it comes to art I stick to the masters," he announces to the room. "Master Michelangelo. Da Vinci. Master Picasso." He crosses the room and cozies up to Peter on the couch. "And my favorite master"—he pauses, drawing out the moment—"Master Bater—only did naked women. Ha!"

"Oh, for the love of—"

"Good one," Peter says, pressing the ice pack tight against his eyes.

"Just a joke," he says, slapping Peter on the thigh. "I know you boys don't like that stuff." He stands up. "No big deal."

He lumbers on, breath heaving. With each step, he looks older and less surefooted than usual. Perhaps there's something wrong with his inner ear, which is affecting his balance. He has been mishearing her a lot lately. There could be a connection. Plating his eggs, she makes a mental note to ask the doctor about it the next time they go in for a checkup.

She serves the food and this time she demands that he come eat. He complies. Perched on a stool, he nudges the eggs with a fork.

"You need to eat with these new pills," she says, pointing at him.

He nods, but before long he stands up, grabs a piece of toast off his plate, and makes his way back to the couch. He taps Peter on the shoulder and asks if he's ever been deep-sea fishing, chewing while he talks.

Breakfast didn't work, but she has other tactics.

"Thaddeus," she says, "it's such a nice day. Why don't you go for a walk?"

He shrugs. It's clear that she'll have to convince him, but it's fine. She knows how to do it.

"Peter isn't feeling well, and I've got all this cleaning to do. You'll just be bored here. Go on, it'll do you a world of good. Go explore the neighborhood."

"Steven won't be back till tonight?"

She smiles and nods. "That's right. We have the whole day to ourselves."

His shoulders slump, and she knows that he's agreed, but she's not going to take any chances today. Grabbing him by the arm, she leads him toward the front door, bypassing the more convenient garage out of fear that something in there would distract him or trigger a comment that she can't walk back. Using the front door presents a logistical problem, however. Three steps separate the living room from the landing for the door. With his balance problems, she's not at all confident in his ability to manage the steps on his own, so she guides his feet, taking great care that he doesn't trip.

He shakes free of her grip. "I can do it."

"I just don't want you to trip."

"Stop babying me!" He blushes, offering an apology.

"It's okay," she says, because saying, *I'm used to it,* would further aggravate the situation, and the priority at the moment is getting him out the door, not her feelings. "Don't forget your hat, and here, let me put some sunscreen on you. I think I saw some in the hall closet earlier."

He presents his arms. "Whatever you want."

She fetches the tube. The cap is crusty and its contents are expired in all probability. But its efficacy is immaterial. The purpose of the lotion is not to protect him from the sun; it's to keep him distracted so he doesn't say or do anything that might offend Peter. It works.

As she applies the lotion, he quietly peeks out the thin windows flanking the door.

"You don't want to be stuck in here all day," she says with a smile. "Maybe somebody's sunbathing by the pool. Or there's a gas station just past the gate. You can buy some lottery tickets. Maybe you'll get lucky and hit the jackpot. Wouldn't that be nice?"

"Lucky." He snorts. "Do you know what I'd do if I won the lotto?"

She shakes her head no and rubs the last of the lotion into his skin.

"I'd buy Gertie a mansion. And a boat for Stevie. Remember how much Stevie liked to go fishing?"

"Very good. Go on now before it gets too hot."

The floppy brim of his hat dips over his thin brow, and sunscreen smudges his nose where she neglected to rub it in all the way.

"Do I get a kiss?"

She could walk away. After last night he deserves it, but in that foolish hat, stretching out those doughy hands and bending that droopy smile, he looks so vulnerable that she can't help herself.

"We'll be all right," she says, pulling back. "Okay?"

He sighs and nods.

"Good, okay." Staring at him, she tears up, but she restrains herself. They are so close now. She needs to focus. Steven will cool off. Peter will help her. "Now, be careful, okay? Don't get into trouble." Then she kisses him again and the kiss lingers.

"Oh?" He wiggles his eyebrows, making her smile in spite of herself. "I'll be careful all right." He reaches lower, but she shifts away.

Patting his belly, she points at the door. "Go."

Heavy, hot air pours into the house. The light causes her to squint, but he steps out without a problem. "Don't stay out too long, okay? It's hot." He agrees and pulls the door shut behind him. The few sips of water he had with his pill won't keep him hydrated for long and he's never done well with prolonged exposure. The first winter they spent in Florida was also hot, and even then, when he was so much younger, he'd taken them all to the beach to escape it.

He was still at the firm then, doing mostly pro bono work, and there wasn't much money, but it didn't matter. On the morning of Christmas Eve he piled them all into the old Buick, the one with the missing rearview mirror and the ice-cold a/c (the car was falling apart but at least that still worked), and made the hour-and-a-half drive out to the coast for the weekend. On the way, they passed through the flat expanse of sawgrass that filled the St. Johns River watershed (low in the dry season), and she marveled at how it continued all the way down to the slash pine flatwoods and cypress hammocks of the Tosohatchee preserve over the horizon. They passed through small towns and a dusting of homesteads before arriving at Cocoa Beach, its glittering shore giving way to the bellowing Atlantic. "We're here," he announced, rolling the Buick through the gravel lot, the parking brake catching with a crunch though it was hardly necessary (the land in Florida was so much flatter than what they were used to up north). Check-in at the hotel wasn't for a few hours still, so they took turns slipping into their swimsuits in the Buick's backseat, and a moment later they raced down the scorching sand and dove into the pounding surf, holding hands.

Only newcomers swam in the winter, but they wouldn't learn that for a few years yet, not until their bodies adjusted to the climate, and anyway, the crisp water felt good on a sweltering afternoon. For the moment, the beach belonged to them, and they didn't know that the water was anything but perfect. They splashed around like seals in the surf, and even though Thaddeus had never been a strong swimmer, he took Steven out past the breakers and showed him how to make his body rigid to ride the swells back to the beach. She treaded water off to the side, keeping a vigilant eye out for the sharks she feared lay in wait to destroy her family. They never came, and over the years she was lulled into believing that they never would. When Steven wasn't bodysurfing with his father he entertained himself by tormenting the jellyfish that had washed up onshore, cutting open their quivering sacks with a sharp bit of broken shell.

A rocket launch was scheduled from nearby Cape Canaveral for that evening, its payload an unmanned satellite programmed to collect atmospheric data over a period of nine months. And huddled together on a large beach blanket spread across the weathered planks of the municipal pier, they anticipated lift-off like they hadn't anticipated anything else in life, because it was vacation and they'd splurged on mahi-mahi sandwiches slathered in tartar sauce and garnished with thick lemon wedges and served in oval baskets of red plastic from the concession at the head of the pier. Steven ran wild into the shadows along the splintered planks, calling out to her every few minutes to see if it was time yet.

"No," she said, and though she could hear his voice she couldn't see his face in the failing light and it worried her. "Come over here where I can see you."

"Come over here where I can see you!" he replied, because even as a child he was willful and didn't like being told what to do. He found a struggling fish on the planks and squatted over it, pulling its fins off before kicking it back into the ocean.

"You'll get snatched," she said, "and don't expect your father or me to do anything about it."

Instead of scaring him into submission as she'd hoped, her words emboldened him. He asked a hundred follow-up questions. Who would snatch him? What would they want with him? Was this a planned or an opportunistic occurrence? When at last she exhausted her ready responses, she conceded to making the whole thing up.

"Nobody is going to snatch you," she said, "just come over here. You're making me nervous."

"I thought so," he said, laughing and running to the edge of the pier. It was a kind of compromise. At least he stayed close to a light. He leaned over the side and shouted back, "Nobody can catch me."

She worried that he might fall in, but she didn't have to worry long because a moment later the giant thrusters erupted in a brilliant silent flash on the horizon, and within seconds a plume of orange smoke arced across the magenta sky, propelling the craft to escape velocity. Steven came rushing to her side. Lift-off resembled nothing she'd ever seen before, and she remembers thinking how wrong it seemed that atmospheric study required such brute force. At least they were spared the deafening roar. Only a dull rumble made it across the water as far south as the shabby Cocoa Beach municipal pier. She was glad for the distance because that small amount of noise made the launch real without overpowering her with its violence. Steven—his skin sticky from all the salt and gritty from sand—squeezed between her and Thaddeus. His black hair smelled like sunscreen and heat, and she breathed it in deep before kissing his ear. Together the three of them watched until the thrusters fell off into the broad sea and the tiny capsule carried on, reflecting the sun's rays that continued to shine uninterrupted beyond the curvature of Earth, until the capsule, too, disappeared, falling into invisible orbit and leaving behind the billowing trail of exhaust that had propelled it so effortlessly into space and that the jet stream was already dispersing into the indigo sky.

They spent that night in a squat, roadside motel with cable television and beds that would vibrate for a quarter. While Steven showered, they made love frivolously like teenagers, Thaddeus tickling her at the same time that he silenced her giggles with playful kisses. She'd forgotten her pill that morning, though she'd always been good about it. She did the math quickly in her head. One skipped pill wouldn't matter and, anyway, weren't they on vacation? The next morning was Christmas and they gave Steven a small Scouts knife that he'd been wanting. Thaddeus surprised her with an engraved locket, which read: *To my wife, Cheryl. You've saved my life.* It wasn't until the car ride home that she realized she hadn't even packed her pills. When she thinks about it now, she wonders if maybe she'd left them at home on purpose.

Back in the family room, Peter sticks his head through the blinds and watches the backyard. Dust motes bandy about in the shaft of sunlight grazing the top of his head. She can't worry about Thaddeus anymore. The heat has zapped her energy. A few dishes remain in the sink, but that responsibility, too, she defers, drifting toward the couch. There'll be time for it later. With a sigh, she sits down.

"You two have such a natural rhythm," Peter says. A forlorn smile plays on his lips, and she wonders for a minute if perhaps he's envious of them, of Thaddeus.

"Give it time. What you call 'natural rhythm' is the result of decades of negotiations and fights."

"I wish I could make Steven stay as easily as you get Thaddeus to leave."

"What makes you think I wanted to get rid of him?"

"It just seemed that way." He turns around and lets the blinds flop shut. His finger lingers on the window ledge. "He's always at that shelter."

"That he gets from his father. Not the shelter bit, but the need to be constantly doing something."

He crosses the room and selects a book from the shelves, leafs through the pages for a moment before returning the volume to its place.

"Is there something you want to talk about?" She broaches the subject carefully, but it did seem odd that Steven took off last night like he did and then offered no explanation this morning. Even at his worst, Thaddeus never stormed off like that, leaving her to guess at his whereabouts.

"Oh? No." He smiles. "I'm just in a funk. Ignore me. I wanted to read the paper, but I'm afraid my headache will come back."

"Well, then listen to the radio. It doesn't bother me. I should take a shower soon anyway." She pushes back a stray hair. She neglected to brush her hair this morning or to even wash her face, opting instead to do damage control with Steven—not that it got her much.

"If you don't mind."

"Of course not. I'm just going to sit here for a minute. Then I'll go up and shower. Play whatever you want."

He tunes in to public radio in time to catch the tail end of a report about the police finding the body of a young Asian male propped up against the obelisk to the Confederate dead downtown, the victim of an apparent strangulation. Between the reporter's baritone and the ceiling fan thrumming overhead, the tension that has built up all morning eases from her body. Showering can wait. It feels so refreshing to stretch out on the couch even if it's only for a second. There's something naughty about the way the body contorts itself during a stretch, makes itself felt, and she can't bring herself to do anything but luxuriate in the invigorating tingle that comes with flexing all her tired muscles simultaneously. If she moves at all, it's to pass an absent hand over her stomach—flat, more or less, even after all these years—while considering Peter. He hasn't even unbuttoned the top buttons of his shirt. Certainly, it can't be for her benefit. Some fashion maven she is. Her hair is a mess and, thanks to all the wrinkles in the fabric, her pants resemble a topographical relief map.

But maybe he expects more from her. Maybe she disappoints him. The thought erases whatever small benefit the stretching provided. *Our decision.* If she disappoints him, he could tell Steven that he's worried about her, that she's not who she used to be, that she's let herself go, and that, maybe, it'd be best to limit the amount of time she spends with Gertie. It would be in Gertie's best interest, and couldn't she understand that? And it wouldn't be a lie. After all, she hasn't even washed her face today. But she stops herself. This is irrational thinking. If he were truly concerned, he'd be scrutinizing her instead of lingering by the bookcase.

He checks his watch, then verifies against the clock on the wall.

"I should at least swing by the gallery," he says, swiveling his shallow-set gray eyes at her, as if asking for permission.

She lifts herself onto an elbow. "Did I ever tell you about Steven's seventeenth birthday?"

"I don't think so."

"Thaddeus got it into his head that he was going to take Steven to a strip club. They'd been fighting about one thing or another for years, but Thaddeus had the notion that a father-son trip to the strip club would miraculously fix everything."

"Sure," he snorts. "I don't see any way that could've failed."

"Thaddeus always looks for the easy fix." Something dry and raspy catches in her windpipe. Sitting up, she tilts her head back and taps her chest, coughing to clear the obstruction, then continues in a husky whisper. "He gets overwhelmed. It's how he's always been."

"Are you okay? Do you need a pillow or something?"

She detects fear in his voice. Fear of her? The notion thrills her. It'd be nice if, for once, someone feared her instead of Thaddeus.

"It's too hot in here, isn't it?" he continues. "I can try opening a window."

A pillow and maybe a cool breeze would be nice, but while she relishes the idea of being feared, his eagerness to please also embarrasses her. It makes her feel old. And that's something else working against her with Gertie, isn't it? Her age.

"I'll live," she says, and takes a sip of Peter's water, which tastes faintly of chlorine.

"You're sure?" he asks, stepping over Gertie's coloring book on his way to the edge of the coffee table. "That couch isn't the most comfortable thing in the world. I can get some pillows from upstairs if you like."

"I'm sure I'll be fine."

"It's no problem. We have plenty of throw pillows."

The whole exchange has begun to feel like an Olympiad of virtue, so she cuts him off with a look. "I believe I was in the middle of a story."

Cowed, he averts his eyes and nods.

"Steven had wanted to go see a documentary about some artist or another with his friends. He didn't want to go to a strip club with his father. It was clear, even then, that that kind of thing... it wasn't what he was into. But you couldn't tell Thaddeus no in those days."

She leans forward with a wince at the hot pinch in her neck, the legacy of a restless night and a hectic morning. Peter doesn't catch her reaction—thank God. The story seems to amuse him, however. He smiles and asks why Thaddeus couldn't be rebuffed.

"He'd hit him. Hard. That's how he was back then." She says it with as little emotion as possible, stating it simply as a fact.

If he's shocked, he doesn't let on, but how could he not be shocked? Nobody hits their children anymore. Certainly Peter and Steven never hit Gertie. Or maybe they do; despite all the time she's spent in this house over the last few years, there's still so much she doesn't know, so much that's kept from her because of Thaddeus. Perhaps Peter himself was beaten at a young age and that's something he and Steven bonded over. It's possible; she knows next to nothing about Peter's formative years. He never talks about them; he never alludes to his family. All she knows—all Steven has told her—is that he ran away from home when he was a teenager and that he lived on the streets for a while, mostly sleeping on beaches near his hometown of Daytona and working odd jobs. He was working at a bar when Steven met him.

Peter wipes the dust from a picture frame, then he checks his watch again. "Thaddeus seems to have calmed down a lot in the past three years."

"He's mellowed. He's been meditating, if you can believe it. He found some videos on YouTube."

He rearranges the picture frame. "Do you think people can really change, fundamentally?"

She doesn't like to look at the photograph in that frame. In it Peter wears a torn purple T-shirt and orange leather wristbands embossed with white stars, and his blond hair is streaked black to match his nail polish. He leans against a cracked wall, presenting an overly aggressive mien for the camera while Steven leans in, pouting for a kiss. She wonders if it was Peter's brazen attitude that first attracted her son, who always seemed eager to rebel against conventionality. While she greatly prefers the current incarnation of Peter and doesn't like to be reminded of what he used to be like, she can't help but wonder if in her younger days—if it weren't for Thaddeus—would she have had the courage to date someone who looked like that? Let alone someone like that with Peter's history, whatever that may be?

"Maybe," she says. "Yes, I think so. I think people can change."

"Does Thaddeus ever act up like he used to?" He bites his tongue, hinting a snarl. It's the only mannerism that remains of the boy in the photograph, and there's something subversive and unnerving about it.

"He's mellowed out..." she repeats, trailing off sleepily, wanting to appear aloof under his inquisitive gaze.

He crosses his arms, narrows his eyes at her, and she thinks it's that quality exactly that has contributed to his professional success, because, suddenly, she wants to confide in him, and isn't that the journalist's most effective trick?

He breaks off the stare and licks his lips before slouching toward the French doors. He floats her an artful nod. "I can't get a bead on this weather."

"I did want him to leave," she confesses. "You were right. Earlier. I was trying to get rid of Thaddeus."

He scratches his ear. "What happened with the strip club?"

He missed a spot shaving this morning. His hair could use a trim, too, and is that the faint outline of an anarchy symbol coming through the thin fabric on the chest of his oxford?

"What's that?"

"The strip club. You were telling me a story."

"Oh, that." She shrugs. "Thaddeus got Steven so drunk that he threw up all over the bar and they kicked them both out."

She doesn't feel like talking for a little while and he seems content to sit with her in silence. The diffused light and the heat that it brings swells the room into a pleasant warmth.

"I got to wonder, though: How'd he even get a seventeen-year-old boy into a place like that? Strip clubs tend to be strict."

She combs back her hair and leans into the couch. "To be honest with you, I don't know how Thaddeus does anything."

They share a laugh. A sallow weariness colors the corners of his eyes. Despite it, he looks relaxed for the first time all morning. "Fair enough," he says.

"Anyway, don't listen to me. I'm probably making him sound like a monster."

"Not at all. It's nice to get a different perspective." He stretches the syllables as he speaks. "Steven, obviously, has his bias."

"I know how sensitive he can be. It was never anything that terrible. Thaddeus... he's just very sure of himself, and he hates being challenged—"

"You seem to get away with it."

She knows that he's flattering her to get her to talk, and she's powerless to resist. She likes confiding in him. "It's different with me. We have a different relationship. But he was a good father. Better than most."

Peter nods. "Steven gets like that, too. I was stubborn myself as a kid, but then my sister beat the crap out of me. I guess that's what siblings are good for."

"It makes you wonder."

"What does?"

She closes her eyes and gestures vaguely. "Oh, just everything."

There's a lot she's wondered about over the last three years, particularly about the fight and what made this one so much worse than the hundreds that preceded it. On the surface, the fight seemed so simple: Thaddeus wanted to celebrate his birthday with a family vacation in the Caribbean and Steven overreacted. Those are the facts, and, really, was there anything surprising about them? No. Of course, it wasn't really about the vacation. She knew that much. The two of them had been at each other like flint and steel for years; this was just the latest spark. But in the past they'd have their fights and then move on. This time, however, it was different. What was it about the vacation that finally drove Steven over the edge? He'd said something about not wanting to patronize an island ensconced in homophobia. Certainly that would be a concern for him; nobody wants to spend their vacation in a hostile environment. But Thaddeus can't even find his way to the grocery store without her help; how could Steven possibly expect him to see beyond the ganja and reggae to Jamaica's complications? He might as well have expected fish to fly. No, Steven would've known better than to expect miracles from Thaddeus. But Peter, with that defiant curl in his lip, wasn't he the only thing that was different this time? Well, maybe, and maybe not, but the more she thinks about it the more she realizes how negligent she's been about digging into his past. For instance, just now he mentioned a sister. Why is this the first time she's heard of her?

"I think I will open a window," Peter says.

Before she can respond, he's crossed the room and cracked a pane enough to permit any passing breeze the opportunity to rustle the blinds.

"There," he says as he takes a seat next to her and crosses his legs. "That should help."

He gives her a smile so well suited to the moment that she thinks he must have been practicing it for just such an occasion.

"I didn't realize how stuffy it got in here. You and Thaddeus must've been sweating bullets yesterday."

"It's just this room. I don't mind the heat. It's Thaddeus who has a problem with it."

"I should get Steven to check the vents. Maybe there's something blocking them." He glances at his phone. "Tomorrow's supposed to be cooler at least."

"That'll be nice."

From outside drifts the sound of a sprinkler spraying against the metal accordion storm shutters. It's joined by the cry of a bird. Combined, they remind her of the low rumble of that rocket all those winters ago.

She smoothes a wrinkle in the knee of her slacks, then looks Peter in the eye. "Why do you think Steven shut Thaddeus out? I mean, really."

He winces and scratches his neck. "Timing? The best I can figure is that he was on edge because we were finalizing the adoption and buying the house. There was a lot of red tape involved all around. He'd just started at the shelter, too, and I think all of it together was just too much. Something changed with him. Things just got out of hand, I guess. But hey"—he smiles—"why dwell on the past, right? We're together now."

A soft breeze sighs through the room, and overhead the fan clanks in its frame.

Time. She nods. "We've just wasted so much time."

"We'll see each other twice as much to make up for it."

"I think we'll have to see what Steven thinks about that after last night."

"Don't worry, he'll come around. Last night was just nerves." He places a hand on her knee. The warmth and weight of his touch differs from Thaddeus's while remaining familiar. "But let's forget about it for now. I'll finish the dishes."

She protests that she can finish them herself, but he insists.

"Then I should really pass by the gallery. Want to come with me?"

"I should wait for Thaddeus to get back."

"Really, three years is nothing. You'll see"

Maybe that's true, but it's not as easy for her to dismiss. Three years ago her hormones were a mess. She did what she could, and no one blames her. Maybe, she thinks for the hundredth time, she could've called Steven after the fight, said that Thaddeus was exhausted and didn't know what he was saying. He was on all these new pills, she could've claimed, and, really, a period of adjustment had to be expected. After Steven agreed to accept an apology it would've been easy to sit Thaddeus down by the pool and explain that Steven was upset because *he* had wanted to take *them* on a vacation—it didn't matter what she said. Any story would do. And couldn't he call to apologize, tell Steven that they'd go on vacation anywhere he liked? Maybe Mexico or Puerto Rico.

It wasn't even about the vacation. The vacation was just an excuse for them to fight. Of course she knew that, but she also knew that she could've easily taken that excuse away from them. If the fight was the only way they could articulate their animosity, then she still could've made them mute. She'd been doing it for so long it was second nature. A thousand possibilities rush through her head. She would've come up with something plausible. Maybe if she had they wouldn't have missed so much already, and she wouldn't be trying to shake this feeling that it was already too late.

Regrets solve nothing.

No, she thinks. They were both adults, and she had herself to worry about because neither one of them was trying to understand what she was experiencing. Neither one of them understood how something like a telephone call could suddenly, inexplicably, make you feel anxious all day even when the caller turned out to be just a telemarketer trying to sell you a new cable plan. Neither one of them had to endure the hot flashes in the middle of a Florida July. And, certainly, neither of them had to reconcile with the fact that at the end of it all the game would be up, she'd be finished in the motherhood department.

Feeling older by the second, she reaches for the water. It's still cold as she takes a sip and the glass sweats. Did they really expect her to go on playing interference forever?

"I was thinking we could all go out for dinner tonight when Steven gets home," he says, sliding a dish into the dishwasher. "Somewhere downtown. My treat."

"Do you ever wonder about the kids down at that shelter?"

"What's that?" he asks, raising his voice above the garbage disposal.

"Those kids at Steven's shelter; their parents just throw them out like trash."

Drawers and cabinets open and close. Silverware clatters.

"Well," he grunts, "lucky for them Steven's always there."

It wasn't so long ago that she could've been one of those mothers. Of course, now... well, that ship has sailed.

"I'm sorry," he says, and pinches the bridge of his nose. "I didn't mean anything by that..."

He mentions something about the office and the gallery and how it's a lot to do on one's own, that he's frustrated, but she doesn't pay attention, not really.

It's a strange sensation, envying mothers who abandon their children, and languishing in this heat that coils around her like a noose, she opens herself, as she has a million times before, to the possibility of abandonment, wanting to know what it feels like to give away a child. Could it be worse than never having the child in the first place?

She was never the gambling type. Not all those years ago after Cocoa Beach when money was so tight, and not as the years passed and things at home between Thaddeus and Steven grew increasingly bitter.

"I'm sorry. I wasn't trying to unload on you or anything," Peter says. "For what it's worth, I think Steven is glad to see Thaddeus."

"It's okay," she says, managing a wan smile. "Thaddeus is much more relaxed now. That's just the way it is."

He returns her smile. "That's good news."

"I had an abortion years ago." The confession surprises him, but she presses on. "I never told Thaddeus about it. The timing wasn't right, and then..." She shrugs. "Well, things just got more complicated. Maybe it would've been different if we had it. Maybe it's just that Steven and Thaddeus can't get along. I don't know. And, anyway, there's nothing I can do about it now."

He looks up from the sink, his long face drawn tight in a strange mix of anger and sadness, a look she recognizes as a cousin to betrayal, and the smallest part of her is glad to inflict this secret on him, to drag him into its conspiracy, because she's tired of enduring it all alone.

"I had no—"

"It's nothing," she says, cutting him off. "Really, it isn't. It's just something I think about from time to time." Rising, she brushes back her hair. "Anyway, I'm going to shower. Let's go out somewhere afterward, okay? I'm tired of being in this house and I feel like taking a drive. Maybe we can pass by that gallery of yours."

"AND OF COURSE ALL THE TOWN HOUSES COME EQUIPPED with hurricane shutters." The realtor, Steven, stood in the model unit's living room and gestured at the sliding glass doors that led out to the patio. "However, you can upgrade and go fully automatic. Be safe with just a push of a button."

There was a wink in his voice. How often had he used that line? Laila wondered. The shutters unfurled, engulfing the bright, well-appointed room in shadow. Silence followed. With only the sterile hum of the air conditioner to give shape to a space that a moment ago had seemed so inviting, Laila felt disoriented. His voice boomed from somewhere nearby: "It's not just a good idea during hurricane season, but for any time you have to be away from home for a while."

He spoke of the ease and the luxury of automatic shutters, his words surrounding her as he crisscrossed the room, rustling drapes, shuffling across carpet. Worried about crashing into furniture in the dark, she clung to the breakfast counter. She focused on the smoothness of the Formica—firm under her elbow and cool to the touch. Something about the way he spoke unnerved her. He seemed to anticipate (hope for even?) the violence of a catastrophic storm. Had she not spent six disheartening months looking at and reject-ing a staggering number of properties on the market in Orlando, she might have walked away right then. She'd rejected other houses for lesser reasons than a creepy Realtor. But something felt right about this home. It fit her well—not so small that she felt cramped, as in her current apartment, but not too large to remind her of the husband and children who had failed to materialize in her life. A two-story one-bedroom town house with a screened-in porch in a quiet subdivision near the pharmacy and within budget: it checked all her boxes.

"The regular shutters are fine," she said.

"Fair enough." With a click the shutters retreated. Steven stood on the far side of the living room. "Something to consider," he said, an awkward smile fixed on his face. "No pressure."

With the return of the light, Laila recognized a shift in his demeanor—a tightening of the muscles, a compression of the features of the face. It was as if she were staring at a hollow shell. In that moment she realized that she wasn't interacting with a salesman at all, but rather the idea of a salesman, a mask—an effigy—ginned up in haste under the scrutiny of a public performance. What had been uncovered in that brief darkness? The possibilities sent a shiver through her.

"Thanks, but I prefer the standard ones." And, she thought, I'll be getting new locks installed as soon as the closing papers are signed.

Now, as she maneuvers a telescoping aluminum ladder into position beneath her bedroom window, Laila wonders if she made the right decision back then or if she allowed fear to distract her from the utility of the upgraded storm shutters. It was partially a financial decision, her stubborn thriftiness winning out over reason. After all, what's a few thousand dollars amortized over the course of a mortgage? Well, she could quote an exact number, but the financial account never considered the urgency of this moment versus the smug frugality of that earlier negotiation. There's something to be said for emotion as the volatile driver of economics. Take, for instance, the present: it's nearly dark with a hurricane approaching and she has yet to shutter her bedroom window because of an aversion to heights. How much would she be willing to pay right now for safety at the push of a button?

She dismisses the thought.

That kind of thinking is a distraction and she's waited as long as she can. A feeder band passed through a few minutes ago. Another one won't be far behind. Then Natalie herself will blow in with the force of the inevitable. What was once some windblown sand off the coast of Africa has grown into a massive weather system destined to pummel America until it exhausts itself somewhere along the banks of the Mississippi. Retribution comes to mind, Mother Nature invoking a righteous correction to the Middle Passage. Yet a more direct image takes precedence for Laila Morales. When she and Alex were children their father would joke that a hurricane brought him to Orlando. "It plucked me off the shore"—not *beach*, because with his accent that word always came out sounding like *bitch*—"and dropped me here. You can imagine my surprise." Laila, of course, was too old to believe the story, but she went along with it, partly because she wanted to preserve something of the gullibility of youth even while ensconced in the nihilism of adolescence, and partly because Alex believed the tale and was terrified of it and she liked to terrorize her baby brother.

Even a hurricane doesn't seem powerful enough to bring Alex home tonight, though. It was silly to expect him. Ever since their father died he's been unreliable, bullheaded, and contrary— worse still in the face of expectations. Viewed this way, his text this morning wasn't vague; it was a code she failed to decipher. It really read: *You're on your own.* Stupid her for expecting otherwise. Esther's unspoken accusation nags her as, grimacing, she clamps her sweaty palms to the legs of the ladder and hesitantly begins to climb; each step is agony. Alex is her responsibility now, whether she likes it or not. And what if he's out there doing something stupid? She flashes to the scene at Cocoa Beach and the reckless storm chasers. He wouldn't be that senseless, would he?

The ground below her is wet, the air chilled. To her right lies the long, curvy street running from her town house to the development entrance. Among the houses lining it only hers remains vulnerable to the storm. At least three of her neighbors opted for the automatic shutters, she notes while steadying herself on the fourth rung. Her palms sweat. Her knees shake. Until the age of thirteen she'd enjoyed heights. The year she was born her father had planted a tree in the yard. The sapling took nearly a decade to mature to the point where it could accommodate her weight. By the time Alex showed up, it had become her refuge, her secret lair, even if the spindly branches and thin leaf cover provided little privacy from Esther's hawklike gaze. Still, it was hers, but then Alex ruined everything, like he always does.

"I wanna climb, too!"

His whiny voice pierced her solitude. It was summer and hot, and all she wanted was to get away for a moment, to go up somewhere shady and cool—somewhere above this strange new family that insisted on claiming her as its eldest child. Alex tracked her across the yard. He bolted toward her as she negotiated the familiar curves and flexible branches of the young tree. He tried to squeeze between her and the thin trunk. He couldn't stand to be apart from her, and even at three he was fearless. But fearless or not, Laila knew better than to let a toddler climb a tree.

"No, Alex! You can't come up here. Get down. Your mom will see you."

"I don't care! I wanna climb!"

"You can't. I'm climbing it. It's my tree. Papi planted it for me."

"No!"

"Go ask him."

"Where's my tree?"

"You don't have a tree."

"I want your tree!" he said.

"No."

But he pressed on and they tussled. Using one hand to fend him off, she gripped a notch in the truck with the other. Despite her efforts, he managed a foothold. The exact order of events occludes in a fog of emotion, but the end result is crystal clear in her memory. She lost her grip attempting to extract him from the tree and fell backward, landing on the sharp end of a small spade their father had forgotten in the garden. Pain registered immediately, followed by a piercing cry.

Esther rushed over to smother her with stepmotherly concern while simultaneously undercutting her. "What did you do?"

Her leg felt cold. Blood stained her clothes and left a dark trail in the grass. The smell of iron and dirt suffused the air. Tears streamed down her face as the wound throbbed. She wiggled her toes. At least she wasn't paralyzed.

Esther kissed her forehead and brushed away her tears. "Tate quieto, it's all right. Félix!" she shouted. "Ven acá. Laila hurt herself."

There was something delicate in the way Esther tried to mother her in that moment, a fragility born not of familiarity or love, or even duty, but rather of fear. The last three years had been rough between the two of them, with Laila sensing that Esther lived in terror of hurting Félix's little girl, his princesa. The fall, then, provided Laila with an opportunity to scare her stepmother and she seized it.

"I'm paralyzed! I'll never walk again."

"Ay, Dios mío. Félix!"

"Haha, Laila fell," Alex taunted from the tree. He'd managed to make it up to the first branch, but when he saw the blood in the grass he, too, started crying.

"You get down from there. Ahora mismo," Esther shouted at Alex, but he refused to budge.

The wound looked a lot worse than it was. Laila had grazed only her upper thigh, but she enjoyed watching the fear on Esther's face too much to let on. "I was trying to climb," she managed between crocodile sobs, "but he pushed me!"

"Your brother se le antoja whatever you're doing," Esther said. "You know that."

So even though she was the one bleeding, Esther found a way to absolve Alex. It was somehow her fault that Alex pushed her off the tree because he wanted to climb, a tree that he had no business climbing in the first place.

"You always take his side!" she shouted. "It's not fair! I could be paralyzed and you're still taking his side."

Félix emerged with a first aid kit in hand, and as soon as Laila spotted him, she pulled away from Esther and thrust herself into her father's arms, forgetting that she was supposed to be paralyzed.

"Come on, no need to cry." Her father soothed her as he cleaned the wound, a small puncture on the upper thigh. "You're a big girl. Y mira, it's nothing. You'll be fine. I have to be more careful about where I leave my tools, that's all." With a smile he handed her a bandage to apply.

"I'm not saying it's your fault," Esther said, as she marched to the tree and plucked Alex from the branch like an apple. When Alex protested, she silenced him with a stern look. "Your brother is three years old. He doesn't know better. You have to protect him."

But who protected her? Alex got whisked to safety, not a scratch on him, while she bled through her favorite jean shorts. Where was her mom to swoop in when danger came near?

Within twenty minutes, she was back in the yard playing... by herself. She gave Alex the cold shoulder for a week. She never did attempt to climb that tree again. And now the county says that tree has to go.

Six rungs up and the physics of her situation loom large. She is a lever that could topple the ladder with a small application of force in the wrong vector. But she's close now. Only a couple more rungs and she'll be in position. She braces herself against the stucco, which is damp from rain but still warm from a sunny day. The irony of hurricanes is that perfect weather always precedes the storm. Touching the house infuses her with confidence. There's a purpose to being up here and it's to ensure her house survives intact. She can do this!

Only she can't.

When not in use, the shutters fold up at either side of the window, compressed like an accordion. In theory, she need only unfurl them along the track and turn the lug nut a few times to secure them in place. In reality, the situation proves more complex. Take, for instance, what happens to metal and plastic bearings in a warm, damp climate. Things that should slide easily seize. Things that should endure are made brittle by the sun. But here, too, physics applies. If she can exert enough force in the right direction the accordion will unfold, but what if the platform from which said force is to be applied is an unsteady ladder supporting a terrified homeowner?

"Fuck," she mutters to herself. "Fuck!" again when she makes the mistake of glancing down.

She closes her eyes and takes a deep breath. The smell of honey-suckle floats in the breeze. A gust tickles her neck. Central Florida is a flat place; when she opens her eyes she can see a long distance. Uninterrupted sight lines are what she used to love about climbing. Perhaps they're what drew her to a town house with a bedroom on the second floor. She likes to survey, to get a lay of the land. From the top rung of the ladder, she can see all the way to the leading edge of the next feeder band sweeping in from the east.

"Fuck."

She needs to move quickly, but trying to force the shutters closed from the ladder is a nonstarter. In a flash of inspiration, she conceives of another option. She can shut them from inside the house. She'll still have to secure the lug nut from the outside, but the brute force of muscling the shutters closed can be done while leaning out a window, with relative safety.

Down she goes as fast as she trusts herself to move. She grabs a can of lubricant from under the sink, then charges up the staircase.

She opens the window. A few quick squirts into the track followed by a firm tug, and the accordion begins to unfold. Before she can congratulate herself, though, she hits a snag. One side flattens without incident, but the other side refuses to budge. Something appears to be jamming the track on the top, but she can't quite make it out from inside the bedroom. She rattles the shutters to see if that removes the obstruction. A thin, armored body with long wings and a stinger emerges from the accordion. Wasps. The obstruction is a nest.

"Shit!"

In a fraction of a second, she slams the window shut and slides down onto the carpet. Two wasps alight on the pane, their stingers scrape the glass. Several more swarm around the disturbed nest. Her knowledge of wasps is limited to topical ointments and epinephrine, but she suspects that the wasps are disinclined to move house in advance of the approaching feeder band. Ordinarily, she'd call an exterminator for something like this, but nobody is going to come out tonight and it's not like she can just leave her bedroom window uncovered—especially with wasps. What if her window breaks and they decide her mattress or her closet are safer places to ride out the storm?

What she needs is pesticide. She rushes downstairs. Under the sink, behind the dishwashing detergent and the borax, she finds an old bottle of weed killer. It's not ideal, but once when she was in high school, Félix took down a pretty beefy rat ensconced in their garage with a bottle of roach spray and a shovel. Weed killer should be enough for a few wasps. Still, she's not about to face off without some added protection. She dashes back upstairs in search of a jacket. Buried in her closet is her dad's old yellow rain slicker. It's several sizes too big but the heavy plastic fabric covers all her exposed skin.

Fingers of pink and umber color an otherwise indigo sky as she creeps back onto the patio. Two wasps remain on the windowpane like sentries. The rest appear to have returned to the nest. Mentally she rehearses the plan. Step one: douse the nest in poison. Step two: knock it loose from the track. Here her plan stalls. How is she supposed to remove it? A broom handle seems the obvious choice, but the last thing she wants is to start whacking at a nest of angry, intoxicated wasps while standing on a ladder. The trick is to remove and contain in one motion, preferably from a safe distance. Knocking the nest into a garbage can might work, but she worries that the can would provide an ideal environment for the wasps to regroup and plan a counteroffensive when she removes the lid—as she must eventually do. Additionally, that plan requires a degree of skill and agility she's not sure she possesses, especially decked out like the Gorton's fisherman. No, a better choice is to suck them up with a vacuum cleaner. It's quick. It's safe—she can extract them from a distance. And, best of all, she can leave them trapped in the bag until they die, even if that takes months or years.

The yellow slicker weighs her down and her hands disappear inside the sleeves, making it difficult to dig through the hall closet to unearth the vacuum, which is shoved in the corner beneath a pile of winter coats. Considering the dismal state of her bedroom carpet, the vacuum doesn't get much use in the Morales household. She resolves to redouble her tidying efforts when this is all over. Hurricane Natalie will be the new leaf she turns for a life of orderliness and cleanliness.

She returns to the patio, dragging the vacuum behind her with one hand and clutching the weed killer with the other. The sentries continue to circle, hovering above her for a moment before alighting once again on the window. The wind had picked up while she was inside. Any minute now the rain will start. She considers changing the theater and mounting the assault from the safety of her bedroom, but that poses an unacceptable threat to the homeland. Should anything go wrong, an angry colony of wasps would inevitably invade her bedroom. No, better to maintain the envelope of the house secure, which means the ladder, a vacuum cleaner, and a rain slicker. Dammit, she thinks for the thousandth time. Where the fuck is Alex?!

She switches on the vacuum and begins to climb.

The ladder shakes under her tentative steps, but the heavy plastic dulls her senses, easing her fears the way blinders calm a horse prone to spook. Her focus remains on the two sentries circling the hive. With the nozzle of the vacuum in one hand and the weed killer in the other, the best she can do is gesture toward a firm grip. Gravity keeps her body in contact with the angled ladder. She climbs higher, regaining some of the confidence of her tree-climbing youth. A gust rustles her hood. The air chills her back. Time is running out. She shuffles up the ladder quicker than before, taking risks that earlier would've been paralyzing to consider.

Before long, she's perched within striking distance of the adversary. Below, the vacuum rumbles, the nozzle sucking steadily in her hand. The sentries swoop in a modified Delta pattern, but she stands firm. Fear will not win the day. They pull back at the final moment. Perhaps it's a defense tactic: warning her off before an attack. Or perhaps they, too, sense the coming storm and are hesitant to travel far from the nest. Either way, their retreat provides the perfect window to take her shot. But she hesitates. How long has this nest been here? Is it possible that these two wasps—that all these wasps—grew up in her house? That they've never known fear of humans and have lived perfectly admirable wasp lives? And these sentries, they could be young kids out on the front line for the first time, subsisting on adrenaline. They must be afraid.

She levels the weed killer on the target. The first squirt will kick off panic in the nest. The sentries will attack; reinforcements will swarm, so it's important to strike with the vacuum at the same time as she begins spraying. The vacuum, she trusts. The weed killer is unproven, a wild card, but the vacuum will not fail her.

The first volley of rain from the quickly advancing band begins pelting shutters down the block, and she tugs on the drawstring of her hood to create a seal against the rain.

It's time.

She pumps the weed killer with a mad fury, atomizing the poison into a cloud of unrelenting shock and awe. She brings down a hard rain of her own against the nest. The first sentry drops from the sky immediately. She stabs at the second with the vacuum, but she loses sight of him in the confusion of the moment. He retreats, beelining back to the nest and disappearing inside. Her first sally and she's beaten the foe into retreat. A primordial scream emerges from her now as she continues pumping the bottle, drenching the nest in weed killer until the muscles in her forearm give out. The wet, glistening thing hangs before her a lifeless catacomb. Her work is done. All that remains is to clean it up. Just as she's preparing to jab at the nest with the vacuum the feeder band arrives. And her ladder shakes.

Her first thought is *earthquake* despite the fact that Central Florida doesn't experience earthquakes. She drops the nozzle and the weed killer. The nest can wait. Her instinct is to get to low ground, to find shelter, but with the shaking intensifying and a howl filling her ears, she no longer trusts her legs to move from rung to rung. Everything is wet and her balance falters. She grasps for the nearest handhold, finding purchase on the lower track of the shutters—right on top of the carcass of the fallen sentry. The stinger pierces her palm. Pain blossoms out from the puncture, throbbing its way up her arm. The physical process takes a fraction of a second, but her consciousness lags, stretching the event. She stares at her arm, as if watching the wave of pain approaching. When at last it registers, she yelps.

The ladder stops shaking. Miraculously, she doesn't fall.

"Careful where you're dropping shit!" Alex yells up at her. "You almost hit me in the fucking head with the vacuum cleaner."

In a flash, the sequence of events rights itself. There is no earthquake. There is no howling. There's only Alex.

"Yo, what you doing up there anyway?"

"What am I—" She scurries down the ladder. Skipping the final rungs, she leaps to the concrete patio slab, nearly landing on him, but Alex slides out of the way just in time. "You have got to be kidding me!"

She kicks at his shin, wanting to punch him, but her hand stiffens around a quickly forming welt. Flexing the fingers sends her into a paroxysm of tears. Cortisone, she thinks. Antihistamines. Epinephrine in the case of severe allergic reaction.

"Yo, damn, Lails, chill the fuck out! That hurts."

She thrusts her hand in his face. "I got stung by a goddamn wasp because of you!"

The swelling smoothes the lines of her palm, and for a brief moment the venom rejuvenates her skin, returning it to an earlier, teenage appearance. But the moment doesn't linger, tilting instead into the grotesque. In the rain, her hand looks waterlogged, puffy, and diseased.

"Gross!" He pushes her hand away. "That looks sick. Get it out of my face."

"Where the fuck have you been all day, huh? I've been texting you since this morning."

He shrugs, then finding nothing to do with his arms, he gathers up the vacuum to push it out of the rain. He moves slowly, his arms and legs uncoordinated, his eyes bloodshot. He's stoned, she thinks. The pharmacology of weed comes to mind, an inhibitor, a blocker of emotional gravitas. To a certain degree it's out of his control.

"Answer me!" she shouts, hoping to pierce the fog in his head.

"I don't know. Out, or whatever."

With her good hand she brushes back her hair, which frizzes in the humidity. The rain does not appear to bother Alex, his purple tank top stretching under the weight of the saturating fabric.

"How do you not know where you were?"

"My phone died. Sorry, damn. I lost track of time."

"Oh, you lost track of time," she scoffs. "I guess that's okay then! I just had to climb the ladder myself and get stung by a wasp because you 'lost track of time.'"

"Do you want, like, a Band-Aid or something?"

"I want you to answer my question, Alex."

"I'm here now. What's the big deal? It's not like this punk-ass storm is gonna do nothing anyway."

"You should've been doing this! That's the point!"

"You're pissed because I didn't get stung by a wasp? Damn, that's cold."

"That's not what I'm saying—"

He rolls his eyes and brushes his tongue rapidly back and forth across his lower lip. The tattoo on his arm twitches—the stupid tattoo that nearly gave Esther a heart attack when she saw it for the first time. "You're being a hella bitch right now—Mom!"

Her eyes narrow into slits. The pharmacy, the wasp—all she wanted was a quiet day to herself.

"You know what? You can take that attitude and get the fuck out of my house!" Her palm throbs as she says it, underscoring a different venom surging through her body.

"Dude, chill out. I'm only playing."

"I'm not. You couldn't be bothered to come home all day anyway—"

"I told you I didn't hear my phone!"

But she's past the edge. She's committed now. Alex may have inherited his mother's quick temper, but Laila inherited something strong, too: their father's stubbornness. Seventeen years of animosity peaks her blood pressure. The bitter taste of bile fills her throat. The first telling shine of a massive migraine flares behind her closed eyes. "There's the door," she says in a quiet voice that builds. "My door that I pay for. Walk your inconsiderate ass out it now—"

"And go where, huh?"

"You wanna act like a grown-ass man, all big and tough, doesn't give a fuck about anybody but himself? Well, fine. Here's your chance. Because you know what? You're not my responsibility. I don't have any kids!"

Alex balls his hands into fists, cracking each knuckle in succession under the broad pads of his thumbs. He puffs his chest to approximate the convexity his slim build lacks and snorts. "Oh, so that's how it's gonna be? All right." He stares her down, drawing on his height advantage. "I didn't wanna be here anyway. I was doing you a favor so you wouldn't be alone or shit tonight. You Gorton's-fisherman-looking bitch—"

She slaps him with her good hand. "I don't need any favors from an arrogant little boy."

"Fuck you!"

He kicks the vacuum into the patio screen, ripping it, and walks right through the house and to the open front door and out into the storm.

For a long time, she doesn't move. Her vision blurs and her neck sweats. Her skin feels clammy. Adrenaline courses through her body and she contracts her muscles to try to control it. The rain helps. Its heavy bombardment ebbs to a steady patter splashing against her slicker.

Calm, she finds herself alone in the indigo-and-gray night.

Alone in the rain.

And the shutters still need securing.

"Fuck."

YOU RECOGNIZE HIM AT ONCE.

At Independent Bar he introduced himself as Alex, and you remember that he prefers vodka and cranberry. You remember because you thought that one day you might see him again and that the knowledge would be useful then; of course, you never expected to see him here, today, so you watch with urgency as he makes his way from the front door to the intake desk, where you sit arranging a row of marbled erasers and sharpened pencils.

Trailing from the waistband of his tight jeans is a purple tank top, cut in the chemise fashion popular with his generation. When dry, it probably billows around him like a sail off the wind; wet, however, it creates a slick of rainwater on the gray carpet. Flecks of azalea, bougainvillea, and mulch speckle his otherwise bare torso in a way that leaves you wondering if perhaps he didn't launch his lithe body into a well-manicured hedge to escape the weather. He may have. Feeder bands have been cycling over the shelter for hours now, heralding Hurricane Natalie's westward track in from the Caribbean coast. The eye will pass somewhere along the I-4 corridor later this evening, but until it does you must endure the raging caprices of its seemingly deliberate slow jog.

You assume he caught the brunt of the last pass before reaching the shelter because every inch of him is sopping, and what initially appeared to be a steady drip is actually a stream originating from his head and traversing his sinewy back before discharging through the hem of his tank top.

None of this, however, affects his slow amble toward the desk. He approaches, taking the time to greet the handful of residents in the shelter tonight individually with a wave, a wink, or a wet hug and a kiss. To your knowledge, he has never been inside this building before, yet he commands the space with a familiarity usually sprung either from antipathy, affinity, or the intersection of the two. It's likely he knows everyone from the clubs, and that complicates your design. You prefer your victims to be unattached, loners—certainly at a remove from you and your sphere of influence.

By the time he saunters up to you at the desk, he's already tread across the kitchen's stained linoleum, navigating the habitually sticky spots unceremoniously, as well as perched atop the tattered arm of the maroon couch in the television corner for a short chat with one of the shier residents. He's taller than you remember and he stares you directly in the eye.

Immediately, he breaches the improbable authority heaped upon the old aluminum desk by planting his palms on the speckled wood veneer, curling his delicate fingers over the lip, and hiking his torso across the desktop. "Hola," he says, affecting a southern drawl. "Whatchu gettin' into?"

He resembles nothing more than a skeletal cantilever, propped up by elbows bowing above a trunk of thick veins, but before anything, however, you need to know if he remembers you.

He brushes a tangle of wet hair from his face with an intimate, effeminate touch that reveals thin eyebrows arched above a pair of eyes light brown in color, bordering on amber. "I'm not homeless," he says, anticipating your first question. "Let's get that straight."

It's both tenacious and hopeless—the hallmarks of a last resort—his coming here, enduring winds and slashing rain to seek shelter within these cinder block walls buttressed, as they are, by generations of cast-off furniture. The roof leaks after an afternoon thundershower, let alone at the height of a tropical system. It's not at all certain that the building will survive the night, and for a moment you allow yourself to feel a bond with this familiar boy and his reckless ego. You slip him a smile.

He smirks.

Separating the work from the individual has become increasingly difficult. You don't come naturally to this type of work. There's no sense in pretending otherwise. The calculated coldness it demands wears on you, and you fear whatever splintered bulkhead remains after two and a half years of breakneck progress may breach in his presence. But almost immediately his hair falls back, obscuring his eyes, and your anxiety recedes. You see him for what he truly is: an entitled faggot—just like all the others—unwilling to help himself. A body better utilized as an example to others.

"I got a home," he says, his voice cracking. "I just need a place to crash tonight."

They all say this in one way or another, and the predictability of this statement—along with the desperate insistence on some minimal level of normalcy it conveys—allows you to marshal the resolve to continue.

You hand him some forms and a pencil. "These are for our records. Fill them out."

You enumerate the rules of the shelter and explain that certain things will be expected of him; chief among these are daily chores and a strict adherence to the curfew. All residents must agree to these provisions, you tell him—matching his gaze—in writing before they are allowed to stay. The rules serve to promote the betterment of the space as a whole and, in turn, the community of residents and staff. Together you help the residents help themselves.

Pointing at the forms, you assure him that his information is confidential.

He shifts positions so that his hip rests against the desktop, then he dries his hands—large, a small callus below the thumb, and free of any hair—as best he can with the moist shirt before grabbing the forms with a sigh. He scans the pages. After a moment, he dismisses them.

"Look, I just need a place to crash tonight." He emphasizes by tapping the desk.

You nod, adding: "Three months is the limit."

"What did I just say?"

Dangling from his small brown nipple is a stainless steel hoop. The lip ring you remember appears to have migrated to his chest. It's an improvement, and hiding your hand beneath the level of the desk so that he can't see, you press your fingers together, recalling the subtle friction of jewelry sliding through a pocket of flesh.

You've felt the sensation hundreds of times, and the memory of it returns with little effort. The nipple, you recall, does a commendable job accommodating lateral movements, but fails entirely when the stress is applied in a perpendicular direction away from the body. It provides resistance in the form of something tough and unaccommodating, like tugging a fork through gristle, and the memory elicits a ghost of a smile from you as you recall the human body's eternal ability to teach you about limitations. For instance, you don't fully appreciate the nipple's pliability until the moment just before the jewelry tears free.

"You still need to fill out the forms," you say, signaling him to take a seat. "Just in case."

"I'm telling you I won't need it." Smiling, he straddles the aluminum chair. All the muted browns and sterile grays of the space unfold behind him. There's a mincing theatricality to the place and its residents, and by scooting his chair so that the room lies over his shoulder, he instinctively separates himself from it as if to suggest a tired tableau that may have once amused him but which no longer does.

Leaning forward, he winks. "Ain't you heard from these bitches? I'm the luckiest motherfucker around."

That may be true if, in fact, he has a home. Those with any other place to go have gone there to ride out the storm. The ones left are the most desperate. You yourself should be at home.

"Fill out the forms."

"Ooh, look at her," he says, dismissing you with a moue. "What's the matter, papi, got your panties in a twist or something?"

You say nothing, and a moment later he draws a bead on you with a long finger.

"I remember you," he says, biting his thumb. "Don't look so surprised. I never forget nothing."

Perhaps, he thinks he can charm you with his bravado. He wouldn't be the first.

Asher and the dozens before possessed a similar confidence, but in one way or another they all failed to go beyond the attitude and embody real change. They lacked the will to strip away every-thing—their entitlement, their families, their very identities as toler-ated members in a failed social order—to strip it all away in service to something larger. They all failed, so you made examples of them. There's no reason this one should be any different. Yet you sense a restrained violence in him that you've rarely encountered. You re-member it from your first meeting at Independent Bar, and, frankly, you find it highly erotic. It's that kinship that you acknowledge now with a slow nod.

Amused, he licks his lips.

"Shit, did I just blow up your spot? Yo, I'm sorry, son." He holds up his hands in mock chagrin. "I wasn't trying to tell everyone how you was trolling the club." He says this last part loudly, then laughs, but even his laughter contains a tinge of forced spontaneity, a terse, lonely hiss, and hearing it you can't help but feel the tiniest bit of sorrow for him and his situation.

But you maintain your silence. He'll think that by recognizing you he's garnered a measure of control over you and the shelter, and, no doubt, he'll seek to exploit it. Allow him the fantasy. You can use it to your own advantage.

Reaching for your hand, he says, "I'm just playing, papi. Damn, don't be so serious."

Squeeze the offered hand until he winces.

It takes only a moment for him to fix his face into a forced smile and squeeze back.

He's strong, but you're stronger, and though you can feel the bones in his hands fold over one another and compress in what must be excruciating pain, he refuses to pull away or flinch.

"You know I was just playing, right?"

"Sure," you say, smiling. "But don't flatter yourself. You're not my type."

At last he flinches and draws back his hand. He massages it as he speaks. "I know you're lying."

For the second time in his presence you're speechless.

He flares his nostrils and the dusting of hair on his arms stands straight up. He flicks the hoop in his nipple before leaning over close to you. "Know how I know?" Not waiting for your answer, he continues. "'Cause I'm a stud and everyone wants to fuck me. That's how I know. And you do, too, Alex." He grins. "Oh, yeah. I remember your name, papi." He bends the corner of the form, then leans back far enough so that you can see the full mischievous glint in his eyes. "It's the same as mine. You told me at I-Bar. I told you I don't forget nothing."

To your left lies a medical supply cabinet. Any prescriptions the residents have must be kept under lock and key, to be handed out by a staff member only. It's one of the rules, and because you need a distraction right now to derail his ego, you stand and inventory the contents, making bullshit notations in the log.

"Not only do I know you remember me, but I know what you're thinking right now, too." Springing to his feet, he wipes the back of his hand across his wet brow. "You're thinking: Oh, he's so hot I just wanna bean him right here." He crouches over the chair and humps the backrest, smacking it with an open palm. "Yeah, you just wanna drive it into me again and again and again!"

Water flies from his sinewy body like from a sprinkler as he ravages the aluminum, grinding its already dented frame further into the intake desk with each successive thrust. Despite yourself, you marvel at the smooth curves of his body, so young and so full of potential, and you feel that old blindness again work its way into you, softening you up.

"Ay, papi, yeah, that feels sooo fucking good! Give it to me hard." He's screaming now, and the handful of residents in the building tonight stare slack-jawed as he grinds and twists and pantomimes any number of sex acts with such theatricality that you seriously wonder if he's ever had sex at all.

When he's satisfied, he sits down with a heaving laugh, breaking alternately to cough or to snap his fingers through the air in a series of explosive cracks.

"Are you finished?" you ask.

He smirks. "Didn't know I could read minds, did you? I got lots of secrets you can learn, but you're scared to 'cause I'm here"—he spreads his arms in disgust, vaguely encompassing everything from the dirty lavender walls to the peeling tint on the windows—"but

I'm not some strung-out loser. Okay, papi?" Leaning close, he bites the tip of his tongue and sneers. "I'm just a lucky motherfucker who needs a dry place to crash. So don't feel bad about wanting me."

Cheeks flushed from the exertion, he corners your gaze. The desk is the only thing separating you, and you wonder if at the moment that's for your protection or his. If you wanted to, you could flip it out of the way with ease. Seconds later he'd be pinned to the carpet beneath his own chair. It would be easy to twist his head until the neck muscles fail and the vertebrae snap. You could have him any way you wanted. You grin. The entire maneuver would take under a minute, and he would deserve it for his hubris.

Instead, you indulge his narcissism. Partly in deference to the space, partly because you don't want a war of wills played out in the open—there are too many variables you can't control—and partly because, despite yourself, you are curious to see what develops.

For a long while neither of you speaks. The residents lose interest and return to the television.

"I like what you do here, you know?" He pulls the chair over so that he's next to you, looking out at the dilapidated shelter. "It's important, and 'cause I'm a selfless guy I'd like to help you out." He slides the blank forms over to you. "You've seen how I got these bitches eating out of the palm of my hand, right? They'll do anything I want, and if I'm working for you that means they'll do anything you want. I can be, like, your representative. A fucking lieutenant!"

Overhead, the fluorescent lights flicker. The power may go out at any moment.

"Why are you here?" you ask.

"Every hotel in town was booked," he says drily. A moment later he recants, looks at you with what passes for sincerity. "Look, I need a place to crash. Just for the night."

"What about your home?"

Shrugging, he picks at the wet fabric covering his knees. "Maybe there are people there I'd rather not see tonight."

For a moment, the ordered surface of the desk distracts him, but then with a smirk he stretches back in his chair until his ribs arch toward the water-stained popcorn ceiling.

"Actually, I have a lot of money," he says. "Does that bother you?"

When he crosses his hands behind his head, the thick cords of veins in his otherwise thin forearms bulge, one side distorting a tattoo of the Virgin Mary.

"No."

"Liar. Everybody's upset when a fine young Puerto Rican has money. It fucks with their ideas. I bet it fucks with your ideas, too."

You pretend to make a note in the log.

"My pops was a famous fashion designer. When I turn eighteen I'm getting it all."

"How old are you now?"

He clicks his tongue, waves a hand. "Girl, what does that matter?"

"It matters."

"Seventeen"—the number a trifle detail he won't be bothered with. "You can ask," he says a moment later while pouting and stroking the faint stubble shading his jaw. "About my pops, I mean."

Your face is stone. Perhaps you smirk.

"Don't be shy, papi," he says, flashing an impish grin.

You could cut that smirk off his face with ease. It would be the simplest thing in the world to grab a knife, flick your wrist and finish the job. No problem. Instead, you shuffle papers, jangle a drawer and feign indifference.

He says nothing. He waits, and in that waiting you recognize something special—a potential in the way he holds back, goading you to act.

It's a tactic designed to unnerve you. You've used it yourself in the past, but tonight you have plenty of time and he's young and impatient.

He eventually capitulates with a sigh. "Fine, I'll just tell you. It's Urbody Couture."

He reaches across the desk for a pencil and brushes your arm. You flinch and a flicker of acknowledgment crosses his face.

"But you should know," he continues, "that I'm only telling you because I think you're cute. I like to keep that shit on the DL, otherwise these putas get ideas, know what I mean?"

Winking, he nibbles on the pencil's eraser and lowers his shoulder, exposing his slender throat. "Don't be embarrassed, papi. You're hot. It's not like I'm gonna bite... yet."

Crack your knuckles.

"Besides, you would've never guessed anyway. It's not really my style—Urbody Couture, I mean." He struggles into his tank top, the wet fabric clinging to his torso like a second skin. "You like my style? Yeah, you do. That's probably what attracted you in the first place. You white boys love this shit."

He slowly traces the length of the pencil with a finger. When you don't respond, he tosses the pencil down.

"Anyway, I don't give a shit about the brand. All I care about is making that coin." He cocks his head and points at the log. "The pen goes from left to right. Write that shit down. I got a reputation to keep."

"Of course," you say.

"There. Isn't that better? For a minute I thought I was going to have to get nasty with you." He slaps you on the thigh as if you were old acquaintances. "See, I'm already doing a great job here. Gotta keep those records up to date, son!"

You smirk, and he seizes the opportunity to flip the chair around so that he's face-to-face with you, spread-eagle. There's a mutual attraction—an equilibrium—that you haven't felt in a long time.

Trash the forms you handed him earlier.

"You can stay for one night." You emphasize the point by holding a finger to his face.

He stretches out his tongue and grazes your knuckle. Then he grins. "Now that's what I'm talking about! Where do I sleep?"

"On the floor. With everyone else."

WITH EYES CLOSED, CHERYL DRIFTS TOWARD THE CASCADE tumbling from three identical showerheads. She merges into the warm water, focusing on the bellows rhythm of her breathing. Heave in. Rush out. Visions of ocean-floor exploration flood her mind. She's in a lead suit scuttling across the desolate bottom of some sea, her copper helmet tethered to the surface by only a thin breathing apparatus. She's been down here alone a long time.

She tips her shoulders first one way, then the other, like a set of scales searching for an ideal balance. She'd like to blame her confession on the mental fogginess that followed a sleepless night, but that's not the case. Upon seeing Steven and Thaddeus interacting again last night, she realized that in three years nothing had changed. All her efforts to triage the relationship had been fruitless. Subconsciously, she resolved then to tell Peter about the abortion. She wanted someone down here in the depths with her.

Blindly, she walks her hands across the mosaic shower tiles in search of her shampoo. Finding nothing along the back wall, she leaves the slick surface for the adjoining one covered in what feels like river stone. The rough humidity calms her, and for a moment she imagines herself in a tropical grotto. Locating the shampoo on a nearby ledge, she works a small amount of the cream into her scalp. She made the right decision telling Peter. He was shocked at first, but he'll come around, and it feels good to finally share the burden of her secret. Already she feels a little less alone, and it's thrilling that for the first time in decades she has a male confidant other than her husband.

When she finishes massaging her scalp, she walks forward into the stream to rinse. The effect is something like total immersion, and, with the force of instinct, she returns to Cocoa Beach, picturing herself as she was all those years ago, no longer young and naive, but not yet a brutal realist.

Treading water, she delights in the lithe silhouette of her arms beneath the waves. They slice through the swells like a ballerina skipping across the stage, the ease of youth in her movements. Unlike now. Now, when she grabs her arms, she finds them corded with muscle from a lifetime of household chores. The skin feels as coarse as a loofah, and it droops from too much sun.

She turns away from the water and reaches for the facial scrub with her left hand, so that she'll be able to squeeze a dollop into the palm of her right hand in the most efficient way possible. There was a time, too, she thinks, when she settled upon the best way to go about washing her face, when the newness of even this routine was fresh, when it was done as an academic exercise, a good habit. Something adults did to hold off the inevitable. There was a time when her beauty shone brilliantly without the aid of creams and masks, before she was remaindered to the utilitarian stacks of aging women.

With a sigh, she leans against the sage tile and scrubs her face.

She wasn't as thin at Cocoa Beach as she is now. Those were her seesaw years. But even when she was heavier there was an underlying vitality to her body, as if the extra weight were a nap her body was taking, one from which she would awaken refreshed. Now, that's changed. Her body feels sluggish. It's slept too long. It's given up.

Stretching into the stream once more, she closes her eyes and focuses on the pitter of water as it strikes her skin and ricochets against the shower door before spiraling toward the drain. The rising steam brings a flush to her cheeks and for a moment erases everything. It obscures the mirror above the vanity, but she pictures the past without problem, feeling things as they were: her breasts firmer, her thighs smoother—everything vulnerable with youth. Her hands travel down.

She shudders, briefly hesitates—has her shower gone on too long already? Will Peter wonder what's keeping her? Perhaps, but she doesn't care. She's spent enough of her life accommodating others. This shower is her time. She steals a languorous touch. Risking a gasp, she opens her mouth. Despite her resolve to be accountable to no one but herself, she feels guilty not thinking of Thaddeus. But in a way she does think of him. Not the Thaddeus who's out there in the real world indulging whatever fancies race by (he's never struggled to prioritize his own needs over the needs of others), but, rather, the idea of him. And ideas, she reminds herself, can take many forms.

She pictures a younger version of Thaddeus, the one from that long-ago trip, but suffused with something foreign, something palpably dangerous that could survive anywhere and that thrives on adversity. Someone like what she imagines Peter was like when he met Steven—resplendent in political tattoos, inured to the world and vaccinated against its violence with sophomoric certitude. That sneer. The younger her and that sneer, what a pair they make!

How would he touch her, this portmanteau of a man? Thaddeus always starts with the shoulder blade, so she turns that part of her body through the warm spray streaming from the three nozzles and smiles. No doubt she would say something flirtatious and hopelessly conventional. *A girl could get used to this,* perhaps. And he would sneer, hearing everything he needed to know about her in just that one line. He would grab her hair, forcing her to catch her breath. *You have no idea,* he would say if he said anything at all, and she would giggle. They are both so young and impatient; he wouldn't linger on her shoulder. He would steal down as quickly as possible, skipping her breasts entirely because she would offer them too readily, and, instead, he would sink his fingers into the warm folds of her vagina, his knuckles lost in a tangle of wet hairs.

The water turns cold, catching her by surprise.

"Dammit," she mutters, adjusting the knob. But it's no use. The hot water's gone, and, anyway, she's probably been in the shower for too long. It's time to step out, to wrap a towel around her body, and to dress.

She returns downstairs to find Peter leafing through the newspaper.

"Good shower?" he asks.

"Mm-hmm." She nods. "Ready to go?"

"Sure," he says, dropping the paper into the recycling. "Let's get out of here. It's too hot."

He leads the way to the car.

Her eyes take a moment adjusting to the dimness of the garage, seeing it the same paradoxical way one hears a piercing silence or burns one's skin against ice. It's disorienting at first. So many objects pile against one another that distinguishing one shadowy space from the next proves difficult, but one by one the outlines reveal themselves. Peter's Mercedes, for instance, dark blue with a worn bumper, sits in the middle of the space clearly enough, and she takes the large rectangle emerging from the far wall to be a system of shelves no doubt housing the mass accumulation of suburban life: things like a hedge trimmer for yard work and a giant inflatable snowman for the holidays. A dank, mossy autumn bouquet, like soggy pine nettles and roasted mulch, fills the air. Maybe there's landscaping work to be done and this is where supplies are kept. In their early years, she and Thaddeus always had a home improvement project on the weekend docket.

"I'm grabbing a soda," Peter says, indicating a refrigerator. "Do you want something?"

The objects come quickly now—water heater, tire iron, bucket, fishing tackle—as her eyes acclimate to the low light, then Peter opens the garage door and brightness spills across the gray space like a firework. She sees a playhouse and a tyke bike, a garden hose and a spare, pool floats and a basketball hoop, a drum kit, a Ping-Pong table, a carton of magazines, a whiteout of plastic grocery sacks. There's so much stuff in here that it threatens to consume Peter's car.

"I got water, soda, and juice," he says.

"No, I'm fine."

"You sure?"

She nods.

He closes the refrigerator and bounds over to the Mercedes, opening the passenger-side door for her. "If you're still up for it, I'd like to swing by the gallery."

"Wherever you want to go. I just need to get out of the house."

She slides into the bucket seat, the cool, soft leather groaning beneath her. Compared to the garage, the Mercedes is austere, with not so much as a stray wrapper in sight. Its age, however, shows in the details: the dash faded from the Florida sun, and a gouge on the tan glove box has been there long enough to turn gray. Still, for an older car there's very little in the way of dust or crumbs. Peter must vacuum the inside on a regular basis. Her lips part and her eyes widen, picturing him in paint-stained shorts and an old T-shirt, rag in hand, taking great care to detail the car. She's in danger of turning his fastidiousness into a fetish, but she allows the indulgence. It's refreshing to spend time with a man without having to be his warden.

She runs her finger along the gash. What caused that? A number of scenarios come to mind, but she settles on one involving a pocket knife wielded in frustration years ago, perhaps after some political demonstration.

"Gives the car some character, huh?" he says.

"What? Oh, yes." At some point he dropped into the seat beside her.

"We've grown up together," he says, stroking the wheel with affection. "Steven thinks I need a new car. It makes sense. With Gertie around, both cars should probably have air bags, ABS, and all those other safety features, but I don't know. Everything is so new around here. I think it's nice to carry a little history around—store it up for a rainy day—don't you agree?"

"I think people have been raising kids for millions of years without antilock brakes."

Her quip elicits a laugh and they share a knowing smile, as if to say, *Aren't all these concessions one makes for family and children the slightest bit ridiculous?* She has the inclination to place a hand on his forearm, but she misses the moment. His fingers fly up. They pull the seat belt across his torso and then flit to the ignition. He flicks his wrist and the car starts with a powerful shudder before settling into an irregular diesel purr. "I bought this used when I was sixteen and spent years fixing her up," he says. "She still runs great." He drops his hand to the gearbox. The car jolts before settling into reverse. "So, we'll just swing by the gallery, then we can go somewhere else."

"Sounds fine," she says. "I'm up for anything."

The glare is so bright in those first moments as they leave the garage that she fails to notice anything odd, but as Peter slowly backs the Mercedes down the sun-bleached driveway it hits her. Something is missing.

"Where's Thaddeus's car?"

PART TWO
The Road to Disney World

YOU HIDE BEHIND THE WALL THAT SEPARATES THE model unit's master bathroom from the bedroom. Shirtless and breathing hard, your brow breaks out in a cold sweat and your knuckles ache. He's on the other side of this wall in the shower and he thinks you're in the kitchen preparing breakfast. You will be in a moment, but right now you inhabit the shadows, spying on him through the sliver of space between the bathroom door and the jamb. Seven short strides separate you. How easy it would be to walk in there, grab his slender throat and squeeze. A simple matter of applying pressure no more difficult than cracking an egg or popping bubble wrap.

"Yo, I been wanting to ask. Not that I'm not appreciative or nothing," he shouts, his reedy timbre reverberating against the ceramic stall. "But why you been letting me stay here?"

Immediately he ducks beneath the shower, not waiting for a reply. His lips look their pinkest and his hair its darkest as the water rushes over his face, diverting around his nose.

You observe how he washes: how he scrubs the thick patches of matted hair forming the points of a triangle slung between his armpits and stretching down to the severe apex of his sex; how he scrubs the crusted tangle of your dried semen from his scant leg hair; how he gargles with the mouthwash you've placed beside the spigot. He spits it out onto his feet, and it looks like he's standing in a puddle of urine until he lifts his heel from the drain and it slides away. He attends to the grit and lubricant caught beneath his fingernails. You've left a series of body scrubs, soaps, and hair care products on the ledge, and these come next. Over the past six months you've learned his routine. His actions have a deliberate purpose, and you observe as, step by step, he trades the insidious stink of sweat and discount cigarettes for an eau of something—something refreshing, something revitalizing with an oatmeal base and notes of lavender.

The shower transforms him.

When he finishes it won't matter what he was before stepping into the stall. It won't matter at all that last night he submitted to leather restraints and answered to "slave"—that all it took to relax his sphincter in anticipation of your fist were a few scant weeks of goading, a dollop of grease, and a hit of alkyl nitrites. Or that later you set a video reenactment of an anonymous political prisoner before a firing squad on repeat so that you could both watch the dissident's impassioned final speech uninterrupted while you dribbled some piss on his face. It won't matter that you asked him if he liked it and that he said yes. *Yes, sir.*

None of that matters after the shower. This morning you are two respectable gentlemen. You indulged the night before, and so what? Nobody got hurt. It took place in the privacy of your home—or in a model home, the show house, which is the same thing. You woke up. You showered. Today, this morning, nobody could look at you and draw a comparison with that other person from last night. That person was a beast, pure id.

This person, you, wears sweaters in muted tones, peeking collared shirts with subtle geometric patterns. You have an aesthetic and that aesthetic is synonymous with anything modified by the term *design* or *sustainable*. You and him. You are the type of people who subscribe to newspapers from other cities, who purchase organic, locally sourced produce and fair trade coffee, and who believe in transportation alternatives. You support health care reform, tougher gun regulations, and amnesty for illegal immigrants. You oppose war. You do not value victory over life. You resent that family values have been consigned to a political agenda because, despite everything, you are a stalwart supporter of the family. You regularly share a table with people who disapprove of your lifestyle on religious grounds. You are tolerated in their homes, and that is enough for you. You lead a perfectly adequate existence and you don't take up too much space.

Except.

Except somebody did get hurt. Many, in fact, and they will continue to get hurt, and you are the one who will do the hurting. You see, the showers accomplish nothing. This morning person doesn't exist. He's a mask. And something else: you enjoy hurting those people, and, unlike last night, with him, it is never consensual. You are angry, and you are not alone. A great many people are angry. A whole country of angry people shouts into the wind. But why take the next step? You've asked yourself this question. Why not trust in the natural progression of things, place your faith in the machinations that have accomplished everything up to this point? Why hurt your own people? The answer is simple: Because the minority lacks a critical mass and is therefore dependent on the sympathies of the majority. Because somebody must be vigilant that those sympathies never wane. And nothing rallies the masses like genocide. Last night you were a monster consumed by your work. This morning you are the righteous mechanism of that work's fruitful implementation. You and him. A narrative of provisional acceptance is unacceptable.

The slapping sound of wet palms brushing across a wet face brings you back. That brief interruption is enough to rally your willpower. Your knuckles will ache, but that's nothing you haven't overcome before. You move to the kitchen, continuing to listen.

The faucet locks, followed by the hollow thump of the stall door releasing from its magnetic seal. A towel shushes off the rod, and as you listen to him dry off, you can almost feel the friction between the terry cloth and your own electrified skin.

Then he's beside you, a towel draped loosely around his waist. He picks at his ear with a cotton swab while the Virgin on his arm dances. "Yo, I asked you a question. You deaf or something?"

"Guess so," you say, quickly slicing a potato for an omelet. You toss it in with the peppers and the onions already in the small bowl to your left.

"Shit," he says, pouting in the sarcastic manner he employs when you act evasive. "Guess I can't whisper sweet nothings in your ear then."

He flicks the cotton swab into the sink along with your peels. There's no garbage can here, because officially nobody lives in this unit. You carry out all the garbage with you when you leave, as well as make the bed, wash and set the dinnerware on the table. The bath products you store in a plastic baggy and place under the sink. Occasionally, one of your coworkers will come to work after a long night and will shower in this unit. It's understood that bath products are kept hidden here for just such an event.

"Guess not," you say.

He presses into you from behind and you can feel the bulk of his flaccid penis through the towel. "That's a real shame."

His arms work their way up your chest until he has you in a tight hold with his naked torso pressed against your back and his hands locked around your neck. Then he begins to massage your shoulders, which are sore from extended hours at the gym and the sustained acrobatics of intercourse with a clumsy teenager. He nibbles on your earlobe.

"I asked why you going through all the trouble of sneaking me in and out of here every night?" His voice threatens the slightest interrogation.

You close your eyes. "Why do you think?"

He doesn't answer right away. Instead, he kneads your muscles until you've shifted some of your weight into his hands. Only then does he stop, and you're obliged to peer back. Follow his movements. With a motion so languid that you have time to notice that the cornice above the oak cabinets needs painting—a new task for later this week—he drops the towel from his waist and tugs on his heavy, hairy testicles while teasing his puckered urethra, which peeks out from the silky sheath of his foreskin.

He sneers. "I think it's 'cause I got this prized Puerto Rican pinga, and it kills you that I might let some skanky-ass putos suck on it a little."

You turn to face him with a smile.

He moves a bit closer, then beckons you the rest of the way with a wink. You oblige. Moaning, he relaxes into a gentle stroking rhythm. Some life slides into his penis and he allows the organ to loll back and forth between his thighs like a sunflower chasing the light. He squeezes it until it gets rigid and points straight at you from within his ample fist. When he's certain that he has all your attention he lets his penis drop and whips his fingers through the air in an explosive crack. Then he erupts in laughter. His penis deflates with remarkable speed.

"Coño," he says, hopping onto the granite counter bare-assed. "You should've seen your face, son! All slack-jawed and shit." He wags his tongue and taunts you with his now soft penis. "Yum, yum, yum," he says, mocking you, laughing again. "But yo, nah, seriously, you don't need to worry about it, papi. Okay? I got standards."

You return to the omelet, which, no doubt, he interprets as a method of mature restraint, and this intrigues him.

"Or maybe it's something else?" He squeezes between you and the counter, his naked bottom shifting to the rim of the undermounted sink. His long fingers pull the whisk from your hand and lay it beside the gas range with an elegant economy of motion. The knife is nearby. "I think you like me, papi. I think you like me so much you wanna be, like, my boyfriend." He bats his eyelashes in an intentionally feminine appeal to your performed masculinity—that tired heterosexual rubric.

"No boyfriends," you say bluntly, surprising even yourself. "I tried that and it didn't work. Monogamy is a hell for straight people."

You ignite the stove and set about combining the ingredients in a pan.

He searches your face for signs of sincerity. Honestly, you're not sure if you believe that or not, but it's a simplifying narrative in regard to your complex situation so you stick with it. He continues to stare, and you wonder if perhaps his anus is sore at the moment, if the inevitable tears sting at present, and if he's acutely aware of the pain.

You flip the omelet, pleased at the browning on the underside. "I understand if you want to leave."

But you know he can't. Where else would he go? Returning to the shelter is no longer an option. Besides, he's too proud for that. He has no home to return to. Of course, he must know that you've determined that by now. No, his only options are to stay on with you or to live on the streets—perhaps he could move to the coast and sleep on the beach.

"Damn," he says after a minute. "I was just playing." He thumbs his nose and hops down from the counter. Sniffling, he rolls his shoulders on the way to the refrigerator to pour a glass of orange juice. "You think I want that either? Shit, no! Too much ass and too little time for that exclusivity bullshit."

You nod, and over the next few minutes the two of you settle into a comfortable domestic rhythm. He pours you a glass of juice and then rearranges things on the table. His unwillingness to let the thread die out is how you know that he hopes that you'll come around.

"This shit works for me the way it is," he says. "If I wanna fuck some other guy, who the fuck are you to tell me I can't?"

"Exactly," you say.

"Damn straight. We don't have to be stifled by all that bullshit."

Grabbing a serrated knife from the artfully canted chock, you slice a loaf of bread and arrange the pieces on a tray. From the refrigerator he retrieves a couple pads of butter. Along with the orange juice, the butter makes the stale bagels and muffins that accompany an open house more palatable, so those supplies are always on hand.

"That shit's fine for some bitches, but me..." He regards you with an incriminating glare, as if monogamy had been your idea, and maybe it had. You've done everything to send such a signal. "Me, I got to keep my options open."

You ask him to pass the salt, which he does. The ground pepper, too.

"And why would I want to be with you anyway? For all I know, you'll go back to your boyfriend. I mean, I appreciate you letting me crash, but we're just chilling. I'm not about to get tangled up in whatever shit you got going on at home."

He has an unnerving knack for extracting information, and despite your reluctance to share anything personal, he's learned that you and your partner are considering a separation and that occasionally you stay here. Up to now, you've managed to satisfy his curiosity while remaining aloof, but if he inquires further, you fear what confessions may come.

"Eat," you say, slipping the omelet onto his plate. "You'll need your energy today."

He raises an eyebrow. "Why's that?"

"I have a surprise for you. Happy early birthday."

"Ah, hells yeah! Now that's what I'm talking about, son! Getting some respect!"

He may be about to turn legal, but he's still a child. You roll your eyes. The option to kill him remains available, if you need it.

A DENTED HANDICAP SIGN STRETCHES OUT OF THE asphalt in front of the squat, whitewashed building. It's the only one of its kind, a survivor of countless bang-ups and petty vandalisms. The whole lot is cracked and uneven like a cooled lava flow and ghostly white where faded lines suggest parking spots. Three older cars cluster together in one corner. These, Thaddeus figures, must belong to the employees of the Little Sunshine Scholars Day Care and Preschool. The only other storefront is a run-down grocery at the far end of the plaza.

He grinds the transmission into park before the Cutlass Supreme comes to a full stop. A strip mall sets the bar low. What do they want Gertie to grow up to be? The least they could do is give her a shot at something better like he and Cheryl did with... with... Steven's name escapes him for just a second. Senior moment. The important thing, though, is that he remembers how they sacrificed so that Stevie would have a leg up. And this is the payoff? They sacrificed for this? So that Stevie could take away his granddaughter, cut him right out like you'd cut a bruise from an apple, all because of an accident (which, truth be told, wasn't even his fault)? So that Gertie could blossom here, in a second-rate strip mall? What a joke. Last night he tried to save her life. But he doesn't suppose that means much. Stevie's always blamed him for everything. He's never understood the sacrifices made, the necessary deferrals. Like a retirement plan, family is an investment to enjoy once it's matured. Thaddeus pulls at the loose skin along his jaw. How did he end up in a position to be judged by people who leave their daughter in a strip mall? At least he and Cheryl never did that.

Staring at the water-stained stucco, he thinks he arrived just in time. That he even got here is an accomplishment all by itself, and congratulations would be in order if he weren't at loggerheads with the folding road map on his lap. A hell of a time for his phone to die. This map and that stoned clerk at the 7-Eleven deserve all the credit. Without them he wouldn't be here now.

Last night Peter mentioned something about Gertie's day care being east of downtown off the 408. He and Steven were happy with the curriculum, he said, and felt lucky to have found a good place nearby. Peter even gave the intersection where the day care was located in that anxious way people do when attempting to conjure an image of a place out of nothing but proper nouns. At the time it meant nothing to Thaddeus, but he remembered the name.

At least he had a direction and a name, but he was hardly out of the subdevelopment when his phone died. It wasn't long after that he got lost. That's when the questioning began: maybe Peter had said Colonial and Semoran. Was it half a block past Washington and Summerlin? Or maybe—and this now seemed most likely—he'd said it wasn't close to the 408 at all. He crisscrossed the city looking for the Little Sunshine Scholars Day Care and Preschool until he ran out of change for the tolls and was forced to find a gas station and purchase an up-to-date map; the one he had, a relic from their first year in Florida, was splotchy with undeveloped areas where now existed a network of communities.

In his haste to exit the car, he tears the map, but that hardly matters with Gertie so close.

The torn map finds its way into the glove box. The seat belt unfastens. The door opens. All of it unfurling smoothly, automatically, because he's focused on that one, present thought: Gertie. This is what it's like to be alive, he thinks, to be fresh.

Even the oppressive afternoon heat cannot wilt his determination. He feels invincible and the feeling catapults him toward the tinted glass door of the day care. Inside, the cracked asphalt gives way to soft gray carpet and a smallish reception area. Potted ferns frame a water cooler. Ergonomic playthings with chipped veneers litter the far corner, and the crisp smell of a/c mingles with a faint citrus aroma, which reminds him of visits to the pediatrician when Stevie was a baby.

A slender receptionist with long, curly auburn hair bends over a row of file cabinets, her skirt taut over her wide hips. This is one worker I could really get behind, he thinks.

The young woman glances at him over her shoulder and smiles. "I'll be right with you," she says in the honeyed lilt of the Deep South.

He returns the smile. "Take your time."

Hanging from a wall in the waiting area, a framed lithograph of an elaborately etched stone vase captures his attention. Though lacking any formal training on the subject, he often ponders aesthetics out by the pool with his pipe. He spends a few moments now debating if the vase is more beautiful because of the etchings or in spite of them, ultimately resolving to ask Peter. The owner of an art gallery should be able to settle the matter definitively.

The receptionist returns to her seat and calls him over. Even from a few feet away, he detects the unmistakable shadow of a bra beneath her light peach-colored blouse, and as with the vase, he wonders whether her breasts are more beautiful because of the brassiere or in spite of it (that's certainly not something he'll be asking Peter).

"What can I do for you?"

The first words out of his mouth must establish an immediate rapport. If he's to see Gertie, she'll need to trust him, but despite his best efforts, he can't move past the bra. The shadow beneath her blouse casts a shadow over his brain. All he can think to do is wink, which has the unfortunate effect of making him look like he's suffering from a neurological tic or a pollen allergy.

She cocks an eyebrow.

He's going to blow this. He's definitely going to blow it because all he can think about is how young and beautiful she is. He winks again and this time she frowns. "You okay?"

Words fail him so he simply nods. His pits begin to sweat. Never before has he yearned so much for something small with which to break the ice, even the most banal of puns would do. He's almost at the desk and certain that he's failed. He'll be found out and then

Gertie will be snatched from him before he's even had the chance to say a proper good-bye. The receptionist moves her hand along the desk and he imagines her reaching for a panic button that will bring the cops in seconds, guns blazing, handcuffs whipping through the air. I just wanted to say good-bye, he'd say, just one last good-bye. But they won't listen. They never do. He'll end up on his knees, beaten. Everyone will cluster around him—Stevie will appear, Cheryl. They'll take pity on him, but it won't mean anything to the cops. He'll end up languishing in a prison somewhere. If he's not shot first.

The receptionist's hand moves under the desk, and he nearly runs for it.

But this is all for Gertie, he reminds himself, for her.

That one solitary thought strikes a flint in his brain. The receptionist with the beautiful hair and the striking breasts sits two feet from him now and he doesn't have time to second-guess. Peering directly at her, he curls his lips into a wry smile and riffs on the flash of inspiration. "The iceman cometh," he says.

"Excuse me?"

Not the reaction he intended, but it's something he can work with.

He stretches his right arm to infinity and lays his left on his breast, in what he believes is a gallant pose, then takes a deep bow across the desk. "A play by Eugene O'Neill," he explains. If he can't think of anything to say, at least he can pretend to be smart.

The gamble seems to pay off. Her expression returns to its earlier softness. "Oh, I, um, I don't know it."

Her hand emerges from beneath the desk. She wasn't reaching for a panic button, only grabbing a pen from a drawer. The rest will go well. Piece of cake.

"Before your time," he says.

"You're a funny one, aren't you?" She points at a candy jar. "Have a chocolate."

"I bet they're not as sweet as you." With the ice broken, he regains something of his usual bonhomie.

"Ooh, I like you." She thrusts the jar at him. "Here, take a couple."

He grabs a chocolate, but instead of keeping it, he offers it back to her. *"Parlez-vouz,"* he says. "That's French. It means 'for you.'"

She crinkles the corner of her lip. "I don't think you got that right, hon."

"C'est la vie. Either way you deserve a chocolate break." He unwraps the bright paper and holds the candy out for her.

"Tell that to my jeans!" But she accepts the offering.

He can afford to take things slower now that he's won her over, so he leans against the doorjamb and crosses his arms on his chest. "Don't tempt me. I'm a married man."

"You're fresh. I like that. You know, most people who come in here—" She pauses to cast a furtive glance over her shoulder, then leans in and says in a husky whisper, "They can be real A-holes."

He cozies up to the desk. "I'm sorry to hear that."

She smiles. "But you seem nice."

"I believe in karma."

"I could tell that right away about you! You have a great aura."

"Is it a purple haze?" he asks, miming a toke.

She giggles and her bosom swells. "Oh, you're bad! You better watch out. You don't want to corrupt the little ones."

"We wouldn't want that."

They stare at each other for a while, unsure how to continue.

She finally breaks the silence by bringing the conversation back to the topic at hand. "So, what can I do for you?"

"That's a good question."

He can't say exactly when he decided to take Gertie. Only that at some point after leaving the house and delving into the anonymous maze of streets that compose this vast metropolis, he knew he had to. He possessed only the purest intentions when he left the house this morning. He simply wanted to see her one time without Cheryl around to stage-manage the situation, just once so he could memorize every bit of her and build up a powerful visual reserve capable of sustaining him through the lonesome stretch ahead. He deserved that much at least after the last three years. But committing Gertie to a mental snapshot, even one that over time would surely aggregate every wish, every desire, every regret he'd ever had or felt into a sort of bittersweet alloy, would, in the end, serve only him. It would be a selfish action, and the more he thought about it the more he realized that Gertie, too, deserved at least one good memory of her grandfather, a pure memory that would stand in contrast to whatever stories Stevie would tell about him.

He beams at the receptionist. "I'm here to pick up my granddaughter."

"Aww, aren't you just the cutest thing?" She has a disarming manner, which, no doubt, suits her profession.

"Hey, now," he says, holding up a hand. "Don't go getting any ideas. Didn't I tell you? I'm a married man."

She laughs, and he melts. There's something so pleasant and light about a young woman's laughter. It rejuvenates him. On some level, he's fallen in love with her.

"I'm sure she's a lucky woman."

"She saved my—"

But before he can finish, she interrupts him. "Are you on the list, hon?"

"What list?"

"The list of approved caregivers—the people who can pick up a child. It's a legal thing," she adds, frowning. "All our kids have one. Are you on the list?"

He hadn't anticipated a list, but he doesn't hesitate. "Yes," he says.

"Perfect. Let me just look you up in the system. What'd you say your name was?"

"Uh, Steven Bloom. And I'm here for Gertie."

She types quickly, her eyes scanning the monitor. "Gertie, you say. Let me just see...Yup, I got it. Steven Bloom. There you are."

He grins and holds up his hands. "There I am."

The flirtation has gone out of her voice, and she's all business now. She gives him a cordial, professional smile. "Can I see your ID, Mr. Bloom?"

"My ID?"

"Sorry. It's a legal thing again. Driver's license, passport. Something like that." She smiles, and he breaks out in a cold sweat.

"Well, you see, that's a problem—"

"Oh?" She leans forward, narrowing her eyes and folding her hands under her chin. She looks sincere but she could be faking. Maybe there is a panic button after all and she's just stalling until the police arrive. He chooses to believe in her sincerity.

"See, I lost my wallet. It was robbed. I was mugged, actually. Right out there." He points at the desolate parking lot beyond the tinted glass. "This isn't a very safe neighborhood."

"Oh my gosh, that's awful." She reaches for the phone. "Should I call the police?"

"No! I mean, no need. It happened yesterday. Not today. Today I'm fine. I just need my granddaughter. My wife, Cheryl, she sent me..."

The kind receptionist scrunches up her nose. Only she's not so kind anymore. "I'd love to help you, but, see, I'm new here and don't recognize you, so I'll need to see some"—she stretches the word— "some kind of ID before I can release her into your care. Maybe I can find somebody else who might recognize you?"

"Notarized," he blurts out. He's thinking quickly on his feet, and it just comes out.

"Excuse me?"

"Notary. I mean, what if I had a signed paper saying I am who I say I am, signed by a notary? Would that work?"

Her eyes widen as her lips stretch into a pained smile. "Do you?"

He scratches his head. "No."

"Well then."

Every instinct compels him to flee before she calls the cops, but the momentum of his lie pushes him forward.

"Not on me, I mean. I have it in the car. Let me just go grab it."

He's out the door before she can respond.

With no time to think, he merely acts. He'll never get another chance like this. If they won't give her to him, then he'll have to take her. It's that simple. Gertie is too important for him to give up now. He's come too far.

He heads for the Cutlass Supreme, but rather than open the door he scurries past it and ducks around the side of the building. He flattens his considerable bulk against the stucco as best he can and surveys the alley. The coast is clear. The adrenaline runs now as he makes his way to the rear of the building. Don't these places always have backyards? He thinks they do. It's not healthy for children to be cooped up inside a strip mall all day long. They need to play outside, and now he's feeling fortunate that he got so lost earlier in the day. Because of that he didn't arrive at the day care until lunchtime, and even though there are many things he's forgotten about raising a child, he remembers that children always go on recess after lunch. He ducks around a dumpster. The back of the long building is shaped like a shoehorn with a notch cut out where the day care is located. A few more steps and he hears children's voices.

Just past the dumpster he comes upon an overgrown yard. Empty cat-food tins litter the area, and growing wild around a rusted chain-link fence are banana leaves and elephant ear ferns. He manages to slither through surreptitiously. Beyond the fence, darting from one plastic playground contraption to another, is Gertie. Seeing her play with her little friends buoys his heart. She looks so innocent and happy, a little child without a single worry in the world. More than anything, that freewheeling innocence is exactly what he needs in his life right now. And, dammit, he deserves it after so long. But Stevie will deny him because his son is hard on the inside in a way that's foreign to Thaddeus. Anger, fury—those emotions he understands, but Stevie inherited his mother's icy contempt, and while that kind of calculated disposition may inoculate one to the types of rage that have defined most of his life, it does so by poisoning the emotional reservoir with spite until sooner or later there's no charitable feeling left.

All right, Stevie, he thinks, you want to play a game? No big deal.

There's only one adult watching the kids. Getting to Gertie is just a matter of distracting her—that and overcoming the fence. The fence is cheap chain link, but it might as well be a ten-foot wall for all his ability to get past it. A terse, surprisingly upbeat jingle drifts through the air, and Thaddeus searches for the source of it. The lone adult. At first, he's petrified, thinking she's spotted him in the weeds and sounded an alarm, but then he notices that it's something much better. The noise comes from her phone. Saved by the bell.

When his luck runs, it races. At the same moment that the woman's phone rings, he spots a gap in the fence where it joins the back wall. It's a small opening, the result of rust and most likely more than one raccoon or feral cat in search of a meal. Probably nobody's noticed it because it's visible only from out here. From inside the yard it's covered by dense foliage, and, anyway, it's all the way on this side of the yard, and all the playground equipment is on the far side.

The woman cradles the phone with her neck and settles into the conversation.

Good, now he just has to get Gertie's attention. It doesn't require much. Apparently tired of the other kids, Gertie grabs an oversized ball and wanders away to play quietly alone. Every now and then she drops the ball and says "poop," but then she grabs it again and continues walking toward the fence.

"Psst." He calls her over. "Hey, Gertie. Hey, beautiful, look over here."

At first she seems confused to hear the plants speak, wary even, but as soon as she spots him through a break in the ferns she shrieks with joy. The day care worker presses the phone to her chest and glances over, but he's well camouflaged and she doesn't notice him. Once she's satisfied that Gertie hasn't fallen or hurt herself, she returns to her phone conversation.

"Hey, beautiful, come over here," he whispers. "Grandpa has a treat for you."

Without much persuading, Gertie approaches the fence, abandoning the oversized ball and lacing her fingers into the chain link.

"Over here," he says, pointing to the gap.

Gertie sees it right away. Such a smart kid! For the first time he's glad that Stevie and Peter chose such a run-down day care. She squirms through and leaps at Thaddeus's leg. And though he could stay like that forever, just soaking up her love, he's now officially racing against the clock.

"Let's get out of here, Hurdy-Gertie. What do you say? Grandpa's got a big adventure planned."

She nods vigorously.

"That's what I like to hear. Now, come on. How do you feel about mice and ducks?" Pulling her by the arm, he doesn't give her an opportunity to answer. "You'll love them! Now, come on, give Grandpa a big kiss. Atta girl!"

HIS EXCEPTIONAL DIGITS ECLIPSE THE SWAROVSKI stemware on display in the mall's atrium galleria. Despite such large hands he manages to avoid looking clumsy or silly while handling the delicate crystal, yet for all his deftness he retains a measure of irreverence in the way he flips the champagne flutes as if they were pistols up for inspection.

"Yup," he says, affecting a drawl. "Gen-u-ine crystal. Woo-wee." You grin.

"Them's fancy fixin' for vittles." He twirls them in figure eights through his fingers.

"You're going to break something," you warn, marveling at his quarter-sized thumbnails and the robust tendons radiating across the smooth backs of his olive hands, the Virgin on his forearm dancing.

He shoots you the finger.

"It's coming out of your allowance if you do."

He laughs and moves away. "You funny, papi, you know that?"

"Sure," you say.

He buries his hands in his hair. Since that first night at Independent Bar he's allowed the close crop to grow a bit, so now his hair resembles the thick coat of a short-haired cat. He looks better shaggy, more at ease, and you tell him so. He accepts this in his customary languid way, then he moves on, elbows akimbo, slouching beneath the fenestrated rotunda.

"So," he says, bending a toothy smile, "whatcha buying me?" A hint of the drawl clings to his words.

"Something respectable. I'm tired of seeing you wear the same ratty T-shirts."

Arching an eyebrow, he asks if you'd prefer him to go around topless. Then he peels back the hem of his shirt, exposing his flat stomach.

"And wearing a collar," you say. "Then we can burn this whole fucking place down."

He grins. "Aren't I a lucky girl?"

"That all depends. Do lucky girls get spanked?"

"Hmm." Meandering deeper into the atrium, he nods in a way that either demonstrates his appreciation or signals the opening salvo to a deep offense. You have trouble telling the difference with him.

"I could use some new kicks," he suggests. "That is, if I get a say."

"Of course. Why wouldn't you?"

"Just checking, sir."

He bends down before a narrow infinity pool to study its ripple-free sheen. From his back pocket, he produces a Moleskine notebook that you bought for him. He jots down a few words, then stashes it away again.

"Let me get a quarter," he says.

"Why?"

"Yo, don't be a cheap ass."

You stare at him, unflinching.

"Come on, I wanna make a wish. You want it to come true, don't you?"

"Sure."

"Well, then give me a quarter and quit being a bitch."

You dig in your pocket and extract a grimy coin. "It's the only one I got, so make it count." As you press it into his warm palm, you ask what he'll wish for.

He makes a quick sign of the cross with it, then tosses the coin into the water. "Can't say."

"That's a raw deal."

He shrugs. "Hey, man, I don't make the rules."

"What about a hint?"

He thinks about this for a minute, figuring his spiritual calculus, then says, "Yeah, all right. I think that's allowed."

In a flash, he's down on his knees barking and sniffing your crotch. The acoustics are such that the crystal across the way rings out. You peel his hands off your pants.

"All right, I think I have an idea. I think everybody has an idea. Get up already."

He quits barking, but he remains on the ground. Laughing, he reclines along the parti-colored tile. It's a testament to the lobotomizing effect of shopping malls that almost nobody notices.

"I like the way the beams look up there," he says, reaching for his notebook again.

"Of all the possible things to wish for."

"A puppy would be nice."

"So would winning the lottery." You help him to his feet.

"Nah, man, I'm serious." He ambles back toward the crystal. You follow a few paces behind. "See, my boy Jose found this bitch on the street. She looked real fucked up, but when he tried bringing her back to the shelter they told him he couldn't have no pets. Ain't that fucked up? I mean, it's supposed to be a place of compassion and shit."

"For people."

He ignores you and examines a picture frame made of Venetian glass, holding it up to the light and bending a few faces into the mirrored edges before continuing.

"So he left the dog at his moms', but she's crazier than Jose, and what that dog needs is a real family." He pauses to look at you doe-eyed. "Someone who can really love her."

"I see."

"And I got to thinking that since I don't live at the shelter no more—and since it's my birthday—maybe that could be me. She's a sweet dog."

"Absolutely not," you say.

"Come on. Why not?"

"Because you don't even have a home."

"Yes. I do." His eyes narrow into slits, and when you don't debate him, he draws his shoulders back and grins. "And, in the meantime, I'm staying with you."

"It's a big risk sneaking you in there every night."

"Well, if I'm such a hassle maybe I should just go."

"Don't get melodramatic," you say.

"Then don't be an asshole."

"I'm being realistic. It won't work."

"You don't know that," he says.

"Yes, I do. Dogs need constant attention, especially abused strays. They need routine and a solid place to live. Considering the circumstances, it's impossible. It just won't work. I'm sorry."

"I thought about all that," he says. "She can come with me during the day and then I'll bring her by late at night when nobody'll see us."

"What about when you go out?"

He bites a cuticle. "I'll figure something out."

"And what if she barks?"

"She won't bark."

"You don't know that."

"Yes, I do."

"No, you don't."

"Look," he says. "She's a great dog. She just needs some love. I can do that. I wanna do that." He reaches for your hand. "We can do that, papi."

You pull your hand back and crack your knuckles. Suddenly you feel very constrained.

"We could," you say. "But I don't want to. I don't need anything new in my life to love."

He flinches. Even as you say the words you know that eventually you'll give in. You always give in. This, more than anything, makes acute your failure. You'll end up a dog owner like you wound up a husband and a father—by inertia.

The argument attracts the attention of a clerk dressed in a navy blazer, pink oxford, and gauche red leather topsiders with tassels. A pained smile creases his smooth face. With Alex's temper running high, the clerk's approach threatens to spark an uncomfortable scene. While you appreciate the purity of your lover's rage and indignation (even when it's directed at you—perhaps especially when it's directed at you), you won't allow his petulance to ruin the day. You've worked too hard reconciling conflicting demands on your time so that you could be here with him to let a temper tantrum derail everything.

Despite evidence to the contrary, you can be remarkably adept at evading conflict. You catch the clerk's eye while he's still a few yards off. He approaches with caution, gauging the situation. To head him off, you float a subtle nod and flit a finger. He pauses, and a moment later he veers back to his station in the middle of the sales floor, where he attends to a thin woman in a floral print dress examining a vase for imperfections. He glances back and you smile briefly before breaking eye contact. The whole exchange is over in a minute.

"He was cute." Alex abandons the crystal wine decanter stopper he's been handling. "You should've let him come over."

"Are we cool?"

He shrugs and heads to the escalators, leaving you to follow. When you catch up, he's at the food court, scrolling through his phone. "I'm hungry," he says. For the moment at least it seems he's ready to forget about the dog.

You volunteer to scout a suitable table, then hand him a wad of cash—much more than he'll actually need. "Find the closest approximation to a salad and whatever you'd like for yourself."

"Keep this up and I may start thinking I'm just your houseboy."

"We wouldn't want that," you say drily.

"Anything to drink?"

"Surprise me."

You find a table by the windows away from all the idle food court chatter and sit.

This talk of the dog has surfaced an ongoing issue that you've ignored for too long. You never fully thought through the implications of removing Alex from the shelter, and now you're at a loss as to what to do with him long term. You can't keep putting him up in the show house. Sooner or later someone is bound to find out. But you can't just let him go either.

Your fingers fumble as you sweep some trash from the table.

Alex drifts from concession to concession, carefully considering his options. For a bit it seems like he'll go for stir-fry, but he ultimately settles on a Latin barbecue stand. It's no surprise; the boy working the counter—a good-looking kid no more than sixteen by your estimation—wears his uniform in the loose, roguish manner you know Alex prefers. A sprouting of wiry hair dusts his upper lip, and a large zirconium stud clings to his earlobe. They talk. The boy smiles a lot, offers an array of samples on toothpicks. And Alex throws back his head in laughter, tastes everything offered. He alternates between flaring out his chest and shrinking back. There's a certain serenity in knowing that, if you wanted it, you could spend the rest of your life waiting at this table while he was off flirting, and maybe that's why you haven't found a permanent housing solution. You have yet to figure out what you want from him.

Eventually, Alex orders, and when he's paid he returns with two plates heaped high with rice and shredded pork and no receipt or change.

"Did you see that fine-ass boy at the counter?" He slides a plate your way. "Oh, and sorry, no salad."

You shift the pork around, then push the plate to the side without taking a bite. "I saw the boy."

He smiles while chewing. "He was hot, right? And he was all up on me. I swear I could've fucked him right there. Bam! Know what I mean?"

"We can do that," you say casually.

He takes a break from shoveling food into his mouth. "Do what?"

"Fuck other people together."

"Yeah?"

"We can do that tonight. Surprise!"

He sips his soda. "That's the surprise?"

You nod. "Tonight we'll go to the club and you pick someone and we'll take him home. Happy birthday."

He wipes some sauce off his lips. "Shit, papi. We didn't need to come to the mall for you to tell me that."

You pick at your cuticles. "You needed new clothes anyway."

"No doubt. Hey, you gonna finish that?"

"It's all you."

He stabs at your plate with his fork.

"HE HASN'T BEEN BY," THE WOMAN BEHIND THE DESK
says, glancing up from a stack of forms. A flat silver bracelet clinks
against the chipped veneer of the desktop as she speaks. Her hair is
pulled back in short, tight plaits. An arched brow gives her face a
permanent look of skepticism. Cheryl estimates her weight at about
four hundred pounds, and even seated she exudes a formidable authority.

"You're sure?" Peter asks.

"Do you see him?" She flips pages at a furious rate, affixing a
mark in the lower right-hand corner of each form, pausing long
enough to peer over the rim of her glasses at them.

"I'm sure he was on today," Peter says, but the woman only sighs.

They're standing in the rear of a noisy warren, talking at a
woman who is actively ignoring them, and they're separated
from the exit by a volatile group of mostly ragged, gender-mud-
dled kids sharing an intimidating look that hovers somewhere
between hunger and misanthropy. Steven is nowhere in sight,
and she's wearing her diamond wedding band and matching
earrings. Perhaps coming here was a bad idea. Peter, however,
doesn't seem fazed by the environment, and she wonders if this
is the kind of place he was living when Steven met him. She shudders at the thought.

"Can you check the schedule?" He leans closer to the woman and
crosses his arms.

The woman in turn makes a show of dropping her pen and leaning back in her chair, resting her hands on her ample bosom. She
cocks her head back and forth between the two of them in disbelief.
Peter returns the stare and smiles.

Bodies seem to close ranks around them and the desire to flee makes Cheryl light-headed. Her mouth feels dry. Somebody coughs and she flinches. The noisome mix of millet and damp that permeates everything in the shelter clings to her clothes. She's supposed to be able to think beyond her reactionary aversion to this bare poverty. She understands the larger socioeconomic factors at play, and she sympathizes. It's something she has always prided herself on, yet at this moment she wants nothing more than to leave, to forget this place and these people even exist. They can find Thaddeus without Steven's help. Coming here was a mistake.

"You really think I have nothing better to do," the woman says. It's not a question, more like a challenge.

"Of course, you're right. We should go—" Cheryl starts to say, but Peter isn't intimidated. He rests his hands on the desk.

"This'll just take a minute, then we'll go."

With a snort, the woman swivels to face a long file cabinet. "Like I ain't got shit to do," she says to herself.

The file cabinet, like the desk, is buried under piles of forms and binders, and as she tears through stacks, her terrifying demeanor becomes something more like bureaucratic frustration. "I had a system," she says, sliding over beside Cheryl to access even more piles. "Excuse me, sweetie."

Cheryl draws closer to Peter. His presence gives her comfort. So this is where her son spends so much of his time. Water stains creep along the ceiling, threatening mold blooms. Windows line the top of the walls; some are taped over with garbage bags—the legacy of Hurricane Natalie this past summer. She had pictured a dark canyon with few creature comforts, yet jangly reggaeton rhythms spew from the too-loud stereo, and the large television in the corner is a barrage of channel surfing. What she imagined, she realizes, was closer to a prison than to a shelter, or at least what she imagines a prison to be like because she's never been in one of those either.

The woman slams a drawer shut. "Nothing. Just like I told you." A steely impatience replaces her fleeting kindness.

Pans crash in the kitchen followed by hollering. The layout of the shelter is such that from the desk all areas are visible, and the three of them turn in unison, immediately identifying the source of the noise as a shy boy—at least Cheryl thinks he's a boy—in a pink sweater and heavy makeup. He's pushing pans around on top of the range while another boy standing off to the side, and looking ill at ease and malnourished, chastises him in a loud whisper.

"Quit making all that racket," the woman yells. When the shy boy doesn't react, the woman plants her hands on the top of the desk. "Sheila, don't make me get out of my chair. What you doing in the kitchen anyway? You know you're not supposed to be in there."

The boy called Sheila gives her a vacant stare. "Sorry," she says in a detached voice. Abandoning the range, she walks to the edge of the kitchen, where she leans against a counter.

"Don't be sorry," the woman says, her bracelet clinking against the desk. "Just don't do what you're not supposed to be doing, then there's nothing to be sorry for. Understand?"

"I guess," Sheila says in a meek voice.

There's something very wrong when such a fragile being is forced into a place like this. Of everybody in the shelter, Sheila is the only one Cheryl feels compelled to comfort. The realization both saddens her and fills her with a bizarre sense of pride. Her thoughts return to her aborted child. All these years she's always imagined it would've been a balancing force in their home, someone who could've mediated a little of the animosity that existed between Thaddeus and Steven, but maybe that was just a fantasy. Maybe whatever second child she may have given birth to would've been as fragile as Sheila, and their home would've been just as toxic as this place.

"These kids don't learn," the woman says, lowering her glasses and talking simultaneously to Cheryl, Peter, and Sheila, who listens from just outside the kitchen like a half-bored waiter eavesdropping on her diners' spirited conversation. "They don't know how good they got it. I been through the system. I been on the streets. She don't appreciate it. I'm telling you I had it a lot harder than them. We didn't have a place like this, *swee-tie*. Nobody was looking out for us. But they'll learn. Soon enough, they'll learn how good they got it."

Shaking her head, she returns her attention to the insurmountable stack of forms on the desk. As soon as she looks away, Sheila ventures back into the kitchen. She grabs a spatula and uses it to push a mixing bowl toward the edge of a shelf, locking eyes with Cheryl as she does so, her vacant expression hypnotizing Cheryl into complacency.

"Now, as for your man," the woman tells Peter. "He ain't been by. If he had I'd be home asleep right now instead of here. Okay?"

The bowl reaches the inevitable tipping point, and now it's as if Sheila is challenging her to intercede, but Cheryl fears leaving Peter's side. Sheila blinks and gives a tiny shrug before pushing the bowl over the edge. Cheryl lunges toward the kitchen, but it's too late and the distance is too great. The bowl topples onto the industrial-grade countertop with a large crash.

"Oh, now you done it, girl," the woman yells. She scrambles to her feet. Turning to Peter, she says, "I got to deal with this. Are we finished?"

"Yes," Peter says. "Thanks—"

In a moment, she's upon Shelia, shouting about responsibility and rules, privileges and community, but Shelia's still-vacant gaze never leaves Cheryl. She could've been a hero, it seems to say; she could've interceded. She had the opportunity and she failed to act.

The unspoken accusation remains with her on the walk back to Peter's car and as they drive away from the shelter.

"I'm sorry you had to see that," he says. "I know it's not very pleasant."

"It was fine. I'm glad we went. That poor—" It dawns on her that Peter isn't apologizing for Sheila or for the shelter. He's apologizing for Steven's absence. "Maybe he just had the schedule wrong," she says quickly. "That kind of thing happens all the time. You look at the wrong week..."

His cheek twitches. "Sure."

"I bet he's back at the house. Maybe you can call him?"

He presses his thin lips into a tight smile. "If it's all the same to you, I'd like to talk about something else now."

"Sorry, of course, whatever you like."

The labored whirl of the a/c compressor and the smooth progression of city blocks serve as a surrogate to conversation. The lights are in their favor as they leave the vicinity of the shelter and approach Lake Eola. He banks left away from downtown, and she scans the surrounding traffic for Thaddeus's car. The muted jostling of the road affords her space to think. Disappearing like this is unlike Thaddeus. He could be anywhere. He probably decided to do something stupid like get Steven a boat even though she specifically asked him not to be extravagant, told him that it wasn't necessary, and, anyway, they don't have that kind of money anymore. But did he listen? Probably not! She can't say that she's surprised. After all these years she's come to accept that level of selfishness from him. But if he took the car then he must've had the keys with him when she suggested a walk, which means he planned to leave. He played her! For all his narcissism and temper, Thaddeus has never manipulated her before. He's always been open and straightforward about his actions—for all his faults he's at least had that one virtue. This, though... this is new. For the first time in their marriage she feels outsmarted by Thaddeus and it frightens her.

She hardly notices that they are miles from downtown, circling the mall, when Peter's phone rings.

"Hello?"

"Who is it?" she whispers. "Is it Steven? Has he found Thaddeus?"

Peter shakes his head and signals for her to be quiet. He begins to say something but is cut off. He snarls, revealing a crooked bicuspid.

"I see," he says.

Snapping his head back and forth on the lookout for traffic, he abruptly switches lanes and heads away from the mall.

"And did anybody check... Was there a call? Listen," he snaps, "what I'm getting at is did anybody even think to call me? Yes, no, I'm aware—look, I'm not going to discuss semantics with you. You know exactly what I mean—"

"What happened?" she more mimes than asks, but he doesn't respond. He drives erratically, cutting people off, tailgating. "Peter, slow down. You're making me nervous."

He ignores her. He runs a red light, nearly clipping a pickup making a right-hand turn. Horns bleat from every direction as he barrels down the road in a chaotic zigzag. He wouldn't drive this way if the call were about the gallery or about Thaddeus, she's certain about that. A sudden dread seizes her. "Is it Gertie? Is Gertie okay?!"

"Forget it," he yells into the phone. His jaw clenches and his ear turns crimson. "I'll deal with that tomorrow when the director is in. No. Obviously, there's nothing you can do now. She's not there now. No. No. You—" He raises a hand as if preparing to pulverize a board.

They nearly swerve off the road, so she does the only thing she can think to do. She grabs the wheel and steers while he powers the pedals. The tacky feel of the worn leather and the slim diameter of the wheel feel foreign in her hands. Pines slip by like pages in a flip-book, interrupted by garish storefronts and derelict tire yards. She can't control the speed, only the direction. She hugs the center lane, slipping between fenders when they ride up on traffic.

"No, don't even worry about it." He's laughing now, spitting at the phone. "You've done enough. Good-bye." He flings the phone into the center console and muscles back control of the wheel. The car swerves a final time, then straightens out.

"That was the day care," he says. "Gertie's gone."

LAILA WEAVES THROUGH THE CROWDED ATRIUM AT THE Orlando Museum of Art. Only five minutes late and the café already hums with a thick lunchtime rush. Esther texted that she'd arrived early, and Laila spots her seated by the plate glass window overlooking the atrium. Of course she managed to find a table all the way in the back of the dining room so that now Laila must push past ornery tourists who'd likely much rather be at Disney World than at a museum. Esther's hair is a shade lighter than the last time they saw each other and it's pulled back into a tight bun that smoothes the worry lines from her brow. She perches on her chair, looking aloof in a black-and-gray tweed suit with raw edges. Instantly, Laila feels self-conscious about her jeans and sneakers. She should've thought ahead and tossed a pair of ballet flats in the car this morning before her shift and maybe a light blazer. Looking around, at least she's not the only one dressed casually. Then again, it doesn't really matter what all these strangers wear, does it? It only matters what Moraleses wears. There's a reputation to consider.

"Oof, so much sun at this table," Laila says, sliding into a chair across from her stepmother.

"Do you want to switch seats? It's not as bright on this side."

"No, it's fine. I brought my sunglasses." She slips them on. She can be aloof, too.

Esther dons a pair of reading glasses. "I can't see anything on this menu. Don't get old. It's awful. Everything goes downhill."

The reading glasses are an affect, the prop of choice for a middle-aged woman of means. She doesn't doubt that her stepmother's eyes are in decline, but Esther hardly needs to read the menu. She always orders the same thing: a candied walnut and beet salad with goat cheese and a light vinaigrette on the side. She's glad for the distraction, though. Pretending to look at the menu affords her a small reprieve from her stepmother's imperious gaze. Neither of them glances up from her menu until a frazzled waiter arrives with two glasses of water.

Only after placing their orders are they forced to finally look at each other. Her stepmother's skin is smooth like a rock polished by a stream, though it pleases Laila to note that Esther's chest shows signs of sun damage. Esther looks her up and down and clicks her tongue, no doubt silently criticizing her outfit. *T-shirt and jeans, and here the museum is hosting a retrospective of your father's work.*

Laila gestures toward the galleries. "Have you been inside yet?"

"I walked through." Esther's focus shifts to the flatware. "I didn't spend a lot of time in there. It doesn't feel the same without your father."

Without her father to do what? Laila wonders, but Esther doesn't elaborate.

"I haven't seen it yet."

"You should. They did a good job."

Their food arrives a moment later. After a few bites, Esther lowers her fork and takes a sip of water. "How is your brother? I haven't heard from him in a while."

She shrugs, choosing her words carefully. "Your son is fine."

But that's not exactly true. She has neither seen nor heard from Alex in nearly six months, not since the night of the hurricane. It's only because of Instagram stalking that she even knows that he's still alive.

"Tell him to call me. Por favor, Laila. Okay? I worry when I don't hear from him."

She picks at her rice pilaf and asks when was the last time Esther heard from Alex, hoping her tone doesn't betray anything.

"A few weeks ago. He wanted money for new sneakers."

And apparently he didn't feel the need to inform Esther of his current living situation. That's something in her favor at least. "I'll tell him to call more often."

"Thank you."

After the hurricane, she intended to tell Esther the truth. She really did, but a mixture of hope that Alex would return and embarrassment that she'd allowed him to go in the first place kept her from following through. Then too much time passed. Admitting the deception became increasingly difficult with each passing day. And for a while it was easier to maintain the illusion than to confess, but lately it's been getting harder to keep the lie going. How many times has Esther called the house phone only to be told that Alex was in the shower? How many surprise weekend visits had ended abruptly with Laila explaining away her brother's absence as an impromptu beach trip or an afternoon at the mall with friends? The scale of the ongoing deception makes it difficult to confess, but so, too, does the fictional history of the previous six months that she's concocted for Esther's benefit. In that version of events, Alex is an ideal roommate, conscientious about common areas and respectful of private space. He works hard at getting his life back on track, and when he stumbles she's there to provide guidance and support like a dutiful older sister. For the first time in their lives, the siblings share a close bond. Laila despairs of abandoning the fiction because the lie is so much more desirable than the reality, more desirable than the antagonistic situation they found themselves in when he was actually living with her.

"¿Que te pasa?" Esther asks. "You're in la-la land."

"Huh? Oh, sorry. I zoned out for a minute. Yeah, totally, everything is fine." She smiles and confidently meets her stepmother's gaze. "I'm just tired. I came straight from the pharmacy."

"You're not pregnant, are you?"

She grunts. "There's zero chance of that at the moment."

"Because sometimes women can be and not even know it. My cousin was that way, or so she said, pero I think she just didn't want anybody to know que estaba embarazada antes que se casó."

"I know what the signs of pregnancy are."

"I know you do. You're the closest thing we have to a doctor in the family." Esther smiles. "Your father and I were always very proud of you for that. How's your food?"

"Fine."

"Do you want my crostini? I'm not going to finish it."

"No, I'm okay."

Esther shrugs and takes a bite of her salad. "You're too thin. You work too hard. I've always said so."

"Can we please talk about something else? I don't want to talk about work or my weight."

"Have you spoken with your mother recently?"

"Wow, okay. Um, no, I haven't, but thanks for bringing her up."

"I'm only trying to make conversation. No es tan fácil with you, you know."

"By mentioning my mother?"

"Well, you don't want to talk about work or your brother, so what am I supposed to ask about, huh?"

"I don't know, like TV or something."

Esther waves away the suggestion. "I don't watch TV. Too many commercials."

"Okay, then movies"—not that she's been recently—"or the news."

"Oh!" Esther places her fork down and leans across the table. "Did you read about that serial killer? They think he's finding guys at clubs. I called your brother and left a message. I know that he goes out sometimes pero you don't think he's in danger, do you?"

"No," she says, too quickly. "I mean isn't it just rumors? Some kid goes missing in Clermont and a few guys turn up dead with enough party drugs in their systems to kill a horse. It could just be coincidence."

"Some of them look like they've been strangled. That's what the newspaper says."

She's hardly touched her food. When the waiter comes to clear away the plates she raises no objections. Nor does she when Esther offers to pick up the tab.

"I wouldn't worry," she continues when they're alone again. "Alex doesn't go clubbing. He mostly hangs out with his friends at, like, the park and stuff. They go out to eat a lot"—at least according to Instagram. "How did we get back to talking about Alex?"

"Eso es lo que quería hablar con you about today. I want to do something special for his eighteenth birthday. Something small. Just family."

She rolls her eyes while sipping her iced tea.

But Esther snaps back. "You might not like me very much, but believe it or not I love you and I care about your happiness. I'm sorry that things are not good with your mother, but I've always thought of you as my daughter—"

"Please stop."

"No, this is important," she says, softening her tone. "Listen to me. Your father is gone." Tears well up, but she blinks them back. "All we have left is each other. You and me and your brother. It's important that we do things together as a family. He would've wanted that."

When Laila doesn't respond, Esther folds her napkin and stands up. "Okay, I'll leave you alone. Me voy. Think over what I said. We still have some time, but we need to start planning soon. I love you. And tell your brother to call me," she says over her shoulder as she walks away.

The animosity will fade before Esther reaches the car. One good thing about her stepmother: she doesn't hold grudges, a trait Alex shares. His temper flares easily, but once he erupts it's over. Laila, on the other hand, cultivates animosity, which explains how she's managed to go most of her life punishing Esther for—for what? She rubs her temples. Why can't her family just be easier?

She finishes her iced tea and stands. The lunch rush is over. Her legs carry her across the atrium to the main gallery of the museum, empty on a Wednesday afternoon. A solid white wall announces the exhibit in heavy block type: FÉLIX MORALES: THE FABRIC OF A LIFE CUT SHORT. A quote from his final interview is stenciled below:

> For the longest time I thought I'd grow up to be a superhero. While my eventual powers, my villains, and my mission remained fuzzy concepts on the edge of my thinking, my costume was crystal clear in my mind. I'd wear an asymmetrical black cape. On my

head I'd wear a cowl like Batman, only with fewer features, little more than a blank shape with mesh slits to see out of. Instead of tights I'd wear pinned trousers of dark gray flannel that belled out mid-shin like the exaggerated points of a military uniform. On top I'd wear an oversized black sweater cut for performance. That's the costume I'd save the world in.

His words appeared in the February 2013 issue of *Interview*, the same month Urbody Couture's most celebrated collection debuted in the tents of New York Fashion Week. Félix, already ill when he gave the interview in November of the previous year, was dead by the time the issue hit newsstands.

The costume was part of her father's first collection in 1986, the year her parents married, and the only unisex garment he ever produced.

Whether Félix's anecdote was the wistful recollection of a man aware of the little time he had left or a complete fabrication—a final attempt to pin an overarching vision to a career widely regarded as uneven—is impossible to tell. He left very little in the way of personal correspondences or diaries. Regardless of the truth, the story was widely disseminated in the months following his death, contributing to the favorable reception of the final collection. The anecdote has become so muddled in her memory that Laila no longer remembers if she'd heard it growing up or if the story had insinuated itself into her conception of her father's professional life like a cultural virus, a revisionist meme. She could ask Alex or Esther (or even her mother) for clarification, but in the two years since his death they've avoided talking about Félix except to gesture at the tragedy of his passing, silence in the guise of reverence being the handmaiden of grief. She could break the silence, and maybe doing so would begin to mend whatever they've allowed to deteriorate in the past couple of years. Motivation surges through her, but the moment fades. How can she broach the subject if she can't even find Alex?

Inside the gallery the air is cool and still. Long black drapes occlude the high windows wrapping the museum's facade; excess fabric pools along the floor like hardened lava. A funerary darkness permeates the space, punctuated by spotlights over the individual dresses. Some dresses stand alone, while others cluster together in loose groupings suggesting a cocktail party or wake. The curator has shown no allegiance to chronology. Taken en masse, the exhibition resembles a solemn, silent parade with dresses from disparate periods accompanying one another through the darkened rooms.

Laila instinctively rejects the concept.

Her father intended Urbody Couture to be a dynamic, evolving brand. The clothes were—are—meant to be worn. Nothing made him happier than imagining a woman dashing out on some errand in one of his dresses. Even on display in department stores her father's work possessed a vitality that the exhibit has stripped away.

Encountering the clothes in this setting, draped over faceless mannequins, lends them a foreign quality that unnerves her. Yet it's impossible to not feel a familiarity with the iconic dresses. There's the now-famous "superhero" tunic, of course, but the floral-patterned secretary dress—alone, seemingly forgotten in a corner of the second gallery like a mistress at a funeral—remained the brand's bestseller throughout the 1990s, even if it rarely garnered notoriety for its designer. The millennial "steeplechase" gown, a commercial disappointment, pivots to gaze across the room at a much more popular "Dubai" from the 2004 collection.

Fashion played an important role at home during her youth, but it was no more important than medicine would be in the home of a doctor or rocks in that of a geologist. Félix and Esther prioritized the quotidian parts of life (another area in which she begrudgingly commends her stepmother).

It makes sense that a museum exhibit would distill her father's life down to the impact his career had within a larger cultural context. Yet the focus feels discordant to her. Halfway through she feels dizzy and has to sit down on a bench to catch her breath. There is no evidence here of the man who mowed the lawn in an old pair of boat shoes and a Florida Marlins inaugural year T-shirt; no mention of the driver who never exceeded the speed limit by more than 5 mph, or the epicurean who preferred guava paste and a slice of Muenster to all desserts. She doesn't recognize the man being celebrated at the Orlando Museum of Art, and what's more, the man she remembers wouldn't either. A central tautology of her childhood insisted that work was work, important only in proportion to how it facilitated the things that actually mattered in life. Not this! Not this fetishization of work. This was a joke, something to get away with and laugh about with your family over dinner: "Can you believe what somebody paid me for a few yards of fabric?"

In her anger, she nearly walks past the final dress in the exhibit without pausing. Nearly. But she does pause and what she sees overrides whatever indignation attended her journey through the galleries. There in front of her, on a podium elevated from all the others, stands the apotheosis of the exhibit's ghostly procession: her mother's wedding dress. She knows the dress from family photos but she's only ever seen it once in person. It was shortly after the divorce when her father was packing up items in her mother's closet to send to storage. She pleaded with Félix to leave her mother's clothes alone. What if she came back and had nothing to wear? Would she leave again? It took a while, but Félix eventually calmed her down by explaining that her mother wasn't coming back, but if she did the clothes could easily be retrieved. She hasn't thought about the dress in more than a decade, but suddenly Esther's question, which seemed unnecessarily cruel over lunch, makes sense. Esther must've seen the dress when she toured the exhibit.

But why is it here? The plaque on the wall says Félix stitched the gown himself. The spirit of the text is celebratory, yet the circumstances regarding her mother's addiction and her parents' divorce are well known. Is the implication that by remaining with her mother for as long as he did Félix somehow became that superhero he claimed to aspire to as a child? It's more mythologizing, but she finds herself susceptible to its effects.

If only she could touch the dress.

Only just to feel the fabric that her father spent so much time stitching, hemming, and embroidering. What does it matter that this dress crowns an exhibit in a museum? It once hung in her closet. She quickly scans the room. A lone security guard in an ill-fitting uniform paces between two adjoining galleries, a bored expression on his face. Aside from a small nod of acknowledgment when she entered the room, he's ignored her. There's no reason he should start paying attention to her now. When he turns a corner she seizes the opportunity. Her fingers slide along the skirt. A dormant part of her brain activates, the part that spent years as her father's constant companion to trade shows and factories, boutiques and studios. She pinches the hem with a practiced dexterity, evaluating her father's stitching by touch and evoking his memory the way a doctor's daughter may recall a sly sense of humor in the curve of an *S* on an old prescription pad. Everything he was at home and at work is preserved in the stitching, the steady, precise stitching. It must've taken weeks to get every detail perfect. Could he have suspected then how everything would end?

"Excuse me, ma'am." The security guard moves toward her, the synthetic fabric of his pants rustling as his pace quickens. "You can't touch the dress!"

She sprints from the gallery.

Outside in her truck she cries for the first time in months.

CAR SEATS ARE TOO COMPLICATED. THERE ARE HOLES for the seat belt, but his hand doesn't bend the right way to pass anything through them, and while he's trying she walks away. He breaks into a cold sweat. The shiny buckle slips out of his wet palms.

"Gertie," he calls, climbing deeper into the backseat, stretching and contorting in the tight space for the best angle. "Stay by Grandpa."

He estimates that he parked the car about twenty minutes ago. Since then the lot has filled up, and from the backseat of the Cutlass Supreme he can just barely spy Gertie crouching between cars, picking at the coarse asphalt pebbles lodged in the tire grooves.

"Poop!" She purses her lips and points at him, but she can't sustain the act for long. A smile wends its way on to her face and she snorts, attempting to conceal her laughter. She hides behind her hands and collapses in a fit of giggles, clearly still amped from playing with the other kids in day care.

"Ha, that's a good one, beautiful. Now, why don't you come back over here?"

She ignores him, and he berates himself for not installing the car seat earlier. He should've had the clerk at the toy store do it when they bought the thing. A skilled professional would've finished the job in five minutes, no problem, and had he done so they'd be on their way to Disney World right now instead of sitting in this parking lot. But he's not doing himself any favors by second-guessing. The situation is what it is. Besides, he's managing all right. All he has to do is buckle in the car seat and it'll be smooth sailing.

Speed is of great concern. Gertie's absence could be noticed at any moment—should've been noticed by now, in fact. That nobody has stormed out here in search of him only proves what an unacceptable place the Little Sunshine Scholars Day Care and Preschool really is.

Sweaty palms aren't doing him any favors. Nor is a shirt that insists on bunching up as he clambers over the seat to grab the buckle. His heart beats erratically, but he's close. He has the buckle in one hand and the clasp in the other.

"Gertie, come stand by Grandpa. We're almost ready, sweetheart."

"Poop!"

All he has to do is pass the belt through the various openings in the car seat, buckle it in place, and he's done. This isn't rocket science. Focus, Thaddeus. As he examines the various passes, Gertie darts toward a raised patch of grass not far from the car.

"Hey, beautiful, if you come back I'll give you ten dollars," he barters in singsong. "I'll give you whatever you want. Doesn't that sound nice?"

She stares at him for a minute—please God, he thinks, don't let anybody see her—then with a shrug she saunters back to the car.

"Good girl!"

She poses with one hand on her hip and the other one out, waiting for the money.

"Just a sec, beautiful. Grandpa almost has this."

She furrows her brow and thrusts her palm toward him. She grunts and it looks like she might scream.

"All right, your grandpa is a man of his word. Ten dollars it is." But in order to reach into his pocket for the cash, he needs to free up his hand. Since he doesn't want to lose the seat belt, he leans over and pins the buckle to the backseat with his chin. "I hope you appreciate this, beautiful." His voice strains as he scratches at the worn denim seat of his pants with his left hand. He wears his wallet on the opposite side, and just as he manages to grab it, he loses his grip on the buckle and it goes flying back into the frame.

"Shit!"

The outburst scares Gertie and she runs away screaming.

A horn honks.

"Fuck!"

Dammit, he shouldn't have yelled. Now they'll definitely come storming out of the day care to take her back. The patrons at the grocery down the way will see him and think he's a stranger trying to steal her; after all, they look nothing alike. She's adopted, he'll plead; he was frustrated with the car seat, surely anybody could understand that—but it won't matter. Someone will call the police and then he'll end up in jail. All because of this goddamn car seat!

"Focus, man!" He lunges for the seat belt and repositions himself for another attempt.

This is about Gertie, he reminds himself. He's doing this for her. He tugs on the seat belt. It scrapes against the worn plastic. Okay, he thinks, now we're cooking with gas. Pass it through and click it in place, no big deal.

Click, click, click.

For a moment he thinks he's found the way through the labyrinth and he rejoices. "Take that, you stupid cocksucker!" He tugs on the car seat and it holds. "Ha!" But then the buckle, flapping batlike, comes flying out of the car seat, nearly smacking him in the face as it recoils into the doorframe.

"Son of a bitch!" He punches the car seat, snapping the plastic headrest and scraping himself in the process. "Gertie, get back over here. Now!"

He wants to rip the whole thing out of the car, throw it onto the hard asphalt, and stomp on it until it's nothing but a million shards of plastic and foam. Then tell him he can't handle a car seat! Ha! But, of course, he can't do that. He understands that much at least. The old rage throbs in his temples, so he takes several deep breaths and chants an *om* as he's been learning to do on YouTube. The rage begins to dissipate. If at first you don't succeed... He straddles the car seat and tries again, this time throwing his weight into the task.

Click, click, click.

The sound confuses him. He hasn't done anything yet. Perhaps it's a miracle. Perhaps he's lined himself up with the universe and willed the buckle into place. *Om,* he chants. *Om.*

Gertie's laughter interrupts the meditation. She stands nearby with a fistful of gravel. Awkwardly, she flings it at the car. Most of the gravel falls to the ground straightaway, but a few stones clink against the paint.

She's throwing gravel, he thinks. No miracle. Sighing, he returns to the problem of the car seat. Something nags at him, however. And because of its incessancy and because it carries the recognizable weight of veracity, he visualizes it as Cheryl.

He pictures her there beside him: Cheryl, wearing a sour look and crossing her arms, trying to get his attention. *Not now, woman,* he wants to say, and he even goes as far as to swipe at the air like he would swat at a mewling cat, but the apprehension remains.

Click, click, click.

She's not by the car anymore, so she must be throwing from farther away. She's got an arm on her, and that makes him proud. He makes a note to tell Stevie to sign her up for Little League. That girl could be an all-star.

Cheryl doesn't rest. *Think it through,* she says.

He's in the car, in a parking lot... His eyelids grow heavy from the strain of thinking. He wants to quit, but Cheryl refuses to leave him alone, so, with a sigh, he presses on. They're in the parking lot. And the parking lot... gives way to a curb! Yes, he definitely remembers a curb with grass.

"Gertie," he shouts, "come where Grandpa can see you, goddamn it!"

His mind rushes ahead. There's a curb with grass, and the curb with grass gives way to the road. Every vehicle on the road metastasizes into one deafening roar.

"Whatever you want," he pleads. Tumbling to his knees he tries to leave the car. Gertie is in great danger. He calls to her again, and still there's no answer. He tries again to climb out of the car, but, again, he's hampered. In all his gymnastics to position his body in relation to the car seat, he's managed to get his shoe caught between the rear bench and the frame, and he can't dislodge it. Confused, he shouts for Cheryl before calling out for Gertie again.

"Whatever you want!" He twists and lunges toward the door. It swings open farther. "Please." But instead of hearing the faint echo of his call bouncing off the back window of the Cutlass Supreme, he hears a solid thud. Something wet hits his face.

Instinctively, his fingers fly to his cheek.

Oh my God, it's sticky! His fingers are sticky, and when he pulls them away he sees blood. It all happens so fast. He remembers a screech, or was it a scream? Then the gravel kicked up against the car. No.

Wait.

He has it backward. The gravel came after the screech. Time stops and everything happens at once.

"I'm so sorry." It's a woman's voice. She bends down toward the gravel several feet away. Her words reverberate.

"Gertie." He can barely whisper. The words won't come. "Cheryl," he mumbles. All he can picture is Gertie's small body crumpled on the street, and he strains with all his might to exit the backseat.

Blond and rumpled, the woman laughs as she approaches.

His heart shatters because of this monster.

"Gertie," he shouts. "Why? Why? Why?" His head and shoulders emerge from the car, but he remains pinned. As much as he wants to, he can't leap out of the Cutlass Supreme and crush this approaching monster's face with his fists.

Just beyond his range, she points at him and laughs. ". . . and it's all over your face."

He touches his face again and feels the stickiness. My granddaughter's blood, he thinks, as tears blind him. His arms lie impotent along the baseboard, and the monster seizes the opportunity to approach.

She touches his cheek and rubs the blood into his skin, playing with it and pulling it away from his face.

"Oh, you're bleeding!"

Suddenly, he feels his foot drop onto the car floor, but when he attempts to set up a lunge the worn sole of his shoe slips on the old carpet. He's wasted enough time already. Using his other foot, he pries off the shoe. Staggering, he hurls himself at the woman and they collapse onto the asphalt. She screams. Gertie's blood binds them. Rage blinds him. He will suffocate her. He will pulverize her. No court in the world would blame him.

"Why?" he screams, pawing at her face. "Gertie!"

And then a tiny voice squeaks. "Poop."

And he feels a tiny hand on his leg.

The roar, which rose so fast and consumed him so absolutely, dissipates. The blindness lifts from his eyes. Turning, he sees her unharmed.

"Gertie! Come to Grandpa!"

He rolls onto his side and reaches for her—inadvertently pinning the woman's hips. Gertie is light, but his arm is weak, so he struggles to shift her weight onto his shoulder.

"Don't worry about me," the monster says. Only now he knows she's not a monster.

He puts Gertie down long enough to scuttle off the woman.

"I'm sorry, I thought—" No. Before he explains anything, he's going to make sure Gertie is safe. Ignoring the sharp pain in his knee, bruised from all the tussling, he pulls himself up to his feet, then plops Gertie into the unsecured car seat. It won't matter for the moment. He closes the door, keeping her safe.

"You could buy me dinner first," the woman says, pulling herself up onto her elbows.

For the first time he really sees her. She's older, closer to his age than to that of the sweet, uncomplicated young women who normally catch his eye, but she carries herself with confidence and her eyes are clear as isinglass. Her blond hair frames her face, and she's dressed in a white linen pantsuit, soiled now in places from being pinned to the asphalt.

"I'm sorry," he says. "I couldn't find..." His thought trails away as he extends a hand down to the woman. "Allow me."

Once on her feet, she thanks him and points at his chin. "Need a napkin?"

He feels the stickiness again, but if it's not Gertie's blood, then what is it?

"You have honey all over your face," she says. Her nose wrinkles. "And it looks like you're bleeding. Now, the first part is my fault."

She kicks at a broken bottle on the asphalt. "I dropped it while I was rushing to get to the car. But the blood is a mystery."

"Honey?" he says, and shakes his head.

"I don't think we're at the pet name phase just yet, big man." She winks, then opens her handbag. "I think I have a napkin. That is, if I can find anything in here."

From his back pocket he extracts a handkerchief and pats down his face. "Don't worry," he says absently. "I always come prepared."

He thinks out the scenario. He struggled with the car seat. He punched it. He lunged out of the car... "I must've cut myself on the car seat trying to get out. I thought my granddaughter—" He swallows, unable to articulate the horrendous possibility. "I thought something had happened."

"And you rushed to protect her." She places a weightless hand on his arm. "What a good grandpa."

He blushes. "It's nothing."

"Well, here. Give me a hand picking up these groceries—what's left of them anyway. I'm afraid I broke most of them running to my car." She indicates a late-model red coupe two yards away. "That's what I get for needing my sugar fix." Picking through her shattered groceries, she shrugs. "I guess it'll be takeout for one again tonight."

"Say no more." He flashes her the mischievous eyebrow, then extracts a twenty-dollar bill from his wallet. "For something sweet."

"Oh, I couldn't." She laughs.

"I insist."

"Keep your money." She accentuates her drawl. "The last thing I need is something sweet."

She's flirty and touchy without being obvious, and he likes that. It's been a long time since Cheryl touched his arm casually or said things that merited a wink. When they started, he remembers, everything had a double meaning.

"Look, you seem like a decent guy," she says, leaning against the Cutlass Supreme. "How about we cut to the chase? What do you say we make it dinner for two? My treat."

"Oh," he says. "I don't know..."

"Now why is that? And don't you dare tell me a man like you doesn't like to eat."

With a laugh he pats his belly. "It's not that." Gertie waves at him from her car seat.

"It's just that I have my granddaughter today—"

"Well, hell, bring her along. She can play with my Buddy. He's a golden retriever and he just loves kids."

She's so beautiful, and he imagines what sharing a meal with her would be like, but he hesitates.

"Hey, Stretch," she says, beaming a high-voltage smile. "I'm out on a limb here. Don't make a girl suffer."

"It's just that..."

"Come on, out with it. What's the matter? Cat got your tongue?"

"You're gorgeous," he says, clasping her hands in his. "A real fox. It's just—"

"You're going to tell me you're married, aren't you?"

He frowns and gives a weak nod.

She pulls her hands back. "Damn, I was hoping widower. Well, nothing ventured, nothing gained, right?" She quickly gathers what's left of her groceries. Before she walks away she slips a business card into his hands. "Let me know if you ever change your mind. Cute kid, by the way."

He listens to the *click-clack* of her retreating heels against the asphalt, wanting to call her back; how long has it been since Cheryl showed him that kind of affection? But he has Gertie now and he shouldn't take any chances.

"Wait."

She looks back, but it's only to wink. Then she's in her car and driving away.

Gertie refuses to cooperate. She clamors over the car seat. She rolls onto her tummy. She squirms, and once, when he puts his finger near her mouth, she bites down hard, then erupts into belly laughter.

The situation and all the new people milling about overwhelm him. To hell with it. He plops her down in the front passenger seat and buckles her in. The shoulder strap crosses her chin and her ankles barely reach the edge of the seat, but it's better than nothing. "We're leaving." He can do this for her. He can give her a roomful of dolls. Stevie won't, but he will. He can take her to the happiest place on Earth.

If anybody's watching, they'll see that he's a good grandfather.

He digs through the glove compartment for his hidden stash. Just a toke. Just a buzz to mellow the jitters of the car seat debacle, something to soothe his nerves and help him find the road.

"Ready for a magical mystery tour, beautiful?" He blows a string of smoke toward the roof.

She coughs and frowns. "Poop."

"The Beatles." He grins. "Before your time. Don't worry, Grandpa will teach you all about them."

She stretches out her open palm and gestures for the ten dollars he owes her. What a memory on her! "In a minute, beautiful. There's no rush. We have all day."

"WHAT DO YOU MEAN YOU DON'T KNOW WHERE HE IS?"

Esther lunges across the breakfast bar like a wave over a breakwater. Laila retreats, but her small galley kitchen provides little shelter. The stove flanks her to the right and the fridge boxes in her rear. A short stretch of tile in front of the pantry presents the only escape. She dashes for it but Esther heads her off. They pause inches away from each other. In the heat of rage, her stepmother's perfume smells tart.

Laila backs off. The slick curve of formica presses against the small of her back. Just out of reach, a glass of iced tea sweats on the counter. She stands firm. "He hasn't come home," she says, as if he were merely out for a stroll. If it came to blows, she could take her stepmother, but her words placate Esther long enough for Laila to shift venues into the living room.

"For how long?" Esther asks, arms akimbo.

"Six months."

"Seis meses!" Esther spins on the balls of her feet and paces, gesturing wildly. She likes to walk when she's mad. Laila remembers that from growing up. "Y me vienes a decir ahora? Jamas en mi vida—oh my God, we have to call the police!"

Laila blocks her path. "We're not calling the police! Be rational."

"My baby is missing!"

"He's not missing. He's just not here."

"Well, where is he?"

"I don't know, but I'm sure he's fine."

"Oh, you're sure he's fine! Cómo lo sabes, huh?" Esther sidesteps her and zips around the living room like a balloon with a leak, coming to rest beside a console table backing the sofa. "You haven't seen him in six months!" As she speaks she slaps the table, causing everything on it to wobble.

"I know it sounds bad—"

"I never should've let him move in with you. I knew something like this would happen."

"Let him? Uh-uh, don't you even try that." She springs forward, close enough to smell the faint halitosis of late middle age. A premonition of her future perhaps, but it's her past that rushes into focus. "You begged me to take him in—"

"¿Yo? ¡Jamas!"

"Yes, you did! You absolutely did. He was standing right there with his bag—"

"That's not how I remember it," Esther says, slowly crossing her arms.

Laila tosses back her long curls. "Why would I lie about that? You think I wanted him here?"

"Is that why you've been lying to me for six months?"

"What? What the fuck are you talking about?"

"You said you didn't want him here, so—"

"You think this is my fault? And who kicked him out first, huh?"

"Ah, entonces you did. You sent your poor brother out into the street, y por qué? Because of this apartment. You want to be alone so much it's more important to you than family. What would your father say?"

"At least I've been keeping track of him, which is more than you've been doing. See for yourself." She pulls up Alex's Instagram. There's his familiar face, smiling in every photo. How can this be the same moody boy they both exiled from their houses? This boy looks happy, well adjusted, friendly, and helpful.

"¿Qué's esto?" Esther asks, digging out her reading glasses from the bottom of her purse.

"Just scroll down."

"I know how to use a phone," Esther says in a huff. Then she's silent for a long time as she works her way through the photos. The screen light ages her—drawing out wrinkles that a practiced makeup brush renders hardly visible otherwise—but it also highlights the small movements of her mouth as she instinctively reacts to the volley of images on the screen: a quick grin, a passing frown; embarrassment, sympathy. Compassion. Laila watches the evolution of emotions unfold, unconsciously mimicking her stepmother's micro expressions. At last Esther looks up. In a quiet, conciliatory voice she asks, "¿Quiénes son estas gente?"

"His friends, I guess."

"If I had friends like that growing up my mother would've locked me in my room."

"I've never met any of them." Her voice sounds sadder than she anticipated. "He never brought anybody over."

Esther sighs. She turns back to the screen, scrolling faster now but pausing frequently to examine a photo in more detail.

"I'm sorry," Laila says. "I should've told you sooner. I thought he'd come back and then when he didn't it just got harder."

Esther rests her forehead in her palm, holding the phone loosely in her free hand. "Where did I go wrong? I tried my best with the both of you—"

"I know." Laila conducts her over to the couch. They both sit.

"—one lies to me and the other one doesn't want anything to do with me."

"It's not your fault. You did a good job." The weight of seventeen years bends her into a slouch. What a waste of time! How many birthdays given over to bitchy glances? Weekends embroiled in useless sparring? How many family functions lost to rancor? So maybe she shares some of the guilt. She stoked the animosity and squandered the good times; this is her reward. And Alex paid the price.

Tentatively she places an arm across her stepmother's shoulders. "I'll find him, okay? I promise. In the meantime, just please don't do anything crazy like call the police, okay? That's the last thing we need." She can see the headlines now: "Son of Fashion Mogul Goes Missing."

"I don't know..." But the endless stream of selfies seems to have alleviated at least some of Esther's fears. She consents.

"Te prometo, okay?" Laila says. "I'll bring him home."

Tears in her eyes, Esther nods, pulling Laila into a hug. "¡Ay, mi'ja, gracias!" She stiffens and recoils. "Ay, pero what about that serial killer?"

Laila resists the impulse to tell Esther for the thousandth time that there is no killer. Instead, she relies on Instagram. "You saw for yourself that he's fine."

"I don't know if I'd call that fine. Some of those friends of his look like weirdos." But there's laughter in her voice, and that's progress.

"WHAT DO YOU WANT TO DRINK?" HE LEANS IN CLOSE to be heard over the escalating EDM beat.

You feel the radiating warmth of his cheek and you hear the pop of his halting syllables, but you can't see anything beyond the pulsing strobe above the front bar.

"Bourbon," you shout, fishing some money from your pocket, but he refuses.

"Keep it." He rolls up the sleeves of his plaid shirt, revealing thin biceps awash in the intermittent fraise and teal hues of the spinning disco lights. "This one's on me, papi."

He squeezes your shoulder, then threads his way through the crowd up to the bar. He looks good in his new clothes: the slim-cut black jeans, the shirt with the mother-of-pearl buttons undone along his breastbone, and the sneakers that you had to go to three stores to find. You're proud to be seen with him.

Your phone vibrates in your pocket for the tenth time since this afternoon, but you continue to ignore it. Last night was a disaster and you have no desire to revisit any of it until the last possible moment. Tonight is about Alex, and you haven't felt this free in years. Even the constant throb in your hands has quieted into a dull ruffle. If any sliver of reconciliation bridges the gap between what you do at night and the ambivalence of a normal life, you're certain Alex is it. Maybe this is what normal people call a midlife crisis.

He lingers at the bar. While waiting you pull a cigarette from your pocket and step away to smoke.

A thin, good-looking guy in a red polo turns to his friend. "He could be here."

"I wouldn't make too much of it," the friend replies. "A few tweakers overdosed. That's all."

You interrupt to ask for a light and the friend wordlessly hands you his lighter. As you inhale a tingle works its way down your pinkie.

"Thanks. I didn't catch your name."

He rolls his eyes. The thin one introduces himself as Jacob and tells you that his friend is named Michael.

"Michael," you say. "What a coincidence. That's my name, too."

"Not really," Michael says, drawing on his cigarette. "It's a common name."

Alex returns with the drinks, and you decide now is not the time. You return the lighter and tell them that you'll see them around. Michael raises his eyebrow in a withering moue.

When you've moved off a bit, Alex says, "Keep it in your pants, papi. Tonight I'm picking and neither of those icy bitches are my type."

"Not old enough, I suppose."

He leads you by the hand to a table outside, and for a while neither one of you speaks. You sip your drinks and share the cigarette. In the mix of moonlight and halogen he looks thicker, more mature and self-possessed than elsewhere. While other boys perch on the edges of their seats, scanning the crowd for an invitation, he sits back in his chair completely at ease. As people filter by he winks or blows a kiss to passing acquaintances, but he never once leaves your side to greet a favorite. He's very conscientious about his role when he's with you, and at times you think he takes you for a social invalid, or some kind of john, and maybe you are.

"Why don't you go see who's out tonight?"

"There's no rush. We can go in later. Let's just enjoy the air for a bit. It's a nice night."

"You can enjoy the air when you're my age." You light another cigarette with the butt of the last. You've officially begun chain-smoking, a habit that's slithered its way back into your life. "Until then you should be in there getting the most out of your fake ID."

He gives you one of his wry grins. "Well, maybe just one lap."

"Take your time. I'll be here."

Before he leaves, he leans over the table and gives you a long kiss, and you can feel every eye at the bar boring into you. When he's gone you raise your drink to the older men looking on with a mix of envy and disdain and then drain it in one slug.

A small stage sits off the patio with access to the main room via a padded door. Sometimes a drag queen performs there, but tonight it functions as a cocktail lounge. You pass through scouting. You bite at the ragged tips of your fingers. If you're clever there's a way to squeeze in a bit of work while Alex makes his rounds.

Scanning the room, your eyes settle on a willowy boy with uneven skin who speaks to your sense of powerlessness. Though a sizable group surrounds him, your instincts tell you that he's the odd man out. How would you go about it? First, you'd approach and offer to buy him a drink or, tapping your nose, "maybe something else?" The idea is to get them to look away from their phones. They usually say yes. Next, you'd suggest a quieter location. Five minutes from here a small lake abuts the commuter airport. The area is deserted at this time. "What's your name anyway?" Let's say his name is David. You grin, feign surprise. "What a coincidence. That's my name, too. So, David, I think you're pretty cute." Suggest a drive. "What about my friends?" he'd protest. "I know a place nearby. They'll never miss you."

Just a quickie. You could be back before Alex notices your absence. But just as you're about to carry out your plan you're stopped by the nagging possibility that willowy David—even with his uneven skin and iridescent blouse—may be the only boy in the entire club who catches Alex's fancy tonight. What then? It's unlikely that of the hundreds of men here tonight that this one awkward teen would be the only object of desire, but are you willing to take the chance?

David's group breaks up, and as you predicted he's left alone, but you can't bring yourself to approach him. Eventually, he drifts away and you head back to the patio to join the coterie of men loitering by the tiki bar. You smoke another cigarette while you wait for Alex.

You wait a long time. Your posture suffers. When at last he returns he has someone with him, whom he introduces as Eddie. He's not what you would've expected Alex to pick. He's jockish, strong but with more mass than muscle. He'll age poorly, and you take some consolation in that. He's taller than you'd expect, too, easily over six feet. Curly brown hair frames his square face, and he's dressed in a striped shirt and light jacket that's too warm for the weather. He looks like he could've arrived from a golf club not fifteen minutes ago. You instantly despise him.

You could've taken David.

"What a coincidence," you say, extending a hand. "My middle name is Edward."

"Right on," he says. "It's a pretty awesome name." He stumbles, and Alex helps him to a seat. Though relatively early, he's already drunk.

"Do you smoke, Eddie?"

"Sure," he says.

You reach into your pack and extract a cigarette. "I'm afraid you're on your own for a light."

"No worries." He places the cigarette behind his ear. "I'll save it for later."

He and Alex fall into easy conversation about the weather.

"So, like, what's the deal with you guys?" Eddie asks, a smile blossoming. "No offense, but you're, like, a lot older."

"Shh, baby. The adults have some things to discuss," Alex says. He pivots in his chair, turning his back on Eddie. "What do you think, papi?"

"Whatever you want. It's your night." You'd prefer someone else, but the sensation in your hands has escalated into a bona fide ache and you want to leave the club before your resistance gives out and you do something regrettable.

Eddie adjusts his ball cap. "What're y'all discussing?"

Alex turns to face Eddie. He drapes an arm over his broad shoulders. "Tonight's your lucky night. We're taking you home. Congratulations."

He grins. "Don't I get a say?"

"No," you say.

"Relax, baby." Alex licks his ear. "It's gonna be great."

IT SHOULD BE AS EASY AS FOLLOWING THE GREEN interstate signs. Except Thaddeus exited the I-4 too soon and now he can't find his way back. With the map open on his lap, they meander through winding residential roads that dead-end or spill out like logs on a flume ride onto causeways with weedy shoulders. Signs announce SPRING LAKE, DOCTOR PHILLIPS, and BIG SAND, but the names mean nothing to him, nor can he track them on the map for all the yawning circumferences of lakes distorting any semblance of a logical grid.

Every sign seems to indicate that the highway and then Disney World is just around the corner.

"If it's so magical," he grumbles, "how come they need so many damn signs? Can you tell Grandpa that, beautiful?" His breath comes in heavy sighs and he's keenly aware of the static weight of his body pressing down into the driver's seat.

Gertie fixates on the seat belt, biting at it, tugging at it where it grazes her face, which is splotchy from the continual irritation. She's an angel. They've been on the road for hours and she hasn't complained once. Finding himself in the turning lane, he steers into an older subdivision. The houses here with their low-pitched roofs covered in asphalt shingles and shabby lawns resemble his own in Apopka, and he catches himself looking for familiar landmarks— the neighbors' basketball hoop, the speedboat sitting in the side yard of the two-story house on the corner. The uncanny familiarity of it strips him of his confidence.

Focus, he thinks. This is Orlando. All roads lead to Disney World. They have to. Just pick one. Just pick any one of these and drive, and eventually...

But isn't that exactly what he thought half an hour ago? And the hour before that? And before that, too? Of course, but he didn't care then. He was in his own happy, magic place. But the buzz, as it must, wore off and now... *hopeless* comes to mind.

"What a pickle. Huh, beautiful? Your grandpa has really gotten us into a mess here. What do you think of that?"

She smiles and claps, happy for the attention. He spots an on-ramp but misses the sign indicating where it goes, but it doesn't matter. It has to be right because Gertie is smiling and Providence won't steer him wrong.

"Just keep on smiling, okay? Can you do that for Grandpa?" He shifts in his seat to better look at her. Traffic zooms. It flies by, magnet-drawn to the interstate. Lights blink from green to red. The asphalt stretches, heating up while shadows arc across it in the nimble cascade of orderly progression.

Thaddeus steers onto the highway. "We'll make a deal. How do you feel about that? You keep smiling and believing in Grandpa, and he'll find his way to the Magic Kingdom. How does that sound? Great! It sounds great."

He recovers a bit of his vigor. The manifest possibility of his plan buoys him in his seat.

Gertie yawns and drops her head to her shoulder. The seat belt rubs across her collarbone and she winces.

"We just have to go a little further along this way. It's all starting to look familiar to your old grandpa. Ha! How about that? We don't need Grandma, do we, beautiful? Not today, we don't. Today, Grandpa is going to find it himself. After all, I found you and you're tiny compared to Disney World!"

He hums—maybe *Cabaret*, maybe something less familiar from *Phantom*—just something casual for background. This is the blinker. That was a lane change. Gas can be purchased over there. And every few yards palm trees crop up in clusters along the median. More often than not, they denote a sparkling new development flanking the highway, invariably given some Spanish name that he practices until he feels confident in his pronunciation.

"Mar y Lago," he says with a heavy tongue that imparts a syrup-slow lasciviousness to the words. If Cheryl were here he would seduce her with this name. "Mar y Lago. The Villas at Coral Gardens." He drifts off into the fantasy. He'll tell them about their journey tonight, and he'll make sure to remember this neighborhood. *Mar y Largo,* he'll say. *Just past that. We went just past there.* He'll tell them tonight when they return, and Stevie will be impressed with his memory and his good taste and will forgive everything again. Gertie had a wonderful time. Couldn't have been happier. Ha! "Isn't that right, beautiful?"

Gertie gurgles something unintelligible, then slips out from under the shoulder belt and presses her face against the car door. She kicks at the center gearshift, grunts, and squirms.

"Hey," he says. "What's this all of a sudden?"

She frowns.

"Why the long face, huh? Don't you like spending time with Grandpa? Come on, let your old grandpa see that million-dollar smile."

The attention buys him a little time.

He's afraid to let the conversation drop because then he would have to admit that they are lost and that her safety rests entirely with him. The fear starts as a cold sensation in the pit of his stomach that morphs into a piercing heat between his shoulder blades. He pulls a hand across his mouth, the skin loose and thin and covered in stubble. He clears his throat, which is suddenly hot and dry. "You know," he says, "in the old days this was all dirt roads and farms. Of course, there wasn't a Disney World then. Can you picture that, Gertie? Can you picture a time before Disney World?"

She stares at him blankly. Impossible to know if she even hears him, let alone understands what he's saying. But she cocks her head and affects the faintest of frowns, which gives him hope.

"Well, it was pretty long ago. And your grandpa was a young man back then when dinosaurs roamed the earth!" His voice drops into a conspiratorial whisper. "Can you keep a secret, beautiful? I liked the dinosaurs. They were good friends of mine. But there was one that was my absolute favorite. Maybe you've heard of him. He was a flying dinosaur that went by the name of Tokeadactyl. He got the highest. Ha! Just a joke for you. Ask your dad to explain it when you're older."

She cries. At first only a little, but then the momentum builds like a tidal surge until the tears stream. Before long a full-blown tantrum transforms the cabin of the Cutlass Supreme into a thundering seizure. She pounds on the door, hot with rage. A semitruck blares, causing the car to shudder. *Whoosh.* Gertie throws herself against the seat, bringing out a creak that Thaddeus knows will remain with the car forever. She squirms out from under the lap belt. Free to move around unimpeded, she turns on the first thing she sees—the glove box—raining on it a torrent of blows.

"Holy cow," he says. "Calm down."

But he barely gets the first word out before she stands up on the seat and starts punching him. Guarding his face with one hand, he steers with the other. With his vision partially obstructed, he swerves to avoid merging traffic, placing his trust in whatever merciful spirit has guided him this long. She wobbles on the lopsided cushion, in danger of losing her balance, but he can't stop the car because now they're in the left lane with nowhere to go but straight. She withdraws, availing her tiny fists against anything they can find, her energy waning.

"What is it? What's wrong?" He desperately looks for anyplace to get off the road, but traffic presses on relentlessly, and he misses every single sign, leaving him with no idea where they're heading. "Please. Whatever it is. You can tell me, beautiful."

She wails. She hisses. Her screams pierce the cabin, a high-decibel cavalry charging on his eardrums. Tears give way to snot and her face glows crimson. She grumbles and finally collapses in a fit of choking spurts that sound like an asthma attack.

They come to a wide shoulder, so he swerves onto it and hits the brakes amid a cacophony of horn bleats. Throwing the transmission into park, he dashes around the car, flings the door open, and clutches her to his chest. She pounds on him feebly. In another time, his instinct would've been different. He doesn't think about it now, but he senses something has shifted inside of him. He could have shoved her, smacked her—anything to shut her up, to calm her down so that he could think.

Pressed against him, her breathing heaves. The tantrum seems to have passed, and her little body shakes with exhaustion and he knows that he would never do anything to hurt her and that this is the shift that he felt inside. She moans into his chest and now she feels fragile in his arms, like a canary. He wipes the snot from her nose with the hem of his shirt.

"Whatever it is," he coos. "Whatever it was. It's okay now."

For a long while they stand like that on the side of the road while traffic stretches by in the burnished haze of twilight. The city is a reckless flat expanse of white volumes and billboards; a hot wind rustles her hair. The median smells of freshly mowed grass. He rocks her to soothe the moans.

"It's okay. Grandpa's here."

She shudders in his arms. Her belly growls and he feels it vibrate against his round gut. She begins to cry again, but lower this time, more resigned.

"Ha! I know what's wrong. You're hungry! Why didn't you just say so? No big deal."

Her face relaxes into an expression of hope.

"Can you keep another secret?" He waits for her to nod before continuing. "Grandpa has the munchies, too." He stretches his face, fakes a faint. She giggles. "I don't know about you, but Grandpa's so hungry he could eat a horse."

She laughs, violently nodding her head in agreement.

"That's my girl," he says. "How does a cheeseburger sound?"

SHE RECOGNIZES THE SONIC DRIVE-IN BY THE EAST-WEST Expressway. They've passed it three times already. They're like balls in a pinball machine, she thinks, bouncing around the metropolis, always ending up in the same spot.

"We're not having much luck, are we?"

"No." Peter frowns. "We're not."

It's been hours since the day care called and explained how a man claiming to be Steven attempted to pick up Gertie shortly before she disappeared. The description fit Thaddeus exactly. The police thought so, too, when they all spoke down at the precinct. She'd wanted to remain at the station following the initial questioning, reasoning that since it was the nerve center of the entire search, staying nearby would allow them to better assist the police should any questions arise. But Peter had been reluctant, claiming that they stood a better shot of finding Gertie if they let the police do their job unencumbered. Plus, he'd said, they could help by conducting their own search. His logic made a certain kind of desperate sense; after all, what parent could realistically be expected to sit idly by while their three-year-old daughter was lost somewhere on the road? But at the same time, she suspected the purity of his motivations. He'd been altogether too accommodating with the police, neither criticizing their bureaucratic coolness nor hassling them to issue an Amber alert. (She was more than happy to pick up the slack.) His entire disposition changed when he spoke to the police; his vestigial scowl was replaced by a servile grin that she didn't like at all, and when he wasn't being addressed he'd been visibly uncomfortable. Despite her reservations, she relented to his authority as the parent, the dueling drives of mother and grandmother silenced for the moment if not entirely reconciled.

"Maybe this was a mistake," she says, but Peter doesn't answer.

The light changes and they continue down Semoran Boulevard. On the last pass she thought she spotted Thaddeus's car. Peter came up right alongside it and rode the horn hard until the car pulled over onto the shoulder. But they didn't find Thaddeus or Gertie inside, only an angry mom with a young child. They apologized. A mistaken identification, they explained, and then they quickly drove away. That's been the closest they've come to finding them.

"I'm glad this happened. It'll show Steven he can't just disappear like this." He pinches the bridge of his nose and sighs. "That didn't come out right. I'm not glad this happened. What I mean—"

She rests a hand on his forearm. "It's okay. I know what you mean."

A wry smile creeps onto his face. For a moment they share an intimacy. She wants to hold his gaze, but the rawness of his stare embarrasses her, so instead she lets her focus drift to the traffic outside. Plenty of cars travel up and down Semoran. Any one of them could be Thaddeus's.

"I feel like a monster for even thinking that."

"You've spent all day tracking down your daughter," she reminds him.

"You're not worried?"

"Of course I am, but she's with Thaddeus, and while he's not perfect, I don't believe for one second that he would let anything happen to her. And the police will find them soon."

She plays with her ring as she talks, glancing at him occasionally. A nervous, desperate sort of expression hangs from his face. Their hands find each other on top of the gearshift. Fine hairs give his pale skin a silkiness she hadn't anticipated, but other than that his hand feels cool and hard.

"Look, Thaddeus screws up a lot, but he always does the right thing in the end. Am I worried? Yes, but not because I think Gertie is in any real danger with him. He won't let anything awful happen to her. You can count on that. I'm worried because I'm always worried when the people I love are out on the streets. It's a mother thing."

He cringes, and she wonders if perhaps she should've left the last part out, if it came across as an insinuation on the depths of his affection.

He switches into the left lane and hunches over the steering wheel to get a better look down a hidden driveway. Not finding anything, he straightens up and speeds along. "I don't think I've ever felt like a bigger failure."

"We'll find them, or the police will."

He withdraws his hand and places it on the wheel. He glances at the instrument panel. "We'll need gas soon," he says.

She tries Steven again, but he doesn't answer. A moment ago Peter indicated that Steven regularly disappears and she wants to ask him about it, but she fears she won't be able to suppress the judgment in her tone and that Peter will feel criticized. She's not willing to take that risk. Men's egos are fragile; they tend to lash out when they feel attacked, then shut down. And the last thing she needs is another man holding her responsible for the failures of this family. They'll find Gertie. She believes that. But as the fuel gauge drops Peter grows increasingly sullen and irrational. He turns down roads with no discernible plan, then speeds through neighborhoods without even a glance. It's as if he's trying to see all of Orlando in a single moment. A few times she prompts a conversation, but the most she kedges out of him is a terse grunt. Eventually, she gives up and switches on the radio. They pull into a station to refuel. He gets out without a word and goes to the pump.

The car jostles and the nozzle makes a muffled clang as it slips into place. A keypad pings in concert with the muted electronic tinkle of a dozen or more digital pumps cycling through the steps of a sale. A receipt prints. A pickup truck starts up. Gasoline flows in a steady chug. Before her road stretches uninterrupted, and though it couldn't be more than ten yards away, she feels insulated from it under the gas station's canopy of bright lights. Just past the far shoulder, thistle and weeds cover an undeveloped lot. They'll build a drugstore there, she thinks, and won't that be convenient?

This area could use it. The police will call soon with good news. Her responsibilities fade away. Soon this will all end. Thaddeus and Gertie will both be home by nightfall.

Peter approaches her window. Stubble shades his gaunt face. His slacks are wrinkled from sitting in the car all day. His shirt fares better—the cuffs buttoned and the collar stiff. On the pump, the gallons slowly tick by.

"I keep thinking about her out there," he says.

"That's normal."

"I don't think I was really prepared to be a father."

She laughs. "Nobody ever is."

He frowns and picks at a loose thread. "It's different with us."

"You mean being a gay parent?"

It's the first time she's ever acknowledged it so directly. She's had her difficulties in the past—Thaddeus and she both have—with Steven's sexuality, but that's all behind them now. She doesn't have a problem with homosexuality. It's just *gay*. The word lacks heft. It embarrasses her to say it with such seriousness. *Gay* is something frivolous and campy, like drag queens and young men in glitter, something innocuous yet bawdy and often in bad taste, an escape, not something burdened with the charge of reproduction and family and all that comes along with a more serious life.

"I don't know how to reconcile everything I'm supposed to be." He pauses before continuing. "I think every man feels that way at one point or another. We just bring it out in each other more, Steven and me, and maybe I'm mad at him because of it. Maybe he's mad at me, too. Maybe we're both just so mad at each other we don't even know what to do anymore."

"That sounds like marriage to me."

He grins and drapes his hand over the window. The sloping knobs of his knuckles hold an ardent sway over her. Her fingers clasp his and the longer they touch the more intense her desire becomes. She flashes back to her fantasy in the shower of his strong, assertive grip—was that really just this morning? She finds herself slipping around the webbing of his thumb and squeezing his palm.

"Sometimes I bolt out of bed in the middle of the night afraid that I've already screwed her up, and on those nights do you know what Steven is doing? Steven is snoring right next to me, and all I want to do is kill him." With a thud, the gas finishes pumping, but he doesn't immediately return to the nozzle. He lingers at her window. "Today was supposed to be a break from everything."

She squeezes his hand and smiles.

"Now you think I'm a monster."

"Don't be silly."

He slips his hand free and tends to the pump, then climbs back into the driver's seat. He fidgets with the gearshift, picking at a bit of residue on the leather cover.

"I'm sorry," he says. "Please don't think bad things about me."

"I couldn't."

His lips are like elastic and she thinks that she'd like to kiss him.

"The truth is having you around has kept me sane these last few days. It's such a relief to spend time with someone I am in no way whatsoever accountable for. I can just be myself. It's rejuvenating."

She blushes. "The feeling is mutual."

"Listen to me," he says. "I'm rambling." Now he's on the verge of tears, "I'm a raw nerve today. And poor Certie... I'm an absolute horrible father."

"Peter, please—"

"How could I have let this happen? What was I thinking?" He casts around, swinging the car keys in the air. "Where could they be?"

"Peter, you really have to calm down."

"How am I supposed to? I've failed my family. This is all my fault."

"Stop." Her forceful tone has the desired result. He regains his composure. "Now, listen. This is not your fault. It's Thaddeus's."

"I'm the father—one of the fathers, at least—it's my job to protect her."

She shakes her head, but he continues.

"I didn't do my job. It's as simple as that."

"No. That's crazy." Her voice is cutting and curt. "I'm going to tell you something, and I say it as a loving mother and wife: you are without a doubt the best thing this family has going. Understand?

Thaddeus and Steven, they are who they are, and they have their strengths, and I love them both, but they're very insular and self-ish. You are reliable. You're the father that girl needs, and she's damn lucky to have you. As for these... these feelings you're having, they're normal."

He smacks his hand across the steering wheel. "But we have to be more than normal."

"Then do it!"

There's not much to say for a long time after that; a pregnant silence balloons between them. Peter starts the car. He merges back onto the road. They look at each other infrequently now, his attention, like hers, more and more focused on the heat wave mirage of the road and the occasional pedestrian beating along the sporadic sidewalks as the day darkens.

"For a while after my procedure," she says sometime later, "I met with a group of women who went through the same thing. It was very informal, but it was nice. The companionship... it helps with those feelings you get of being isolated." She fidgets with her ring, unsure of what to do with her hands. "It was only for a little while. Just long enough to understand, to really know where it all fits in. People overlook that, that humans need to fit in." She smiles weakly. "I've always believed you can cope with anything as long as it has its place."

He nods and a weight seems to slide off him like water. She pats his thigh.

"You're probably right," he says. "I don't think Steven knows how to compartmentalize like that, though. Between the shelter and Gertie, he's crippled by fear."

"Does he say that to you?"

He shakes his head with a faint smile. "He never would, but I can tell. He's just petrified to make a mistake with her, you know? To teach her the wrong thing or set a bad example. We both are. No offense, but neither one of us wants to emulate our own childhoods, so it's tough figuring it out."

"That's how everybody feels. I'd be worried if you didn't feel that way. It just means you're being good parents."

He switches on his blinker and passes a truck, then slips through an intersection as the light turns red.

"I get stressed out but I can manage. At the end of a long day when I'm just too tired to care about Gertie, or Steven, or any of it, I can fall back on the work and say, 'Well, Peter, you've worked your ass off today for your family,' and I can feel better about myself. In the abstract I can still care even if in the moment I'm being selfish. I don't know if Steven feels that way, too. He never talks to me about that stuff. He just disappears some nights. I worry about him, and not for the reasons you're probably thinking. We have an arrangement—"

"I don't need to know about that," she says quickly.

They come to a stoplight, and he brakes. She surveys the opposing traffic as it streams by, but there's no sign of Thaddeus. *An arrangement?*

"At any rate," he continues. "I don't care what he's doing. I just need to know where he is in case of emergencies."

She grunts. "He's being very irresponsible. Just like his father."

"He's scared and insecure. I don't suppose I can blame him for that."

"And you're being too understanding."

Peter shakes his head, and she recognizes the softness in his expression. It's the same softness she has for Thaddeus, and it's a softness that forgives too easily.

"He's threatened," Peter says. "That's all. We both are, I suppose."

"By what?"

He shrugs. "Assimilation? Losing something essential?"

She rolls her eyes. "Yeah, well, that's life. You make sacrifices."

An arrangement?

SHE SCROLLS THROUGH AN INFINITE FEED.

Unfocused. Scanning. Awash in images and silent video. Her consciousness comprises little more than light striking rods and cones. No need for the brain at all. Until something familiar—a curve of an elbow? A shadow on skin?—in the cascade of bright pixels triggers her attention and she pauses to investigate.

Nothing important.

Just a colleague and his wife taking in a baseball game in Tampa. She resumes scrolling. The higher functions of her brain again recede. All the knowledge she's acquired over the years, all the reasoned opinions, all the nuance, switches off. The animal brain takes over, filtering through the endless data in search of a signal in the noise: Alex.

How many times in the past week has she tracked the engagement of a post, comparing stats across platforms in the vague hope that doing so would reveal some clue, would point her in some fruitful direction? Everybody leaves digital footprints. Tracking somebody down should be far easier than this. A fleeting sympathy for the NSA colludes with a push notification on her screen to disrupt the animal mind. Bill Philips has left her yet another voice mail. That makes five since she skipped a shift two days ago without bothering to call in.

She ignores the voice mail and resumes scrolling.

Every dinner. Every night at the club.

Every catch from every weekend fishing excursion.

This far down the stream the images are digital fossils. Still, she returns here with some regularity, always uncovering something new interspersed among familiar posts. Algorithms are impish things.

No telling when they'll surprise you. If asked to she could construct a comprehensive chronology of several people's recent lives without the aid of time stamps. Where others might count sheep, she's developed a game of recalling certain snapshots in proper sequence. The game offers no challenge. It merely passes the time as she lies in bed, trying in vain to sleep.

For all its insidious creep, vast tracts of a person's life escape the social media dragnet. This is especially true of Alex, whose lax attitude toward his digital brand puts him at odds with his peers. His posts, when he does post, tend toward sketches of clothes he hashtags #urbodycouture and #thesecondcoming. The son of a sort of celebrity. How many others in his position have parlayed a tangential connection to fame into a career? Khloe and Kendall. Jaden. Miley. Alex Morales, reality TV star. A frightening prospect, but at least then she'd know where to find him. Just follow the drama.

Instead, she sits in her living room in the dark, pupils shrunk in the blue light from her phone, and slightly cold as the a/c nears the end of its brief cycle. Old take-out containers stand sentry on the coffee table. Junk mail speckles the counter in disorganized piles. Pairs of jeans dominate the floor like drunks at the beach. Nearby her purse trawls a string of items including birth control, wallet, and earbuds across the carpet. In a few hours it'll be Alex's eighteenth birthday and she's no closer to finding him.

She fires off a text. The seventh today. The seventh he'll ignore.

Feeling philosophical around lunch, she sent him a long message saying she understood his silence was an outcropping of the deep sense of loss he feels for their father. **Our grief**, she wrote, **is shared, so too must be our healing.** He ignored it.

Her loquacity devolved throughout the day:

I'm sorry. Please come home.

In addition to feeling fruitless, the stream makes apparent the uncomfortable reality of her solitude. Her contributions to the feed consist chiefly of reposted baby animal videos, inspirational memes, and, most depressing of all, photos of whatever pharmacy she happens to be covering on a given day, often bearing a caption that is some permutation of "stop by and say hi if you're in the area." Nobody ever does. The techs in the district tease her about her lack of a social life, assuming she puts her career before dating. It's true she's a hard worker, which makes dating more difficult, but not impossible. She's hardly the only pharmacist with a demanding schedule. She seems to lack an aptitude for men. The closest she's come to a serious relationship was the year she spent fooling around with a married guy, and even that ended three years ago.

In her memory, Sean appears with sly, downcast eyes and lips parted just enough to allow a seductive peek of his tongue. A former high school and intramural athlete, when they met he was settling into the body he'd likely carry through to middle age—neither in shape nor overweight, but bearing shades of both. A transitional body. He captured her attention immediately despite the inconvenient fact of his marriage (or, perhaps, because of it). He was enigmatic and she liked that, too. She knew his name, his age (twenty-eight, her age now), and his preferred sexual positions. Little else was forthcoming. He knew nothing about her beyond her phone number, her address, and that she was willing. Nor did he seem interested in learning more.

At the start of their affair she regularly inquired about his tastes and opinions, his profession and aspirations—in short, his life—but he gingerly deflected her queries. What little he did offer came only under duress (which is how she came to learn the bit about his athletic past). His aptitude for deflection outpaced her appetite for hectoring, and fearing above all breaking with the illusion that she was an unsentimental girl who preferred casual hookups to relationships, she eventually abandoned her efforts, reconciling with the fundamental mystery of him. Clearly, privacy figured prominently in the hierarchy of his desires. His reasons simply remained beyond the scope of their relationship.

Despite her resolve to not dig into his past, a tension remained between them. Her fundamental nature demanded an intimacy he refused to supply, and that imbalance excited him. Their most passionate trysts occurred when he'd show up at her door unannounced in the middle of the night after she'd worked a long shift and was looking forward to sleep. "I'm outside," he'd say, his voice oozing through the speaker on her phone. "I'm coming in." A month into their relationship he'd asked for a key to her house for this express purpose. It was *that* kind of a relationship. She'd listen, heart racing, as the front door opened and shut, followed by his quick steps across the living room. Waiting under the covers, she struggled with conflicting desires, wishing that she'd had some notice and could've tidied up before he arrived but also delighting in the fact that she hadn't. She liked to imagine herself as the kind of person who held nothing back from her lover: *This is my mess, take it or leave it; I don't care one way or another.* But, of course, she was the exact opposite kind of lover. She did care. She cared a great deal.

From the bedroom door he'd lock eyes on her, his stare seeing right through her even in the darkness. If he was an enigma, then she was common and plain as conventional wisdom. "It's late," she'd say, and he'd smirk and grunt, "Mm-hmm." Then he was on top of her and she felt her body responding to his touch, rushing away from her. More than once she came before him, her body drawing him in deeper until he finished.

"Do you have to get back to your wife?"

He'd lick the sweat off her neck and then get up and dress. "I'll see you again soon. Wear black panties."

Then he'd be gone and she'd spend the next however many nights sleeping in nothing but black panties, waiting for him to return.

She spends too much of her life waiting on men, she thinks as she thumbs through the endless minutiae of other people's lives. But her efforts pay off. In the middle of the epically mundane something amazing happens: a familiar face surfaces.

She shoots up on the couch and brings the phone close to her face. The analytic mind spins up all its faculties.

There on a crowded dance floor, shoulder to shoulder with a brawny boy, is Alex.

Her brother looks sallow in the club lights, but the angle of the photograph flatters his sharp features. The boy he's with wears a dopey grin while tossing a sturdy arm across her brother. A proud sneer adorns Alex's face. Her brother has many gifts, but humility isn't among them (though he's not as confident as he'd like to appear either). In the photo he's trying too hard. Not that it will matter: the boy looks half gone already, bleary-eyed and drunk, probably tripping. A Venn diagram of toxicology comes to mind and she hopes that Alex knows better than to party irresponsibly. She's never known him to do more than drink and smoke pot, but six months is a long time in a teenager's life. Troubling, too, what a hormonal teenager might do to impress a would-be lover, especially on the eve of his eighteenth birthday.

He's young, this boy. Not much older than Alex—twenty-one, twenty-two max. A college student for sure. The longer she examines the picture the more familiar he becomes until she's convinced she knows him from somewhere. But from where?

Her phone pings again, reminding her of Bill's voice mail. She dismisses the notification blocking her screen. Bill and the pharmacy can go to hell.

Ah, but that's it! The boy. She recognizes him from the pharmacy! From the time she covered for Josie at the store by the university. He came in with a prescription for a fungal infection. She frowns. What is Alex doing with this guy? Where did they meet? Are they dating? The stream doesn't offer much context. No location is tagged and the only commentary is in the form of two emoji hearts and a thumbs-up. The post has eighty-three likes.

For all the world it's young love, but in the final moments before her baby brother's birthday, Laila doesn't agonize over the boy's identity or his suitability. Nor does she obsess over matters of safety. No, the burning question concerns the ease with which Alex can find someone while she herself struggles. What is his advantage? Perhaps, as with everything else in life, finding a man is simply easier for men.

Rousing herself from the couch, she resolves to clean the apartment in the morning. She'll call Bill, too. Apologize and explain the situation, or, at the very least, concoct a plausible lie. On her way to bed, she adjusts the thermostat. It's chilly, and with just one person the house won't heat up that quickly overnight. She sends a final text before turning in:

Happy Birthday

Then a quick follow-up:

Be safe!

"I'VE CHANGED MY MIND ABOUT URBODY COUTURE," HE SAYS.
His bare shoulder presses against the wicker bookcase, its shelves decorated minimally with a conch shell and a leather-bound volume that nobody has ever opened let alone read. You wouldn't be surprised to learn that its gilt-edged pages were printed upside down or simply left blank. Like the plastic areca palm in the corner, this book is a prop designed to sell an idea.

"What about all your sketches?" You reach for the bottle of bourbon. The seal is broken from plying Eddie with a few shots before he headed for the shower. "Are you just abandoning them?"

He throws himself onto the couch, messing with his phone for a second before shoving it deep into a pocket. "Don't be stupid." He pouts and shields his eyes with his hands. "I just wanna focus on my own thing."

You sip the bourbon to get the taste of it, then cut it with some water.

"Check it out, papi. I'm gonna start my own line called Balas de Cariño—bullets of affection! It's all about peace, love, and ass." He sits up, cocks his head at you. "That's tight, right?"

"Sure."

He regards you with hooded, vulnerable eyes. It's taken a long time to earn his trust, but he's finally dropped his adolescent bluster and allowed you a sincere glimpse of his ambition. Your hands twitch. If he were any of the others, you would seize the opportunity to destroy him, but the thought makes you queasy. So instead you focus on aesthetics. "What's the artistic vision?"

"Simple, clean lines." He slinks over to the counter, pulls the bourbon from your hand, takes a sip, and bites back a cough. "I want to do something fun. I'm tired of complicated and dark."

"He'll be out of the shower soon," you say, referring to Eddie. "Then we can have some fun."

He shrugs.

"What's the matter? Don't you want him anymore?"

"Nah, he's hot. I don't know." He scratches his scalp and yawns. "It's getting late."

You light a cigarette, then toss him the pack. The smell of smoke will linger in fabrics and resist attempts to eliminate it, but for now you're not worried. "Go ahead," you say.

He draws a languid puff, exhales a quicksilver filigree that rises like a cobra from the basket of his mouth.

"How do you intend to finance it?"

He takes several quick draws before grinding out the cigarette in the sink. "I don't know yet."

"What if I could find someone for you to talk to—an investor?"

He picks at a pimple on his neck. "That be cool, I guess."

"That's something I could do. I could ask around with some people I know... There's a lot I'd like to do for you. A lot I could show you—"

He cuts you off with a kiss. His breath tastes like menthol. "I don't want to talk about it right now," he says.

"All right. Whatever you want. No big deal." You place his hand on your cheek and massage his knuckles. "I think the shower just went off."

"Good."

A moment later, Eddie emerges from the master suite in bare feet and dripping on the carpet, his thick athletic body wrapped in a towel.

"We're just getting started," Alex says.

Eddie assesses the situation, gazing badger-like between you and Alex. "That shower really did the trick." He forces a laugh. "I'm not so shaky anymore."

"I'll get you something to help you relax."

Alex entertains him while you pour a bourbon, stirring in a few drops of the GHB just to loosen him up.

"Why don't you drop that towel, baby?" Alex says.

Eddie hesitates.

"Come on. Don't be shy."

"I'm not," Eddie says, but he makes no move to remove the towel from around his waist.

Alex pauses. "You have done this before, right?"

"Of course." He responds too quickly.

"What about a game?" you suggest, pressing a tumbler into Eddie's hand. "Do you like games?"

"I guess," he says, scratching his clavicle. "What kind of game?"

You and Alex exchange a glance while Eddie stares on, cow-eyed and nervous.

"Let's play Control," you say.

Eddie sips his bourbon and winces. He puts the glass down. "What's that?"

"You'll like it," Alex says. "It's fun."

Your hands throb. Tonight is Alex's night, not yours, but wrapped in that towel Eddie looks so innocent and maybe even egregiously naive. He looks at you with expectant eyes. You encourage him to drink up. After a few more sips there won't be any hesitation. Like all of them (except Alex), he's too eager to comply, to simply go along. While you struggle to control the throbbing in your hands, Alex moves in and kisses his bare shoulder, which is splotchy from the hot shower. Eddie places a hand on the back of Alex's head, roughly guiding him toward his nipple, and you think how driven by instinct men are, how ignorant of even the possibility of a delicate touch or of equivocation.

"The rules of the game are simple," you say, focusing Eddie's ecstasy. "I control you in every way. You must do what I say; otherwise, you get punished."

"Oh." His voice is foggy and he giggles. "I don't know if I can do that."

"Nah, baby," Alex says. "You'll be amazed what you're capable of."

The drugs do their job. Eddie shudders at every touch. He acquiesces in a fit of nervous laughter that flexes the muscles in his throat. The throbbing in your hands escalates to a thumping.

"Okay," he says. "If you think it'll be fun."

"Oh, yeah, baby, I do."

Alex toys with him, nibbling his lips and teasing out his tongue. Deep white grooves mark the broad surface of Eddie's tongue like irrigation canals. Alex murmurs something that you don't hear, but it doesn't matter what he says. Eddie is too far gone to resist. Alex's eyes roll back like a shark's eyes before an attack.

You slip between them. "It's time to play."

Eddie kisses you. When you don't resist, he kisses you again. Emboldened, he reaches for your pants. The veins in his neck bulge. You grab his hand.

"Slave," you say, pointing at Alex. "Dog," you say, pointing at Eddie. "Master," you say, pointing at yourself. "This is how we play."

"Yes," they both say in unison. "Yes, sir."

The bedroom is nearby. You pin Eddie to the mattress so that his head hangs down the soft edge. His feet reach out toward the wall. He slips closer and closer to the blurry line of consciousness. If you wait too much longer he'll be a limp doll, no use to anyone.

Alex crouches beside you and Eddie nuzzles into the front of his jeans like a good pup.

"Suck his dick," you hiss at him. Without hesitation he pulls Alex's thick cock out and begins licking it.

Alex stretches his head back, cooing encouragement. You share a smile. *Happy birthday,* you want to say, but you're afraid of ruining the mood, so instead you order him to fuck Eddie's mouth. "Show this dog who's in charge."

While he does you rip at your leather belt. Your vision blurs as you watch Eddie's throat expand with each thrust. He coughs, but Alex pushes on, choking him with his cock. Eddie sputters around the organ in his mouth. Tears form and his eyes bulge, but he doesn't resist. The cheap, rough comforter rasps against your shins and the top of your bare feet as you get into position. It probably burns along his back. He struggles, but you order him to draw his knees into his chest and then you hold his arms down.

Alex withdraws a little just as you jam your dick into Eddie's ass, eliciting a glorious howl. Eddie takes it all in stride, and that's how you know that he's done this before and that earlier he was just being coy, and if he's done this before then he's just like the others. When he asks you to slide over a bit, to hit his sweet spot, you slap him.

"Dogs can't speak!"

He could've spoken up at any point in his life, and maybe if he had this wouldn't be necessary now, but he hasn't and the time for talking is over, and now you have to take action.

You never intended to involve Alex in this. That's the truth. You always intended to protect him from the work, but he's here now. He's here now and your hands are on fire. Staring into his eyes you silently ask for forgiveness before your logic fails and your brain slips into a more primitive mode, and nothing remains but the work.

You tear Eddie's ass, pounding recklessly.

"Fuck his mouth, slave. And you, dog, take it and shut the fuck up!"

Alex presses his hard cock farther into Eddie's mouth, and you act quickly. Vacating his ass, you straddle his chest and pin his arms to his side with your knees. "Keep fucking," you order, wrapping your hands around Eddie's vascular neck. Your grip starts off tender, but soon his pulse is hammering against the ring made by your fingers. His heart beats faster. The circumference expands and contracts as Alex slides in and out of his throat.

"How does that feel, slave?"

Alex can only mumble. His fevered, serious expression belies a man focused on a task.

"Good," you say. "Very good. This is a dog. Use him."

Alex accelerates his thrusts. Eddie tries to scream, but you clamp down, silencing him.

"It's him," you say. "He's responsible for everything."

"Yeah," Alex says. "Yeah, yeah, yeah."

"Good. Talk to him. Say what you want to say."

"Ah, it feels so good. You like that Puerto Rican dick? Yeah, you do. Take it, bitch!"

"Fuck him harder!"

Eddie's eyes widen, snot leaks from his nose. You keep Alex focused on your face, encouraging him to fuck harder.

Bruises are forming. You relax your grip long enough to place Alex's hands on Eddie's throat. "Squeeze," you order. "Make Daddy proud."

Alex obeys. His large hands easily wrap around Eddie's muscular throat. He can likely feel the murmurs and gurgles now, but he continues to pound away at Eddie's face. You lay your hands over his and squeeze. Together, you squeeze harder and faster than you ever have alone. Eddie bucks his hips and tries to flip you off his chest, but you have him pinned, and his screams are muffled by Alex's cock and, of course, by the pressure of four hands on his throat. He tries to bite down, but you hold his jaw open with your thumbs. It's enough to give Alex pause, but you're too close now, so you redouble your efforts. There's nothing he can do anyway, he's too gone on sexual bliss to really complain. Eddie's eyes flutter. His struggles cease and a glob of Alex's spunk drips out the corner of his mouth.

You release your grip and Alex collapses back into an armchair. He pats himself down with Eddie's towel. He's panting, and his smooth, tanned skin glistens. The Virgin on his arm twitches. He falls asleep in the chair in that position. You smell his sweat on your hands, and dropping back onto the bed, you finish yourself off. It's unclear how much time goes by before the throbbing in your hands subsides and your vision returns to normal. Somewhere in the back of your mind floats the realization that it's past midnight and therefore Alex is no longer a minor. Everything he's done tonight was done as a legal adult. Only then does the extent of what you've done crystallize.

A long time passes before Alex stirs in his chair. He rises and slouches across the carpet to Eddie on the bed. He lies in the same position, his skin already cold.

"Hey," Alex says, tapping Eddie's shoulder. "Yo, get up, son." He tries to rouse him for a few moments more while you pretend to sleep.

"Hey, papi," he calls.

You open your eyes and fake a yawn.

"Yo, get up. I think something's wrong. He's not moving."

You smile.

THE ROAD IS EVERYWHERE.

Thaddeus whistles a tune while peering up at the red traffic signal rocking from a cable. After so many hours on the road, he's come to appreciate Gertie's quiet company. They're like two astronauts barreling through space—everything around them the russet hue of a fading sun. Her long silence allows his mind to wander back to the lady from the parking lot and her business card pressed against the instrument panel.

He imagines entertaining her poolside with drinks and witty conversation. For all his sexual bluster, what he desires most is to talk to an elegant woman, somebody who isn't always looking at him like he's failed at something he didn't even know he was supposed to do. Maybe his frustrations with Cheryl boil down to friendship. They were once best of friends, but lately they've become acquaintances propelled by inertia.

"Poop."

"Just a little bit longer now, beautiful. You've been a real trooper, sticking by your old grandpa all this time, you know that?"

She pulls an old movie ticket stub from the crease between the seat and the armrest and fans it at her face. The a/c is inconsistent, and after a long, sunny afternoon heat radiates off the asphalt, making sitting at a traffic signal a sweaty affair. He adjusts a well-worn plastic vent. The air blows across his chin and he grins, but the second he moves his finger the slats droop again. His lip twitches into a momentary frown. "Just a bit longer," he repeats.

She crosses her arms. "Poop."

When the light turns green he accelerates. He creases his face into a doughy smile for Gertie's amusement. "I know exactly where we are. Just gotta have a little faith in your old grandpa."

She rolls her eyes and he reaches over and taps her chubby thigh, directing her attention to a passing drug store. "That's where your grandma picks up my pills. Did you see it?"

Sighing, she sinks farther into her seat.

"Not impressed, huh?"

She gives the glove box a few exploratory kicks.

Another drug store zips by. Maybe that's the one where he has his prescriptions. And isn't that over there the grocery store that sells the blueberry muffins Cheryl likes? Landmarks sweep through his memory like the yellow glow of a lighthouse. Buried among sun-bleached CDs in the armrest is an emergency stash. He wrestles a joint from a crack in the plastic and punches the car lighter.

"Grandpa really has a good feeling about this now. I really do. Just another few blocks now, Cheryl—I mean, Gertie. We can still make it for the fireworks. You'll love them."

The plan for Disney World is over. He knows this, yet he doesn't. The road is all that matters now, the act of driving, of continuing on. Everything will fall into place if he follows through. Yet a growing doubt urges him to pull over and place a call from any of the stores slinking out of view in steady procession. It could all be over. Time on the road weighs him down. He's tired and he's tried, and isn't that the important thing? That he tried? But when he looks down at little Gertie, her delicate face and stubby hands, her straight black hair, he feels rejuvenated. He won't do it. For once he can't bring himself to take the easy way out, to simply toss up his hands and leave Cheryl to sort out his mess. That's what he did with Stevie for all those years and look at the results. No. Gertie may be a little bored but she's safe. He fed her. He played with her. He is in control. Nothing can stop him. Thaddeus Bloom is invincible.

By now the day care has certainly noticed Gertie's absence, but as long as he remains on the road he's safe.

He takes a puff.

Gertie coughs and bats away the smoke.

"You got the right idea there, beautiful. Don't follow your old grandpa's example. This stuff is bad medicine." He lobs a grin at her, then returns to scanning the road. Somewhere out there a turnoff waits to change his luck. It's bound to be close. That palm tree. Yes. He's certain he recognizes the reticulated crook of that particular palm tree. "This stuff." He brandishes the joint, indulging with a smallish drag before continuing in a choked-up voice. "This stuff is only for grandpas, and only when things get a bit too wacko. Do you understand?" But she's not looking at him.

A cold sweat seizes him, and he reaches out for her hand. He squeezes it hard, too hard maybe, but he can't afford the luxury of consent. He squeezes until she looks him directly in the eye and then he lets her go.

"Listen to me close," he says with measured lucidity. "One day you're probably going to be offered a lot of it when you get to school, high school that is." He stifles a laugh. "You'll be offered a lot, but you have to promise your old grandpa that you'll just say no. Don't make the same mistakes I did. Can you do that? Hmm? Can you make your grandpa one little promise?"

Slowly, she nods.

"Yes!" He spreads his arms wide. In his excitement, he slams his hand against the dome light and sends the joint flying under the dash. "Oops." Deftly he bends over to paw the floor mat. "Of course you will"—his voice cracks from the effort—"because you're a real winner."

Gertie screams as they sway into the neighboring lane, but the sway lasts for only a moment before he finds the joint and regains control. He takes a puff and smiles at her.

"A real winner, just like your old man."

He wiggles his eyebrows and sticks his tongue out at her. She crosses her arms. But he knows her laughter is hiding in there, waiting to make everything better. It's just a matter of bringing it out, so he pulls a dozen funny faces. With each one she squirms a bit more freely, twists her fingers, and pulls her hair a bit more anxiously. Eventually he coaxes it out of her. Eventually she drops her concentrated stare and erupts in belly laughter.

"That's right, beautiful. You go ahead and laugh at your old grandpa. He's got a few screws loose, huh? But that's okay. He gets by. But you! You're going to be a big success. Maybe the first Oriental president, who knows? What do you think about that?" He doesn't wait for a response. "I'll tell you a secret. You won't repeat it, will you? Of course you won't. You didn't get those brains from your grandpa's side of the family. You get that from your grandma Cheryl and your daddy Peter. And you know something else? I say God bless them. People like your grandpa here are lost without people like them."

His gaze drops down to the business card on the dash, and suddenly he feels guilty.

"I don't mind telling you that. I'll tell the whole world. Your grandma saved my life. I haven't always been the best, but she kept me from being a lot worse. That's a fact. She's the greatest woman in the whole world. Well, at least until you came along."

Gertie giggles, covering her face with an arm.

Outside, the soft pink-and-orange glow of the evening sky gives way to a starker halogen as streetlights blink on. The road is illuminated for miles, a vast network of asphalt curving and bending into an impossible number of subdivisions and culs-de-sac and driveways. It occurs to him with the precision of weed philosophy that in all his years of driving, no matter where he's been, he's never left this road. The stucco. The trailers. The grocery stores, the car dealerships, and the retail plazas anchored by a bar or a restaurant or a gas station. All of it piled alongside the road, all of it vaguely familiar. He wonders if there's a woman for every confused man in each of these places.

The turnoff could be anywhere.

"Do you know why melons always have big weddings?" He softens his eyes. "Because they cantaloupe! That's a good one for the junior audience, huh? Fruits getting married. Not that I mean anything by that, Stevie, er, beautiful," he stammers. "Hey, you know, just a joke."

Sweat beads his brow and he roughly wipes his forehead with the back of his hand. He glances in the rearview and spots a police cruiser keeping a steady distance.

Gertie frowns.

"Yeah, I know. Poop! Lay off, would you? It was just a joke. You have no idea how lucky you are to have two devoted fathers." He takes a toke. "Not everybody gets that, you know? Your parents, they're A-OK. Couldn't do any better by you. Wonderful people. And Cheryl. That grandmother of yours, boy, did you luck out... All of them..." He dabs at his suddenly misty eyes. "Hey, what are you doing over there, cutting onions? You got my allergies going. Look at me, I'm blubbering like a whore on payday. Ha!"

The cruiser advances, and he swerves the car to miss a neon traffic divide, cursing it as he careens back onto the largely deserted road. The effort momentarily sobers him. He blows his nose into a crumpled napkin and drops it on the floor before drying his eyes with the collar of his shirt. Gertie whimpers.

"No big deal," he says, straightening his back, smiling—the very picture of calm. He kisses his fingers and taps her head. If this is the end then at least it's been better than nothing. "I know exactly where we are now. We're almost there. What about one last joke? Would you like that?" He puckers around the roach end of his joint, and she coughs. "All right, all right. I get the hint. Your grandma doesn't approve either; gives me the same shitty look."

With the push of a button he lowers his window. Rushing wind drives out the smoke. The wind licks at the business card, too, peeling it off the dash and sending it sailing out of the cabin.

"There. Happy? It's gone!" he shouts, but he can't bring himself to toss the joint just yet.

The road screams through the widening gap of the window, jostling candy wrappers and ashes from all the hidden corners of the cabin, roaring toward an elegant equilibrium, an equilibrium of... of everything. His fingers and scalp grow clammy in the buffeting wind. The temperature drops. His ears pop. In his anxiety, he misses when the police cruiser—which was an ambulance anyway—turns off the road. He swerves into the oncoming traffic lane, slowly gaining headway over a rollicking tractor-trailer carting a cargo of logs. Ahead of them approaches a car.

"Hey, it's okay. Just a joke, you know? Relax, and anyway, I wasn't going to call her. You believe me, right, beautiful?" His hands are off the steering wheel now; one holds the joint while the other juts out the window, surfing on the palpable waves of pressure, skating across some invisible, mellow ether.

"It's a funny one, this joke."

Her stare is the coldest thing in the world.

Presenting two crossed fingers, he bows his head solemnly. "Scout's honor," he says before once again—his final recourse—bending an exaggerated frown. "We simpatico, beautiful?"

The approaching car blares its horn. Beside them, the tractor-trailer decelerates, honks to signal the all clear. It all happens in another world. Right now, this instant, his only concern is Gertie. He wants that smile. He needs that smile. If he can get that, then the cops can have him. He sticks out his tongue. Blows a raspberry. Rolls his eyes dizzily in their sockets. If he really focuses he could probably make out faces in the approaching car.

Gertie blinks. At last she smiles.

"Now that's what I'm talking about. Ha! Okay, here we go." He shifts in his seat. He pinches the roach end of the joint between fat, tender fingers and inhales with great relish before grinding the butt into the ashtray, then flicking it out the window. Like a needle finding its groove, they slide between the reflectors and overtake the trailer in time to wave at the screeching car disappearing in the rearview in a halo of fishtailing brake lights.

"Two old friends," he begins, screaming above the wind, "a rabbi and a priest..."

"HOW FAR COULD HE HAVE GONE?" PETER ASKS.

They sit idling in a strip mall in an unfamiliar part of town. Burger wrappers litter the floor mats. A carton of fries sits on the console between them. The greasy aroma of onion, mayonnaise, and ketchup recirculates through the vents. He rests his chin upon the wheel and gazes out the windshield. "We've looked everywhere. Haven't we?"

She scours a cuticle and sighs. A hundred shopping plazas containing a thousand stores beneath a million stucco arches litter the landscape. Thaddeus could be at any one of them.

"We tried," she says. "Maybe we should leave the rest up to the police."

He slams his fists into the pitted dashboard with such force that the whole car shakes. Then he throws himself into the seatback. He pummels the soft center of the steering wheel. The horn bleats.

"Stop it! You're going to hurt yourself. Peter!"

He carries on. He's a machine fueled by a deep well of guilt, but she knows what to do in these situations. She knows the right way to squint and pucker to convey a sense of authoritative empathy. The technique has kept Thaddeus in line for decades, and maybe Peter isn't that different—maybe no man is. She looks into his gaunt face with its premature lines and already a dusting of gray in the stubble, and she calibrates her expression.

"We're calling it a night," she says. "Maybe Steven will be home by now."

He smirks, but she holds his gaze until she feels a shift in his mood. Sighing his consent, he reaches for her hand. Their fingers entwine and he gently bounces their hands against the gearshift. His fingers are much rougher than Thaddeus's. They feel nice. She holds on until he regains some equilibrium.

He looks down at his knees and laughs. "I don't care if he ever comes home."

"Steven? No. You don't mean that."

"I'm thinking of leaving him."

"Because of today?"

His head drifts toward the window and his eyes are closed. "It's not just today."

"Steven's never mentioned anything to me about this." She picks at a loose thread on her pants. "I always assumed... Oh, Peter, I'm so sorry."

"We don't want the same things. I'm not even sure we understand each other anymore." He sighs. "This kind of life—a family—it's not for him."

"Well, have you talked to somebody about it?"

"Yeah, and I think that's what it comes down to. We just want different things. And because he can't give me what I want I think I resents me for wanting it. It's kind of fucked up." He fiddles with the angle of the rearview mirror, keeping his eyes away from her. "Anyway, I've been thinking about it for a while. I've held off because of Gertie, but that's kind of a cliché, isn't it?"

The color drains from her face and her arms feel heavy in her lap. All she can muster is banal advice about how difficult it is to know what the right thing to do is as a parent. "You just never really know." When she hears her voice it sounds like it's coming from a thousand miles away.

"I don't think he'd fight me for custody, but there's stuff—in my past—that if he wanted to be vindictive, and then after today..." He trails off.

"But you wouldn't want to deny him some rights, would you?"

"I don't think it'd come to that."

A breeze rustles the stand of azaleas and cabbage palms abutting a nearby retention pond. A stray napkin spirals across the parking lot.

"Sorry," he says, sniffling back tears. "I didn't mean to put you in the middle of this."

She manages a wan smile. "These things happen. I'm glad you told me." But she can sense him retreating. It's as if a wall has gone up between them, and she feels ashamed that she allowed her shock to get the best of her and now Peter will believe that he cannot confide in her.

"If the problem is with Gertie, Thaddeus and I... we'd be willing to watch her, indefinitely, if you two need some time to work things out."

The wry grin that always hovers on the edge of his face deepens. "I appreciate the offer," he says, "but she's our responsibility."

"Maybe I'm making a big deal out of nothing, but it's just that you said— Never mind. I'm sure you know what you're doing."

"No, please."

"It's just... is it something I said?"

"I don't think I follow."

"Well, you said neither one of you wanted to emulate your parents. I know this family can be very selfish. Thaddeus has his things—I've indulged that, so it's partly my fault—but we're good parents. We raised Steven right, even if we don't always agree on everything."

"I never questioned your parenting skills, Cheryl."

"No, I know..."

He sits up in his seat and squares his shoulders. "Did I miss something?"

A late-model Chevrolet rumbles out of the drive-through and stops for a moment before merging onto the road. The commotion flushes an egret from the retention pond.

She worries her hands in her lap. "It's just, you say you're unhappy, but you don't want my help. You never even leave Gertie with me."

"It's not you—"

"But what if it was just me?" she blurts out, afraid to lose her nerve now that she's started. "Or just me and you?"

"I don't follow."

"It's Thaddeus and Steven that are always causing the problems, but what if we didn't need them." She reaches for his hand

and presses it to her breast. "What if it was just you and me and Gertie?"

"Are you suggesting—"

"An arrangement." She looks at the prominent bulge of his knuckles and feels the warmth of his skin against her chest. "Like what you have with Steven. We can be a family. The way it should be without all this animosity."

"You can't be serious." He pulls his hand away and drops the transmission into drive.

"Don't do that," she says. "Don't be silent. We're both adults here. Can't we just discuss this like adults?"

He needlessly adjusts the mirrors, then grabs his phone from the center console. The Mercedes coasts toward the road. "I don't think there's anything to discuss. I'm sorry I bothered you with our private affairs."

"Who are you calling?"

"The police. Maybe they have some news."

AT FIVE A.M. SHE STOPS PRETENDING TO SLEEP AND gets dressed. She laces up her sneakers in the dark. Her phone, always nearby, is quiet. No text messages. No missed calls. The only activity a couple of notifications reminding her to return to games in progress, which she ignores. She slips the phone into her hip pocket and creeps downstairs, mindful to make as little noise as possible.

She doesn't need the caffeine today but she prepares a quick cup of coffee anyway for the sake of her nerves. While the coffeemaker cheerfully percolates, she sorts through the contents of her purse by feel, electing to rely on the penumbra cast by the streetlamp just outside the living room window rather than risk losing her resolve in the rational brightness of her kitchen fluorescents. Her shame has made her a cat burglar in her own home. She may not be proud of what she's about to do, but the possibility of it kept her up all night. Every time she closed her eyes she saw that image of Alex out at a bar with a stranger, a stranger she recognized. A familiar stranger she could trace. But she hesitated. Was she the type of person who stalked men? It would seem she has become that type of person.

Buried in a purse pocket she finds her pharmacy keys. They confer immense power. These keys allow her to do everything from voiding a transaction on the register to accessing the controlled substances kept behind bulletproof glass. Today, however, their greatest power is one that will be available to any customer in a few hours: they allow her to walk through the front door. These keys give her the power to time travel. Not the kind that allows her to go back and change what happened between her and Alex, or to save her father, or even to set things on a different path with Esther, but it's the power to do the next best thing.

When she's working the keys remain easily accessible in her lab coat pocket, but she won't be wearing a lab coat today, so the pocket of her jeans will have to do. In they go, distorting the contours of the fabric and digging into her upper thigh. She whispers a quiet apology to Félix; he hated anything that ruined the line of a piece of clothing. A happy tune signals that her coffee is ready. She rushes to silence it, then pours herself a travel mug—cream, no sugar—and secures the lid in place with a quiet hiss. But for the lack of light, today could be a regular morning. She moves through the kitchen amazed at how little thought is needed to go about her routine.

Patient privacy is paramount, and to demonstrate good corporate citizenship some policies will have to be revised in the wake of the breach. Onerous new procedures that accomplish little will be instituted. With a twinge of regret, she thinks of Cecily at Sanjay's store and all the other techs in the district, and all those who will one day replace them. They will bear the brunt of it. Her silent legacy shall be a quotidian frustration for these people, busywork in the guise of security. For however comprehensive a policy, nothing can protect against somebody going rogue. She takes a sip to calm her nerves, then walks out the door.

An early-morning chill slices through her thin hoodie. Shivering, she jogs over the dewy lawn to the parking lot and climbs into her truck. The windshield is frosted over, so she switches on the defroster, which blasts cold air until the engine heats up. While she waits for the view to clear, she tucks her hands under her thighs and calmly watches her breath dissipate in the warming cabin. The important thing now is to stay focused. If she allows her thoughts to wander she might reconsider, and she doesn't want to reconsider. She wants to carry through with the plan. Nothing but an overwhelming familial obligation can justify her intended course of action, which is to say she has no choice in the matter.

When the windshield clears she shifts the transmission into gear and presses the gas.

More than geography, what separates her from the pharmacy resembles a bell curve of anxiety as a function of desire and logistics—the admixture refining with each sip of coffee and every green-lit intersection disappearing in the rearview mirror. The road is never completely empty, however. Even now decisions must be made whether to pass or to fall in line. Those on the road this morning are not commuters but, rather, fellow travelers, spurred on by duty or vocation. Their destinations—like hers—concealed by the darkness. They share a sisterhood of obligation. In solidarity, she breezes through the usual bottlenecks, unobstructed at this hour.

Out of habit, she parks on the side of the building and walks toward the entrance.

For a moment, she indulges the fantasy that her actions can remain anonymous, but, of course, she knows better than that. Security cameras along the well-lit perimeter record everything. The silent footage will speak louder than even the slam of her car door, which reverberates off the concrete and stucco of the deserted parking lot before fading into the tangle of foliage surrounding the drainage canal behind the property. The cameras will help create a narrative of intent—evidence already submitted for a crime not yet committed. Nothing she does can erase the footage. Were she to lose her resolve and flee, the footage would remain. Perhaps she should leave. The possibility nags at her with increasing vigor. She could climb back into her truck and go home, retreat under the covers and pretend this was all a nightmare. In a few hours she could call Bill and apologize for her absences and her lack of communication. As a pharmacist she knows of many sudden illnesses that might provide a convenient excuse. Without a crime there would be little chance of anybody checking the cameras. But her presence here, at this hour, remains recorded, suspicious nonetheless. It's another kind of time travel, a fait accompli initiated by an earlier iteration of herself and carried out by a future version, the present existing only to bridge the gap.

She sips her coffee and stares beyond her translucent reflection in the glass door.

As soon as she turns the key corporate will be notified. Rusty, the store manager, will be contacted. Most likely corporate's call will wake him. He'll be groggy. It'll take a moment for him to process what's happening, to consider whether he forgot to inform corporate that he granted one of his staff permission to enter the store early. That moment won't last long. Checking the cameras will come later, when the bureaucracy has had time to process the request. In the meantime, alarms do go off for no reason. He lives nearby. He'll volunteer to drive over and check out the situation. The whole movement will take ten minutes at most.

She turns the key and the timer starts.

First she weaves through a snarl of shopping carts clustered near the entrance, a deterrent that fails to slow her down. In less than twenty seconds she reaches the office and punches in the alarm code. Success. The first hurdle cleared. But there's no time to celebrate. She sprints for the pharmacy at the back of the store, careful not to spill her coffee. In her haste, she drops the keys and they slide across the floor, coming to rest under a shelf of adult diapers. Retrieving them eats up precious seconds. But, at last, she fishes them out and flips through the keys with lightning speed. She unlocks the heavy pharmacy door and slips in, slamming the keys down next to the register, where she'll remember to grab them on her way out.

Once inside she makes a beeline for the computer. This is her known unknown, her wild card. Sometimes it boots up instantly. This morning it takes longer and she impatiently glances at the time on her phone. Eight minutes left. The delay gives her time to formulate a defense. As head pharmacist at this location, she can claim prerogative to enter the pharmacy as she sees fit, but her recent absence undercuts that argument even if an utter lack of precedent didn't. Executive prerogative is perhaps the best she can muster, but it's far from a good defense. She'll need to come up with something more convincing for Bill if she's going to save her job. Confessing the truth occurs to her as the computer wakes up, but she dismisses it as a no-win strategy. Even as her fingers fly over the keyboard pulling up patient files, she knows Alex's disappearance doesn't justify breaking into the store and violating privacy laws.

If she's honest with herself, she knows she chose to enter now rather than wait till normal business hours because she suspects that she's already lost her job. Unexplained absences do not bode well for a pharmacist's career. Everything grinds to a halt without the pharmacist, which means no revenue and angry patients. And the techs who did show up as scheduled? They must get paid, which means the pharmacy actually loses money simply because the pharmacist isn't here. Imagine several days of that. Imagine if your pharmacist refused to answer her phone, if she neglected to return the district manager's calls or listen to his increasingly frantic voice mails. If she walked in here during normal business hours they wouldn't let her anywhere near the computers. Nope, couldn't risk it, she thinks, pulling up Eddie's file. This information is too valuable to her. She snaps a photo with her phone of his patient record, including his address, and shuts down the computer. Three minutes left on the clock. Just enough time to lock the pharmacy, engage the alarm, and slip out the front door.

She guns it out of the parking lot with thirty seconds to spare. The pharmacy recedes in her rearview mirror as the sun breaks over the eastern sky.

She did it! The celebration is short-lived, however. As the realization of what she's done fixes in her mind, she feels queasy and her vision blurs. She's just thrown away everything she's worked for. And for what? So that she can play Sherlock Holmes with her brother's lover's data? Her stomach churns and she veers onto the shoulder, braking hard. She jams the transmission into park and scrambles out of the truck just in time to hurl all over the weeds sprouting through the gravel on the side of the road. Tears stream down her face. Nobody even slows down as they pass the lone woman hunched over by the roadway, shuddering in the first blush of dawn.

THE ROCK SKIPS FOUR TIMES BEFORE SINKING. A SERIES of concentric ripples upset the otherwise still surface of the lake.

Inevitability hews a queer course.

Yo, how can you be so chill about this?

After everything you still ended up in this park tonight, this park like a forgotten tidal eddy across the highway from the commuter airport. The streetlights burned out long ago.

What choice do we have?

How many times have you been here before? How many times has a clueless boy sat where Alex sits now? More than you care to remember.

"Do you think anybody misses him?" He speaks to the water, his shoulders slumped.

"What's that?"

"Eddie." In the pale light from the shrouded moon he absently picks at a pimple on the corner of his lip.

You manipulated him into agreeing that involving the police was a bad idea. Police only complicate matters. Even if they believed that Eddie's death had been an accident, there would be an inquiry that could turn up troubling facts. Once Alex relented, all that remained were logistics. For that, too, you had a plan. A man found dead in a public toilet would garner a sensational headline or two, but would quickly fade into obscurity. He can't see that now, but one day he will realize that obscurity is what will save him.

"It's too early for that." You move down the small dock, which is blocked from the road by the restrooms on one side and dense foliage on the other.

The same foliage hides your car from view. Anybody passing by would have to be looking to find you. You're potentially visible to anybody driving along the highway, but nobody looks this way as they approach the tollbooth a quarter of a mile away.

"I bet nobody'll look for him." He traces filigrees in the water with a long twig.

"That wouldn't be such a bad thing."

Several people saw the three of you leave the club together. Your anonymity and his transience can protect you to a point, but sooner or later people may start asking questions. In a sense, questions are exactly what you want, what this work has always been moving toward. Questions lead to outrage, which leads to justice. But how can the work raise a cry for justice while simultaneously creating the very conditions of the injustice it seeks to condemn? The paradox vexes you. Perhaps you came to this place to work out a solution.

He clicks his tongue and tosses the twig into the water. "That's fucked up. You know that, right? Please tell me you get that."

Overhead stars shine in a patchwork of clouds. Across the lake the blue lights of the airport glow uninterrupted. And all of it reflects on the placid waters, which stretch out from the muddy banks like silvered glass.

You sigh. "Yeah."

"It probably don't mean shit to you."

"That's not true."

"Whatever."

This is your fault. He was supposed to remain insulated. Your carelessness involved him and now you don't know how to proceed. Perhaps the best option would be to leave right now, to go home and forget about everything you've done, forget about him, reboot and start anew. You could do it. You could start your mornings with a grapefruit and toast and the local paper. You could shower and dress, make plans with your partner that, somehow, overcome your hectic schedules. You could drive your daughter to day care and then arrive at the office with a box of doughnuts for your coworkers. And you could afford to eat them because you spend forty-five minutes of your lunch hour at the gym and the other fifteen eating a cup of cottage cheese, a few points of pita and a dollop of organic hummus. You could go to the grocery store as a family. You could vacation on the coast as a family. You could put your daughter through college, support her as she struggles to make a life of her own and start a family of her own. You could be a grandparent. You could grow old with your partner. You could die and have a minister intone bland niceties: you trimmed the neighbors' hedges, you beautified your community, you were compelled to civic responsibility. You could do it. You could do it, and after a while you'd go numb and even forget about all of this—about the work. It would be just one more suburban secret. And perhaps that's another reason you came here tonight. Wouldn't the narrative of a strangled student in a public restroom resolve neater if the body of a spurned lover were also present—some stranger, a drifter, a kid with no place, someone who a population eager for neat resolutions could believe was responsible for other recent deaths? A brown body to blame.

"I'm sorry," you say, and rest a hand on Alex's knee.

He turns his head and with downcast eyes asks, "Would you look for me if I went missing?"

A private jet, edging in between the blue lights, comes in for a shaky landing. Without hesitation you say, "Of course."

"You fucking better."

How many times have you been on this same dock before this same view, always watching the planes taxi and take off, or the wobbly landings of new pilots mastering their craft? How many times have you drawn inspiration from them, used the display as a convenient backdrop to your work? Other boys have sat where Alex sits now, transfixed and easy prey. The only thing separating them is a nascent empathy in your character.

"Come on," you say, "I'll take you home."

"No way am I going back there. I'd rather sleep here."

"Listen to me, there's nothing there anymore. It's like nothing ever happened. You're going to have to forget anything did. This is important. Understand?"

He shakes his head. For a while you both are very still.

"Okay," you say. "I know another place."

PART THREE

"You'll stay with me, Papi?"

"WOULD I LIE TO YOU, HONEY?'" HE CROONS. "'WOULD I lie to you?'" His face floats in shadow, a stubbled chin and drooping lips suggesting more than is visible. The latter, curled into an exaggerated grin and further distorted by the faint blue glow from the dash, looks cadaverous. "That's an old Eurythmics tune. Before your time. One of your dad's favorites as a kid. But it's true. I wouldn't lie. Not to you."

She yawns, curls her knees to her chest and drapes an arm across her face to block the light from the neighbors' halogens. Disney World failed, so here they are in the driveway in Apopka. The road was never meant to last forever. It was just a place to work out his next move.

"Oh, no you don't," he says, roughly poking her. "Grandpa promised you an adventure and we're going to have an adventure."

She rolls into the light and frowns at him. He consoles himself with the knowledge that kids don't have much in the way of attention spans, and it's been a very long day.

"So, all right, it's no Disney World, but this is better, beautiful. Grandpa's got something even better." He leans into the light, reaching for her. "How does swimming in the middle of winter sound to you? Pretty special, huh? Not just anybody can give you that."

She squirms, and he tickles her chin.

"Look." He points at the tent covering the house. There must be something she likes in his tone because she quits fussing and sits up. "It's just like the circus. Well, the flea circus maybe! Ha! You ever been to the circus?"

She squints, gives him an embarrassed smile, and shakes her head no.

"Well, what are we waiting for? You'll love it!"

He moves quickly to capitalize on her good graces. Over the course of the day he's learned how fickle her mood can be. Yanking on her arms, he drags her past the gearshift. She howls at the rough treatment, but he presses on. Next door a light flickers, a curtain parts. He smiles, waves at the figure in the window, and the curtains overlap. The lights go dark.

"All right, settle down." Once she's cleared the center console, he sits her on his lap like a rag doll. "See? Everything's fine. Grandpa's got it all under control. Sorry I had to be so rough."

She whimpers, and he kisses her forehead. "You're breaking my heart," he says. "It's okay. Everything's okay. You're just tired, but Grandpa promises it'll all be worth it."

He allows her a moment to calm down before opening the squeaking door and climbing out of the car. Knees crack. Bones ache. No big deal, he thinks, and, anyway, she seems to enjoy his struggle until her feet catch on the running board. She whines and kicks his shin as soon as she's free.

Wincing, he says, "That's some leg you got there. Maybe I'll tell Stevie to take you out for soccer." With his other foot, he rubs the sore spot, but she kicks again.

"Hey, all right, I get the hint." He grips her firmly by the armpits and with a loud huff slings her over his shoulder like a bag of mulch. Her hip rests against his collarbone. "You're getting bigger by the minute," he says, short of breath. "What have those parents of yours been feeding you?"

She pinches his ear, and when he shouts, she giggles.

"Okay, pretty good, but let's save something for the pool, huh?"

With the tent in place, if he wants to get to the pool he has to go the long way around the house. He cuts across the front yard. The wet grass surprises him. But then, of course, the lawn still needs watering, even if they're not around to enjoy it. Flowers can't survive on sunshine alone. He remembers that Cheryl keeps the sprinklers on a timer.

"How's this for adventure?" he whispers.

A shadow crosses the neighbors' window. With the shades drawn he can't make out anything further. Something crinkles the grass nearby. Probably just an armadillo looking for a quick termite snack. He presses on.

The change of scenery calms Gertie. She sucks her thumb and rests her head against his shoulder blade.

He passes through the side gate. Wet grass gives way to uneven flagstones. He stumbles and reaches for the wall for support, but with Gertie obscuring his view, the best he can do is hope he makes contact before toppling over and crushing her against the a/c compressor. When he feels tacky vinyl under his fingers, he breathes a sigh of relief. The wall is his only guide through the side yard. Over the years, areca palms, crotons, and azaleas have been left to grow wild. Now the walkway is thick with vegetation, which would eclipse the lone spotlight, were it on. A warm breeze rustles the fronds, teasing his tired, bloodshot eyes with shades of night. A low shadow darts away.

"Your grandmother convinced me to get these pavers. I didn't think we needed them, but she nagged me until I gave in. Women, huh? You always know how to push our buttons, but we just can't say no to you. Anyway, I guess she was right."

She squirms down his chest and he readjusts his grip to support her. She points at something in the dark.

"Just an armadillo, beautiful. Nothing to be scared of." He palms the vinyl. "The pool heater is somewhere around here... Your grandma was afraid of walking through the grass. She was afraid of the mud and the lizards. That's why she wanted these pavers." The memory brings a smile to his face. He cries out when his fingers brush a bump in the tent. "See? Right where I left it." The tent lacks a convenient opening, but the vinyl is baggy enough to allow him to push open the pool control box underneath the surface. He jams his finger into the panel until he hears a motor kick on. "Ha! Your old grandpa's still got a few tricks up his sleeve. Now we'll have warm water for our swim."

HE WAVES A HAND BEFORE YOUR FACE. "HELLO?" HE SAYS in singsong, but the words register only dimly.

Years have passed since you were here last. It looks more run-down than you remember, but otherwise the same. The hedge overgrows its border, obscuring the path to the front door. Were the door visible under the tent, you're certain it would be in need of paint. Time has succeeded where you have failed.

"Hey, are you listening? I asked you why there's a tent."

You blink. Shake your head to clear the images from your mind.

"Don't worry about it," you say, conducting him through the side yard. "It doesn't matter."

Clouds completely hide the moon. Drawing close to him in the darkness, you feel his heat; the smell of sex still lingers on his tawny skin, prompting a replay of the night's events. Your mind races in a free fall of disaster. Nothing went according to plan.

"I thought you said you were taking me someplace where I could stay?" He tugs on your sleeve as he talks, his eyes darting nervously among the three houses ringing the backyard. You don't have to remind him to keep his voice down; he intuits the need.

"This is better," you say quickly. "Nobody will think to look here."

"But where the hell am I supposed to sleep?"

You point at a simple shed near the back fence. "There."

"You're kidding, right? I might as well have stayed in the park." He whispers, but voices carry in the backyard and you worry about neighbors spotting you.

"It's just for tonight." You take hold of his arm and lead him past the pool. He resists at first but then relents. "Tomorrow we'll go to Cocoa. I'll fix everything. Sorry," you add, "I know it's not ideal."

"I—I don't know if I can... It's just gonna play over and over in my head all night." His cheek twitches and he chews his lip.

You drape an arm across his thin shoulders. "Hey, come on. You gotta stay strong just a little longer, okay? We can't change what happened, but I promise that you'll forget all about it on the coast. You'll see. I know a hotel where we can stay for a while. It'll be safe. You can go swimming every day. It'll be a fresh start."

"You'll stay with me, papi?"

"Yes," you say. "We'll go together."

Sniffling, he dries his eyes with the heels of his hands and considers the shed again. "Shit," he says. "Okay. Does it at least get Wi-Fi?"

SHE TAILGATES BEHIND A LATE-MODEL TOYOTA THAT peels off to the left as soon as it clears the gate. Once inside she follows the signs for building seven to the rear of the development. The street curves past a large courtyard housing two pools, a hot tub, a barbecue pit, and a gym. Three-story beige apartment buildings fall into place like apostrophes. Ten years ago she lived in a similar if less opulent version of this place when she was in college. It's 7:45 and the development is quiet except for a trio of pale, shirtless men noisily facing off against a pair of young women at the volleyball courts. The pharmacy has been open for almost an hour and she still hasn't heard from Rusty or Bill. The silence troubles her; it's a bad sign. By now, corporate has examined the security footage and discovered her transgression.

Following her pit stop on the side of the road, she headed north, putting some distance between herself and the pharmacy. In need of coffee, she eventually stopped at a Dunkin' Donuts. When rush hour started, she headed toward the university, her truck an anonymous contributor in the rising tide of commuters.

She parks and kills the engine, then deletes the photo of Eddie's patient file from her phone and the cloud. At least she had the equanimity to refrain from printing anything. Her presence in the pharmacy is not debatable, but her purpose is another matter. The pharmacy cameras monitor the registers and the inventory, not the computers. The system allows surprising latitude in terms of usage. (No doubt that will change as a result of the breach.) Maybe she was checking the week's schedule or referencing the district personnel directory for another pharmacist's contact information. She could have needed to know how much personal time she's accrued—she's been ill, and that's why she hasn't been at work. In the hours since her break-in she has yet to settle on the best lie.

Standing next to the truck, she strips off the hoodie that earlier did a lousy job of keeping her warm. She tosses it in the backseat and closes the door. Across the parking lot a sleepy-eyed young woman dressed in scrubs drops behind the wheel of an older Mazda. She yawns, sitting comatose, the seat belt strap paused midway across her chest. Her eyes betray a mental fog. Morning has not yet arrived for her. Laila pegs her for a med student, maybe nursing. The work is grueling, the studies challenging, and the long hours made all the more debilitating, no doubt, by her insistence on enjoying her youth well into the late hours. Laila was once that sleep-deprived young woman—dedicated to her studies, fast-tracking her pharmacy degree in six years. She applied the same discipline to her career. That, and a bit of luck, is how she ended up the head pharmacist at the age of twenty-eight. The young woman snaps out of her reverie. Her eyes automatically dart around, assessing the situation. Perhaps she's wondering how she arrived behind the wheel of her car. Laila gives her a kind smile before moving on.

Eddie's apartment is on the third floor, overlooking the pool. She strolls along the breezeway, passing a rusted bike chained to the railing, its seat missing. Not far from that a clay flowerpot overflows with cigarette butts next to a threadbare welcome mat. The walkway comes to an end in a dark alcove stacked high with Styrofoam coolers in various stages of disintegration. Taken together they form a kind of impromptu sculpture: *Still Life with Bros*. A crushed beer can tops the assemblage.

She stands before number 307. Eddie's apartment.

Her nerve abruptly flees. Her legs feel heavy; her head, light. She steadies herself against the railing.

What if Alex isn't here? What if he is?

When their father died she felt similarly indecisive, which is how she knows she can overcome it. Uncertainty can be an immensely generative force if you're willing to embrace it.

Holding her breath, she knocks on the door.

Nothing happens for a long time.

A third possibility occurs to her: What if nobody answers?

As the moment stretches she breaks out into a cold sweat; her arms tingle.

Light-headedness, tingling limbs, and sweating are hallmark symptoms of a panic attack—the result of adrenaline flooding her system and constricting her blood vessels—but knowing the patho-physiology doesn't halt the progression of her anxiety. Her heart races and she's short of breath; instantly she regrets the steady intake of coffee she's been having since five A.M. Elevated caffeine levels do not help the situation. What is she doing here? How would she explain herself to anybody asking? A neighbor, say, or a security guard. Can she explain? She muscles down the instinct to flee. All anybody can see is what she chooses to share. (Something else she learned following her father's death.) Appear serene and be serene, she reminds herself. To the larger world all proceeds apace. She is simply an older sibling come to visit a student, to treat him to breakfast. She likes this story. It sounds authentic. Not least of which because it is, in part, true.

She knocks again, firmer this time. With authority. This sister does not question her right to stand in front of the door at eight in the morning.

Bare feet shuffle over carpet on the other side of the door. A deadbolt snaps back. The doorknob squeaks, then the gummy seal between the door and the weather strip along the jamb breaks. A pale, skinny boy with blond hair and dressed in a black T-shirt and boxers greets her, stifling a yawn.

"You must be Eddie's roommate," she says, immediately directing the conversation. "Nice to meet you. Is he up?"

"I'll see if he's home," the boy says. He pads off deeper into the darkened apartment, leaving the door open behind him. She follows him in, not waiting for an invitation.

A dartboard hangs across from a black light poster. Well-worn paths map the graying carpet. Empty cans of soda and beer share the glass coffee table with a large pizza box, a crushed pack of cigarettes, and a sweat-stained baseball cap. Socks and tank tops compete with dust bunnies for real estate. The cold smell of a/c and cheap air freshener mask—just barely—the stench of garbage emanating from an overflowing thirty-gallon trash can.

Down the hall beyond the kitchen the boy knocks on a door. "Yo, Eddie, man, there's a girl here to see you."

Girl. She rolls her eyes, allows herself a moment's ire at everyday misogyny, then puts it aside. Other priorities demand her immediate attention.

The boy returns. "I don't think he's home. He's not answering."

"Mind if I just pop my head in to check?"

The boy shakes his head. "Door's locked. I already checked."

"Locked?"

"Yeah, so, like, he's not home. Unless he's got somebody in there with him." He falls into an armchair and yawns. "Sorry, you probably don't want to hear about that stuff. You his sister or something?"

"I didn't see his car when I pulled in." It's not a complete lie, though that hardly seems important at the moment. She's well past sly semantics.

"His spot's right out front." He hops out of the chair and lopes out to the breezeway in bare feet. His arms and back flex, supporting the weight of his cantilevered torso over the grimy railing. His pale triceps and calves are blinding in the early-morning light. "Huh, I don't see it," he calls back.

She approaches the door. "Does he park anywhere else?"

"Maybe the visitor parking, but that's all the way in the back." She doesn't step out of the way as he reenters the apartment, forcing him to squeeze past her. "He probably crashed at somebody's house," he adds, dropping onto the couch with a yawn. He's done as much as he's willing to do. That much is clear. "Honestly, I don't really remember last night. Not gonna lie, I was pretty wasted. We had a party..." He kicks an empty beer can off the coffee table and plants his heel in its place.

Crossing her arms, she peers down at him. "Was Eddie at the party?"

"For a while, yeah, but he took off at some point. That's kind of his thing, you know?" Balling his fists, he looks away.

"I know he went to the gay club," she says.

"Oh, cool!" He relaxes his grip. "Yeah, like, I didn't know if you knew or not. He brings guys over all the time. Well, not, like, all the time, all the time, but, you know, sometimes, or whatever. Everybody's always super chill."

"But you don't remember if he brought anybody over last night?"

He shrugs and reaches for his phone. "I can text him."

"Don't worry about it." She pulls out her phone. "I'll just text him—oh, shit, this is a new phone. I don't have his number."

"No worries, I got you." He swipes around on his screen for a few seconds, then reads out a number to her.

"Awesome, thanks."

"Sure thing. Listen, if you hear from him remind him he owes me twenty bucks for beer last night."

She sighs. "He's only twenty. You know that, right?"

"Oh, shit. I mean—"

"Go back to bed. You look like hell."

Walking back to her car, she fires off a quick text:

You owe me $20 for the beer last night, dude. Where u at?

He won't recognize the number, but with any luck he'll write back. How hard could it be to impersonate a college student?

THANK GOD A NEIGHBOR HAD THE PRESENCE OF MIND
to phone when Thaddeus pulled into the driveway with a little girl.
In retrospect it seems so obvious that he would've taken Gertie back
to the house, but it never occurred to her because she'd spent the day
obsessing over a gay man half her age.

Peter shifts the phone from one ear to another. At this hour who
knows what remedial police academy rookie they have manning the
phones at the precinct.

"Maybe you should hang up and call back. I can try Steven again.
He might answer this time."

He slowly drums his fingers on the wheel and stares straight
ahead.

A scar stretches away from his wrist. Though faded now, the
wound looks to have been deep—and intentional. He catches her
staring and she quickly shifts her gaze to the rear bumper of the car
in front of them.

"Figures we'd hit traffic now," she says, brushing a strand of hair
away from her face. She taps her ring against the exterior door panel
to the faint beat of reggaeton drifting in on a hot breeze.

He clears his throat but remains silent.

"Listen, what I said... it wasn't right. I don't know; I can't explain
it. I was caught up in the emotion of everything you were saying.
You know all I want is what's best for Gertie, right? Peter?"

He cranes his neck out the window and taps the horn. She allows
him a moment longer, but it's clear that he doesn't plan on responding. Instead, he settles back into his seat and places his free hand
firmly on the steering wheel, the scar bulging over the tendons in
his wrist.

"This is ridiculous. Will you just say something to me, please?"

"There's a wrecker up there now." He points with his chin. "We should be moving soon."

"Okay." She nods. "At least that's good news."

He moves his head and she can't tell if he's agreeing with her or simply shifting his gaze.

Outside, a crow pecks at an empty bag of potato chips on the shoulder.

"I'm sorry, Peter. I truly am. I wish I could take it back. I hope you can believe that."

"Get your arm in," he says, reaching for the a/c. "I'm putting up the windows. It's starting to move again."

THADDEUS SHUFFLES ACROSS THE DECK AND TAKES
Gertie by the arm, which is wet and smells of chlorine from splashing
in the scummy water along the pool ledge. She squeals but doesn't
fight. "Why don't you get back from the edge, huh, beautiful?"

With her free arm she reaches back toward the pool and traces
a smiley face on the milky residue coating the blue tiles. The un-
derwater dome lights create a brilliant shimmer. Leaves float on the
surface, some dead bugs. Still, it's beautiful and he can see why she
would be attracted to it. The filtration system cycles on with a thud
and she pulls against him, drawn to the sound. Gently, he tugs her
back from the edge.

"Do you ever go swimming in that big pool your daddies have?"
He strains to speak as he slowly lowers himself to the ground one
knee at a time.

She shakes her head no in an exaggerated sweep from shoulder
to shoulder, her straight black hair whipping across his face. Her
hair smells like weed.

"Maybe we'll do some diving," he says, tapping her head, "get
your hair nice and wet before taking you back home."

She giggles, nods.

In addition to the weed, he smells the night-blooming jasmine
Cheryl planted either last season or the year before. The confluence
of aromas makes him think of hookah bars and stallions gallop-
ing on hard-packed trails past a silhouette of minarets. He pictures
himself in that far-off place, just Cheryl and him and the sun setting over a woozy desert. And he smiles. Maybe they'll do that.
Maybe they'll go on a vacation. A romantic getaway could be just
what they need.

His grip slackens and the moment it does Gertie squirms free and runs back toward the pool. He's too exhausted to chase her down again. If there's trouble he'll be able to get to her in time, but for now he'll just watch. There's no sense in wasting his energy. She dips a finger in the water, then brings it to her mouth, goading him to intercede with an impish smile. When he doesn't, she quickly pops the finger in her mouth. Almost immediately, she scrunches her nose and spits.

"Not so good, is it? Maybe next time you'll believe it when somebody warns you not to do something." He waves her over. "Why don't you come sit by Grandpa instead?"

She shakes her head and squats by the pool. She slaps the water and laughs at the hollow, wet sound. "Poop!" she shouts, and startles herself with the slight echo. "Poop!" This time she listens for the rebound, her face splitting into a grin when she hears it.

The stone deck is warm, and his legs begin to sweat inside his pants. He rubs his eyes. The skin below is dry and loose. He sighs. Time marches on, he thinks. No big deal.

"Some pool, huh? But the water's still too cold for little angels. We don't want you to get hypothermia. Why don't you come over here and keep me company for a bit?" He brushes a spot clean for her, going over it a second time to make sure all the dirt is gone. "Come on," he says. "Sit over here and tell your old grandpa a story."

She studies him, considers the pool, then considers him again. Eventually she ambles away from the water, but instead of sitting beside him she ducks alongside a large clay pot and holds a finger up to her lips, signaling him to be quiet.

"Hide-and-seek, huh? Okay. No problem. Whatever you want." Straining, he rolls himself onto his side before using whatever momentum he can leverage to haul himself up onto hands and knees. A dull pain radiates along his shin from where she kicked it earlier.

She covers her eyes, her dark hair mushrooming over her fingers. Slyly, she grins at him.

He stifles a yawn. "Oh, no. Where'd Gertie go?"

It's not Disney World, he thinks, but at least it's an adventure. Anyway, she seems happy enough even if, in the end, he's brought her here to see an inferior pool to the one she has at home. It won't be long now till the police arrive. Tomorrow will not go well.

She squeals, and he refocuses his attention on the game. "I just don't know where she could be," he says. "I guess I'll have to call the police."

"Ha!" she says, popping out from behind the planter. She waddles over and kisses him on the nose.

"Oh, thank you. Grandpa really needed that." When he reaches for her, though, she darts back to her hiding spot. These seem to be the rules of the game. She hides. He gives up. She laughs and then gives him a kiss before hiding again.

"Are you going to remember this when you're older, Hurdy-Gertie?" A sharp pain shoots up his leg. The stone is unforgiving. He winces attempting to rearrange himself, but every position hurts. "Are you gonna remember the time your old grandpa took you on a wild-goose chase?" He reaches back to rub his knee and nearly loses his balance. He opts to sit, but Gertie has other designs.

"No!" She crawls, demonstrating what she wants from him. An armadillo makes a racket near the shed.

"Okay," he says. "You win, but you'll have to give Grandpa a minute. Never get old, beautiful. Okay? Can you make me that promise?"

She nods. Her pink shirt is smudged from where she's been pressed against the planter. When she stands he notices that she's bow-legged. They'll make fun of her for it, he thinks. But he's barely finished the thought before she's running toward him in a whirl of exaggerated elbows and knees. She stops just short of his face.

"Daddy," she says, and points at him.

He laughs so hard it turns into a cough, but he doesn't want to frighten her, so he reaches up and gently clasps her arm. "Bless your heart," he says. Vaguely, he registers a scurrying in the grass and curses the armadillo out of habit. "That's a good one."

"Daddy," she says again, still pointing.

"I'm honored, beautiful, I am, but let's not get into a habit, okay? If Stevie heard you, he'd flip his lid. And Grandpa doesn't need to get into any more hot water."

She huffs and wiggles her arm as if it were made of spaghetti. "Daaah-aah-addy!"

Behind him, the armadillo hisses, and the hissing is a kind of scream that sounds like flesh sliding along denim.

"Come on now," he says. "We were having such a good time. Look, Grandpa's ready to play again." He rolls himself onto his elbows and knees. "See?"

From this angle it's clear that she's not looking at him at all. She's staring behind him. He reaches for her, but stretching in his position puts too much pressure on his injured knee, so he stops and slumps onto the ground. She looms over him, framed by glowing clouds slipping across the sky. "Daddy," she says, pointing at something he can't see. A new sound joins the hissing, the sound of feet scuffing against stone. The armadillo pauses right behind him. And it kicks his foot.

He turns in time to see a bag of mulch swinging toward his head. "Stevie?"

Then everything goes black.

YOU DRAG HIM PAST THE DIRTY LOUNGE CHAIRS, THE rusted barbecue, the canisters of gas, and the withered ferns in their mildewed planters, refusing to allow his weight to slow you down. Despite your best intentions tonight has been a colossal failure.

"Daddy?" Gertie cautiously peeks out from behind the planter where she hid when you hit Thaddeus with the mulch, likely scarring her for life.

"Stay there," you order.

Once he's inside you may still salvage the night, but her presence here is troubling. It indicates that something has gone very wrong at home and you curse yourself for not paying more attention to your phone throughout the day. It was stupid.

Sweat beads on your brow in the warm night, but you're almost to the tent. All you have to do is keep pulling and remember to hold your breath. The police will find Thaddeus inside the house and will assume he succumbed to the gas and fell (which explains the bruise on his temple from where you hit him with the bag of mulch). The only mystery will be what he was doing in the house in the first place. Maybe he wanted to show Gertie some bauble, and in his excitement he forgot about the gas. It wouldn't be the first time he's acted irrationally, ignoring the consequences of his actions. Many people can testify to that.

He starts to slip so you pick up the pace.

"What the fuck?!"

You whip your head toward the commotion and spot Alex sprinting for the pool. Gertie teeters near the edge. He slides across the grass, scooping her up just as she's about to topple headlong into the water. She shrieks. A light snaps on in the neighbors' window.

You dive for shelter under the patio overhang, dragging Thaddeus along. You huddle over his body, panting, counting the seconds until the light extinguishes. When it does you hustle.

You know the old couple next door and you know that at their advanced age eyesight can't always be trusted. It can play tricks. For instance, where there's a large man you've known for decades lumbering around a pool, you may see the impossible sight of a lithe Latino teenager charging across a lawn. These things happen, but everyone makes mistakes, sees things that, perhaps, aren't really there. The truth, no matter how improbable it may seem at first, can be ascertained. It's a simple matter of substituting in what you know must be true and forgetting the rest. If you and Alex disappear swiftly enough, leave no evidence behind, how hard would it be for a mature, rational mind to let the substitution stand? But first you must get Thaddeus inside the house.

Thaddeus rolls his head. His eyelids flutter open and he moans.

"Hey, where you going?" Alex calls out.

"Watch her," you command, and he complies.

In a second you've reached the tent. You tear open the Velcro, letting the flaps rest together gently while you shoulder his bulk into position. Then you take a deep breath and drive forward.

It's warm inside. A humid fog stings your eyes and burns your nostrils. Grommets in the tent fabric occasionally align with a window, admitting a weak beam of light into an otherwise perfectly dark space, but you know this house like a rat knows its maze. You easily drag him past the kitchen table to rest against the island. Your work done, all that remains is to unhitch yourself from his bulk and slip back out into the fresh air.

Before you can he comes to.

"Stevie." At first he whispers, but as he revives his voice regains its familiar timbre. "Give me a hand. I can't see anything."

"Shut up!" you hiss, and immediately clap a hand over your own mouth. Just disappear. Leave him! But, of course, you've always known that you can't do that. This house, his very existence, the sentiment of family and its insistence on deference: it's all a quagmire imprisoning you. It demands a response. Your hand slowly drifts down to your chest, where you feel your heart racing.

"Come on." He coughs. "Do your old man a solid."

His arm windmills for leverage, crashing against the porcelain jars lining the edge of the counter. It would be the easiest thing in the world to take his hand and help him to his feet. No big deal. It's what anybody else would do in this situation. You want to help him, actually, but you won't. You can't. You must harden yourself against him. This week was a mistake. You took a chance against your better judgment. Even though you've been on the cusp of something grand, even though you've been more productive and have felt more truly yourself these past three years than at any time before, you were convinced on the grounds of family to give reconciliation a shot, and because you did everything has been ruined. Somehow he got a hold of Gertie and brought her here, and by doing so he has not only placed her in danger, but he has also compromised every separation you've endeavored to maintain. You can't forgive that kind of blind entitlement. You won't.

His fat hand slaps against the old countertop. He struggles to breath.

"Stevie?" He breaks into a coughing fit. "Are you there?"

You're so close to him that you can feel his humid breath. It won't be long, you think, till he suffocates. And you know, without a doubt, that this is the last time you will ever see him.

"Stevie? Son, please."

His pathetic voice and labored breathing cements you to the spot. He's so much weaker now than you ever imagined possible. You press your lips to the top of his head, fearing that he's grown too fragile these past three years. "I'm sorry," you whisper. Your eyes burn from the gas, they tear, so you close them. You have to leave. There's nothing else to say. You cover your nose and mouth with a sleeve and make your way out following the same path you took to get in, the path you know by heart—never looking back.

On the patio, a breeze builds and you forget yourself for a moment. You cough out all the gas and smile.

Alex has calmed Gertie. They play together nearby.

"You like playing horsey, huh?"

Alex's high, sweet voice drifts across the yard. She crawls around to his side and pushes. He allows himself to topple.

"Oh, no! You've knocked me over."

She laughs, claps, and lunges for his stomach.

You squat down because you're afraid that if she sees you she'll cry again, and right now all you want to do is watch them play.

THE FADED TENT SLOUCHES AT THE HEAD OF THE driveway like a melted candle.

"That's Thaddeus's car!" Cheryl points frantically.

"Yeah," Peter says, his eyes narrowed into slits. He pulls into the driveway going too fast, jams the transmission into park, and is out the door before she removes her seat belt.

"Wait for me." Taking a misstep exiting the car, she falls onto the concrete and howls in pain.

He's halfway to the side gate and hesitates for a moment before coming to her aid. "Are you okay?" he asks. The animosity is gone from his voice.

"I think so." Her knee stiffens, causing her to wince as he helps her sit up, but she's put up with worse.

He nervously glances at the house.

"Go," she says. "I'll be fine. Go get Gertie."

"Are you sure?"

"Of course I'm sure. Go!"

"SHE LIKES YOU." YOU SPEAK AT JUST ABOVE A WHISPER to avoid waking Gertie.

"Kids always like me." He repositions her head on his lap as she snores.

"It's not just kids." You come close but he pushes you away.

"She's yours, right?"

You nod.

"And that was your old man? This your house?"

Again you nod.

With his tongue he probes the corner of his lip and juts his chin toward the tent. "He gonna be all right in there? Or do I not want to know?"

"You probably can't stay here tonight."

He braids a lock of her hair through his fingers while she drools on his jeans. "Yeah, I kinda worked that out for myself."

"I have to stick around and deal with this, but afterward we'll go somewhere safe." He's helped with your work and now he's met your family. You scoot closer and again he gently nudges you away. "Lay low tonight and tomorrow, then we'll be out of here. Just you and me. I promise."

He shakes his head slowly and frowns. His eyes remain locked on Gertie. "Nah, don't worry about it. I can take care of myself, papi."

A cold sweat breaks out on your neck. Nausea washes over you. Your head hurts and your bones ache, possibly from the gas, and all you want is to lie very still for a long time somewhere cool and quiet.

He plucks a blade of grass, then scratches his ashy elbow. He rises to his feet, cradling her. "I'm tired of running. I'm gonna go home."

"Take the car," you say, your stomach clenching. "Go to Cocoa. Get out of here for a while. I can meet you out there in a few days. This is just a setback."

He slips her small body into your arms and you worry about her breathing in the poison on your clothes. Then he presses his lips to yours, letting them linger. He sniffles. "Take care of this little girl, okay? She needs a dad."

Please, you want to say, *it's just that things got muddled and I temporarily lost focus; everything will be better. I can be better.* But you don't get the chance because he's gone, leaving only a faint trail through the wet grass, and for the first time in a long time you feel like crying.

An entire lifetime passes like this. You with the child, here by the pool: that is all that exists. A small universe. Your hands throb as you brush them through her hair, but that is to be expected. And, if you're being honest, you welcome it. The throbbing is your most authentic self. It creates order and is rational; it marks the passage of time.

A familiar gait brings you back to the larger world.

Bags anchor his eyes and his clothes are rumpled. Combined, the effect is one of run-down sexiness that you recognize but haven't seen for a while. Something cracked in him today, regressed. You smile.

"Oh, thank God! You're safe." He sprints across the lawn and you release Gertie, who has stirred and wrestles against your grip, wanting to go to him. He swoops her into his arms and showers her with kisses.

You roll a blade of grass between your fingers, watching the reunion. "That's new." You indicate his rolled-up sleeves. You can't remember the last time he willingly showed his scars.

"She smells like... what is that—smoke?" He takes a deeper whiff. "Jesus, Steven! You've been smoking pot around her?"

Your real name on his lips is like the peal of a faraway bell calling something long dormant to attention. You perk up and become defensive. "I didn't smoke around her. That wasn't me."

"Where's your father?"

You shake your head. "I couldn't tell you. She was in the yard when I got here."

"Alone? Never mind. We'll deal with that later. At least one of us got here in time." He fixes his weary gaze on you. "Do you want to tell me where you've been?"

"What do you mean—"

"Because today can't be the first time you've lied to me about being at the shelter."

You examine your nails. Your cuticles are inflamed. You really must stop biting them.

He pinches the bridge of his nose. "Tell me something, Steven. Please."

A warm breeze ruffles the loose fabric covering the house. Any minute now the police will arrive and find Thaddeus inside, and then your separate lives will crash into each other, reconciling—for better or worse—into something unified. You meet his gaze, a confession perched on your lips. There was a time when he was all you needed; maybe he's still the only thing you want. Have you ever looked as content as he does right now with Gertie in his arms? For a fleeting moment with Alex, you did—with all of your boys in their own small way. Maybe what you've been doing at night hasn't been about redemption at all, or, rather, it's been entirely about redemption and not at all about retribution.

"I can't," you say at last. "It's better this way."

"Well, um, I don't know how you expect me to respond to that."

"I don't."

"Fine." He shrugs. "Your mother's out front. Go wait with her. I'll bring Gertie up. I just need a minute."

You nod and struggle to your feet. Slowly you make your way to the side yard.

"Steven," he says. You stop and turn to look back at him. Gertie gently bounces in his arms, sucking her thumb. "I love you."

"She shouldn't—" you start to say. He intuits the rest and pulls her hand away from her mouth. "I love you, too."

When they find the body inside the tent you'll act shocked. A tragedy. And just as things were improving... Who could've predicted this turn of events? But, of course, in retrospect, there were signs. He hasn't been well; he's been acting erratic. Last night he nearly choked her. Thank God it wasn't worse—that we got here when we did...

You can work with that.

IF SHE CAN GET TO THE CAR SHE'LL BE ABLE TO HOIST herself up. It's just a matter of perseverance, and that she has in abundance. Time is her limiting factor yet again. What if Thaddeus has gone and done something stupid? What if he's allowed something to happen to that beautiful little girl? He can barely even swim. What if she's fallen into the pool? The thought sends a shiver down her back. No, she can't—she won't—take that chance. The car is nearby, and she just has to crawl.

She wastes no time pulling herself to her feet. A little worse for wear, but the knee is bruised, not broken. She massages it while catching her breath.

A familiar voice rings out from the yard. She rubs her leg one final time and presses on. "It's just a charley horse. Get it together, Cheryl." With each step she feels her strength returning. By the time she reaches the side yard, the pain has dulled into a steady throbbing.

A decade has passed since she was here two nights ago to set the pool controls, and there is a great deal to navigate quickly. Voices volley but the dense foliage strips away the words, leaving only tones and cadence, which makes it difficult to identify the speakers.

Somewhere near the air conditioner, she runs into Steven. "You're here!" She latches on to him and sways side to side. His clothes smell like ash and spice—pleasant at first, but then soon too sharp and she has to turn her head. Her nose stings and she tastes it in the back of her mouth. But her baby is here! He's safe. It doesn't matter that he's been missing all day. He came back when he was needed, like he always does.

"I've been trying you all day. Where's your father?" He stiffens at the mention of Thaddeus, then squirms out of her grip. "Is Gertie with you?"

"Everything's fine. Peter has her."

As he pulls away, the air freshens, and because of that and because Gertie is safe, she breathes a sigh of relief. She closes her eyes and leans against the a/c, thankful to God or the universe or whatever that everything has worked out and that her family has made it through in one piece. "Come on, let's go see her."

"No!" His hip twitches, and for a moment it seems as if he may bolt over the fence, but then he squares his back and fixes his face into something approximating a smile. "I'll wait by the car. You go on ahead, if you want, and be with Peter."

"Alone? Why?" She stands up straight and swallows hard.

Peter wouldn't have told Steven what she said in the car, would he? No, it wouldn't make sense. Not with Gertie in danger. But then again, maybe he would. He could want to hurt her, and isn't that what she's feared all along? After today Thaddeus is out of the picture for sure, and now Peter has the perfect excuse to cut her out as well.

She studies Steven's face for any indication, but he betrays nothing. Under scrutiny, he hardly even blinks. The only motion is the curling and uncurling of his fists, which come in rhythm with his slow breath and of which he seems unaware.

"Did Peter say something to you? What's going on?"

"Nothing's going on," he says, his voice pitching up and sounding a thousand miles away like it did when he was a child and had done something wrong but knew she couldn't prove it.

She presses him. "Where have you been all day?"

"My phone was on do not disturb. I came as soon as I realized—"

"Where's your father? I need to talk to him." This time he flinches. She sees it clearly even in the low light of the side yard. "Why are you doing that every time I mention your father?"

"I'm not doing anything."

"Don't lie to me, Steven Bloom. I know you too well. Every time I mention your father you flinch. And you're telling me you don't know where he is but his car is out front and yours isn't. Did you take Gertie out of day care? Have you been with him all day?"

"No!" He slaps the side of the tent. The vinyl emits a hollow groan. "I told you everything I can."

"Jesus Christ, Steven! What is going on? What are you not telling me? Where is your father?"

"Sorry. Look, it's been an emotional day for all of us with Gertie missing—"

"But you didn't know that because of your phone."

"What?"

"You couldn't have known Gertie was missing all day unless you checked your phone. Or if you were with your father—"

"No. What? That's not what I meant..."

He attempts an explanation, but she knows not to listen. Instead, she watches his face. It will betray him sooner or later; it always does. His eyes dart and his lips twitch. His posture slumps the longer he speaks. He bites at his nails, but immediately snorts and pulls them away. Practiced desperation creeps into his voice, but it passes quickly, as she knew it would. He lacks shame, and true desperation can't endure without shame. This is what she's always known about her son, what she's always been afraid to admit to others, even to Thaddeus: Steven doesn't feel things like other boys. His eyes water and she doesn't know why she didn't notice that earlier. Hives have formed along his forearms and the insides of his elbows are red as if from struggling with a great weight. The wind shifts and the tent quivers. She catches the sharp scent of ash and spice, the same she detected on him earlier—

Her voice catching, she interrupts him. "Where's your father, Steven?"

His expression hardens. A dark smile plays at the corners of his eyes. "I couldn't tell you."

BROWN CLOUDS SWIRL AROUND A YELLOW MOON IN A
purple sky. Stevie dragged him into the tent. He remembers that. But
instead of waking up inside, Thaddeus finds himself floating high
above the house. Down below, Stevie plays with Gertie. He alights
on the patio next to them. All his pains are gone.

"Good to see you, Pop." A faint aura obscures Stevie's features.
"Have a good flight?"

"Sure, sure. Listen, I don't want to waste any more time. I've got
a surprise for you." With one hand he scoops Gertie up and with the
other he pulls Stevie toward the planter where Cheryl hides his pipe
and weed. "Come on, our little secret. We won't tell your mother."

"Well, all right. I don't see any harm in that."

"Look at us all together at last. The Three Amigos. Ha!"

The world creeps forward at a sluggish pace, but he doesn't
mind. He's a man who can appreciate the moment, and this is one
hell of a moment. His granddaughter curls up in his arms, a giant
smile plastered on her slumbering face. His son sits beside him, and
they're dipping their feet in the cool waters of the pool while passing
the pipe back and forth. "Do you remember when you gave me this
pipe?" he asks, taking a toke.

Stevie claps a hand on his shoulder and kisses him on the cheek.
"This guy," he says. "I love this guy."

"Right back at you!"

Together, they stretch out on the patio and gaze up at the heav-
ens. The clouds part to reveal a universe in motion. Stars blink. Gal-
axies swirl. A neon meteor shower passes overhead, coaxing the
damn termites out of the house. They funnel into the sky where they
form a bold, arcing rainbow.

"Will you look at that?" Thaddeus says. He wants to wake Gertie to show her, but she's had such a long day already. It's better to let her rest, and, anyway, there will be more nights like this, many more opportunities now. "Have you ever seen anything like it?"

"Once or twice."

Serenity washes over Thaddeus's face. What a wondrous life his son must live if he's seen something like this sky before.

"But I'm glad we're seeing it together, Pop."

"I'm a lucky man to have a son like you. I'm proud of you, Stevie."

Stevie's eyes are half closed from the pot and his lips are a happy wobble. He thanks Thaddeus, then chuckles. It's contagious, and before long they both erupt in giggles. He tries to stop for fear of waking Gertie, but he can't, and his inability to control himself only goads Stevie. They laugh so hard that tears begin to form.

Stevie manages to quiet down first. He sits up and reaches for Gertie. Thaddeus slips her into his arms. His son and granddaughter: the picture of happiness under that gorgeous swirling sky. "I hope you're not mad," he says, "about today. I just wanted to take her on a little adventure."

Stevie snorts, waves away the words. "Please. We're family. I couldn't stay mad at you."

"Speaking of family, what do you say you, Peter, and Gertie come back in a few months when it's a little bit warmer and we have a big pool party? It'll mean the world to your mother."

"Gertie'll love it."

Thaddeus smiles, but it quickly turns to uncontrollable sobbing. "I'm sorry, Stevie. Whatever it was I did, I don't remember. I know it must've been bad, but I just don't remember. Honestly, Stevie, I don't. I have trouble remembering a lot of things these days. But I'm sorry anyway. It's not worth all the time we've wasted."

"No sweat, Pop." He shakes it off like it's nothing, dries his father's tears, and then stands. "Water under the bridge." Reaching out a hand, he helps Thaddeus to his feet. "And speaking of water. What do you say to a little dip?"

"I'd say we're getting along swimmingly!"

"Good one." Stevie turns to Gertie: "Your old dad still has a lot to learn, gorgeous. Guess you could say I'm a little wet behind the ears!"

"Ha!"

A tall, thin boy enters from the side yard. Scars cover his body, but his tranquil smile and serene demeanor put Thaddeus at ease. Peter and Cheryl follow close behind.

"Oh, good," Stevie says. "Right on time."

The boy and Stevie hug while Peter and Cheryl stand off to the side.

"I couldn't leave without saying good-bye," the boy says. "You have such a lovely family."

Thaddeus wrinkles his brow as the stranger approaches.

"Just a friend of mine, Pop," Stevie says, placing Gertie in the boy's arms. "He's going to watch her while we swim."

"Does Peter know about this?"

Peter grins. "It's all right, Thaddeus. It's not a big deal."

"Yeah, Mr. Bloom," the boy says. "Relax."

Peter whispers something to Stevie and they exchange smiles. "Enjoy your swim, Thaddeus."

Cheryl will join him. She bends over and unlaces her shoes.

"Ready?" Stevie asks, helping to unbutton his collar, which has suddenly become very tight.

Sluggishly, Thaddeus nods.

The boy bounces Gertie in his arms. "Say bye to Grandpa," he says.

Yawning, she claps one hand at Thaddeus. He returns the gesture. Everything suddenly feels heavy. Then Peter touches him on the chest and gives him a small push. "Don't worry about a thing," he says. "I'll take good care of her."

Thaddeus doesn't fight. He lets himself fall into the cool splash of the pool, which is refreshing on such a warm night.

A BANK OF DULL GRAY CLOUDS OVERTAKES THE STARS.
He hears a splash and feels himself bob in the wake, and then she's beside him, holding his head above the agitated surface. Her hand is warm—so, too, her lips on his forehead.

"It's okay." Her voice trembles. "It's going to be okay." She calls for someone to bring her an aspirin, then she pulls him to the shallow end of the pool. He attempts to help by pushing along the bottom. "Just relax," she says. "I got you." So he does, and the transit goes much smoother. His arm aches, and he winces when she accidentally knocks it against the railing while attempting to drag him up the steps. "It's okay," she says, cradling him. She coughs. "We'll just wait here."

"Gertie?" he asks.

"She's fine. Peter has her." She strokes his head, kisses his forehead, then spits. "Save your energy. Help is on the way."

"I'm not worried." Despite the pain in his arm, he rolls onto his side and gives her the mischievous eyebrow. "No big deal."

She stifles a whimper. "What were you thinking, huh?"

He lacks the strength to explain about Disney World, so he settles for a wink.

"Oh, God, Thaddeus." She hugs him tighter, and he feels like a hot-air balloon freed of all its ballast. He's soaring.

"Best high of my life," he says, pressing into her breasts.

"What was that?"

But he doesn't repeat himself; instead, he gives her a closed-eye smile.

"Stay with me, okay? Help will be here any minute."

Her hand moves away for a moment and he hears some hurried talk over the gurgle of the filter, then her hand returns and she's tilting his head back.

"Here." She places something chalky in his mouth. "Swallow this. Good. Okay. Now, you just relax, okay? Just relax; I'm right here."

The pill sits on his tongue, the flavor mildly unpleasant as it dissolves. It's the best he can manage, but then, it should be enough. It's just a little pain. "Cheryl," he says, wheezing. "You saved my life."

"Shh," she says. "Just relax and think happy thoughts." She kisses him and he can feel that she's crying. He wants to make a joke about getting her wet, but it's amazing how much it hurts to speak. "Remember," she says, "how much fun we had—the three of us—that first summer in this house?" She shakes him a bit, keeping him focused on her voice. "We bought Stevie that badminton set and the two of you spent the whole day out here hitting that... that—oh, what's it called?"

Shuttlecock, he thinks, but she's already moved on.

"You and Stevie stayed out here all day hitting it back and forth to each other. I had to drag you both inside when the mosquitoes started up. I was so afraid you'd get encephalitis..."

Her voice trails off. The heater's really humming now, he thinks. He can't even feel the water. There's a new sound, a low-frequency drone building in pitch. He wants to ask Cheryl about it, if it's the ambulance approaching, but when he opens his mouth to speak he finds the words absent. Well, not exactly absent, just too difficult to dislodge. He shuts his mouth. That's something, he thinks. She saw that. That's something.

"It's okay," she says. "Just relax. I'm right here."

No problem. Easy as pie. He sits still, allowing the water to bear his weight. It's much easier to keep his eyes closed now. Good, good. Cheryl is here. The ambulance is on the way. Gertie is safe. That's the important thing, that Gertie is safe. And Peter is taken care of. And Stevie... He smiles. Right here—right by this pool—they shared the pipe. The drone is louder now. The drone is everywhere. Out from the depths of his memory rises something that he can't quite grasp, but the drone overpowers it. Something he had to do. Or maybe something he wanted to do. He's having trouble remembering. What's the difference anyway? Oh, well. And then it's gone. That's the important thing. The paramedics must've arrived and put a respirator on him because his face feels boxed in. But they haven't turned on the oxygen yet because he's having difficulty breathing, drawing only on every other breath. "Just a little bit longer," she says. "Stay with me." And they must be carrying him by his clothes because he feels tightness everywhere. Soon they'll turn the oxygen on and the air will start flowing. Soon. Not yet, apparently, but soon. No problem. He's waited a hell of a lot longer for more important things. No big deal.

CONVENTIONAL WISDOM FORBIDS RETURNING TO THE scene of a crime, but you find it necessary to flout convention. Eddie was a mistake and now he's a loose end. The risk was minimal with the others. But Eddie leads straight back to Alex, and you must protect him.

An empty stillness clings to the parking lot at this hour. Later people will drive here from nearby offices to enjoy a solitary lunch overlooking the lake. For now the sun only pinks the horizon, suggesting the bustle still a few hours off. Still, it's brighter than you prefer. The risk of detection has increased. As a precaution you pull a hoodie over your head. Moving quickly, with purpose, you retrieve the body from the bathroom. Even with the stiffness that comes with death, it's a simple matter to shove it into the backseat. A blanket softens the silhouette. You could be transporting a crate of LPs or plush carnival prizes.

Before you slip behind the wheel, you empty Eddie's pockets. House keys, wallet, phone. A hemp bracelet adorns his wrist. This you remove and place on your wrist as a memento. Like the scrubs from the first one, the bracelet will serve as a reminder to be more careful in the future. The wallet and keys are irrelevant. You will part with them when the time is right. The phone, though, presents a logistical problem, one you turn over in your head as you shift the car in gear and drive east. A message from an unknown number glows on the screen:

You owe me $20 for the beer last night, dude. Where u at?

You feared this would happen. Already his disappearance has attracted attention. Like all devices, this phone can be tracked. Sooner or later the police will trace it, so it's imperative to dispose of it with all deliberate speed. It must never lead back to the body because the body must never be found. With the others you preceded cautiously, planned things so that even if you lost yourself in the moment contingencies were accounted for. None of that happened last night. You were eager, and now this body contains DNA that leads directly back to Alex. The phone poses a threat, but it represents potential as well. Perhaps it can save Alex. Salvation has come in stranger packages.

Scrolling through recent messages, you absorb Eddie's style. Does he favor emojis? (He does not.) Does he abbreviate? (He does.) What is his preference in terms of capitalization? (He defers to autocorrect.) When you feel comfortable impersonating his prose style, you fire off a response:

Met up with some ppl. Hitching a ride to the beach. Get you back later

The response is instantaneous: **No worries. What'd u get up to last night?**

Nothing. Just drinks. Pretty chill night

Did you hook up?

Your thumb hovers over the screen, primed for a response—you're channeling this boy now, feeling his life as your own, tasting the drinks consumed last night, reliving the sex—but you stop yourself.

Something feels off about this conversation. Who is this person you are texting with and why is their number not in Eddie's phone? You read over what's been written as you drive. The thread feels hectic, forced—laying claim to a familiarity not borne out in the anonymous nature of the exchange.

Who is this? you ask.

Silence. Not even an indication that the other party is typing a response.

Enough.

You've risked too much for one night already. You toss the phone onto the passenger seat. Better to go radio silent and stick to the plan. The road is long between here and Cocoa Beach, and the slash pine flatwoods and cypress hammocks of the Tosohatchee preserve present plenty of opportunities to dispose of a body. Alligators will eat anything.

The phone, of course, will continue on to lunch at the Cocoa Beach municipal pier: an outgoing tide, beautiful bodies all around, a mahi-mahi sandwich with a thick lemon wedge and steak fries, served in a red plastic basket lined in checkered wax paper, #blessed #foodporn #sunsoutgunsout. How easy it would be to reach for a phone with greasy fingers, to lose your grip on the thin device and have it slip, and what bad luck to scramble to recover it only to accidentally knock it over the edge of the pier with the toe of your flip-flops. A shame, really, but hardly the first thing lost to the wild, wide freedom of the sea.

All that comes later. For now you drive. You drive on into the rising sun.

THE ROAD STRETCHES BEHIND HER LIKE A RIBBON STRIPPED from a spool.

Silence.

She doesn't dare respond to Eddie's text. Either Alex is with him or he isn't, but she's reached the end of her road. She turns the truck toward home. Traffic grinds on as expected and the drive gives her time to think. Neither Bill nor Rusty has attempted to contact her all morning. For a moment, she fantasizes that everything that has transpired since last night is a figment of her imagination. Perhaps she is having a nightmare and at any moment she will wake up alone in her bed, safe under the sheets. Why stop there? Maybe the last six months have been a nightmare.

She's not that lucky.

Reality demands its due. The life she's known and worked hard to build is over. She may still salvage something of her career, but it will take time and a fair bit of luck. In the interim she might make a good receptionist at a doctor's office. She could enjoy gallery work, or perhaps something in real estate.

Her focus shifts to practical matters. How long will her savings last? Will she lose the house?

The possibilities keep her occupied until she pulls into her parking spot. Climbing out of the truck, her legs feel heavy in the thick atmosphere of a bright, humid morning. She's exhausted and all she wants is to nap, but afterward she'll take herself to the pool and allow the sun and the water to drive away everything enslaving her spirit. She failed Esther. Alex crossed over into adulthood. She didn't do her job well. But there it is: sometimes you lose.

She opens the door and steps into the cool cavern that is her town house. A familiar scent greets her.

"Lails?"

"Alex?" The blinds are drawn, the lights are out, and her eyes have not adjusted, but yet she charges forward into the living room. "Papo, is that you?!"

A quiet voice answers: "Yeah." (Has she ever known him to sound so glum?)

As soon as she enters his line of sight, he scrambles off the couch and rushes her. In the span of a breath, he's wrapped his long arms around her and buried his face in her neck. He's taller than her and has to hunch over to make it fit, but he does so. He smells like boy, like heat and sweat; a cloying cologne lingers along his hairline. It smells nothing like Eddie's apartment. Hot tears wet her skin, dulling the scratch of his bristly cheek against her neck. He shudders and his knees buckle, but she props him up. She soothes his scalp with her hand and hums into his ear the way Félix did when she was little and the world seemed so large and scary.

"Shh. Hey, it's okay, papo," she says. "Everything's going to be fine. I'm here." And it's all she can manage, even as he falteringly apologizes for everything. "I'm here," she repeats. "I'm here. I'm not going anywhere."